MORE ACCLAIMED FICTION FROM
HESH KESTIN

THE LIE

"A provocative thriller about a dynamic Israeli lawyer—famous for defending accused Palestinians—whose views are tested when her own son is taken captive by Hezbollah. *The Lie* is what great fiction is all about."
—Stephen King

"Engages us with authentic detail….A nail-biting thriller that will stay with you."
—*The New York Times Book Review*

"An utterly riveting thriller that is likely to rank as one of the year's best…*The Lie* has everything: memorable characters, a compelling plot, white-knuckle military action, and an economy and clarity of prose that is direct, powerful, and at times beautiful."
—*Publishers Weekly* starred review

"Not a single word is wasted in Kestin's masterfully wrought and mercilessly readable novel of intrigue, and terror. *The Lie*'s political, cultural, and personal insights are matched only by its breathtaking action and suspense. Quite simply, the best thriller I've read in ages."
—Jonathan Evison, *New York Times* bestselling author of *West of Here* and *Lawn Boy*

"Knuckle-gnawing, heart-stopping, sleep-suspending….The plot is compelling; the writing taut, lucid….Simply superb fiction."
—*Washington Jewish Week*

THE IRON WILL OF
SHOESHINE CATS

Gold Medal for Literary Fiction, Independent Book Publisher Awards

"*The Iron Will of Shoeshine Cats* just may be the best book you never read. Think *The Godfather* on laughing gas, or *Catch-22* with guns. It's also as good a novel about life in the sixties as you'll ever pick up. Witty, sexy, thrilling, and all story. You can't put the damn thing down. If you're still one of the blessed who reads for pleasure, get this book, because it's a pleasure to read."

—Stephen King

"A vibrant, hilarious addition to the genre of mob tragicomedy.... Kestin's richly layered characters—a monstrously obese German organized crime attorney named Frit von Zeppelin, a Jewish Texan who speaks in malapropisms, a dentist who anglicizes or Yiddishizes his name depending on his mood—are straight out of Dickens; his vivid attention to the details of place, New York, and time, 1963, is like poetic journalism; and his snappy, concise prose and dialogue is on par with Raymond Chandler."

—*Publishers Weekly* starred review

BASED ON A TRUE STORY

Bronze Medal for Literary Fiction, Independent Book Publisher Awards

"Kestin's clear knack for clever banter shines throughout the piece. What could have been stock characters in a classically clichéd Hollywood plot are rendered genuine, fleshed-out individuals through Kestin's skill with language. These characters have gumption, they have heart, they have panache. And they're not afraid to talk back. Another bonus: *Based on a True Story* is frequently hilarious. This gem in Kestin's collection makes *Based on a True Story* worth checking out."

—*NewPages*

"These three superb novellas by a former foreign correspondent are some of the best short fiction this reviewer has seen in years."

—*Kansas City Star*

"*Based on a True Story* is witty and funny. It is also sad, wise, and wistful. Parts of it are heartbreaking. The language is masterful. The knowledge it took to write these three novellas is clearly evident on every page—not just Kestin's knowledge of the human heart, but also his large grasp of world geography, his understanding of the history of the various locations he uses to ground the stories, and his notable use of the languages spoken by various characters, from the natives of Atu-Hiva to the people of Mombasa to the Latin spouting Fritz von Blum in Hollywood. It's an opulent read created by what is plainly a simmering talent, a bountiful mind."

—*Perigree*

"Hip in a manly, intellectual way."

—*The Lit Life*

"A !@#!%&#! masterpiece: War, passion, greed, fear, nobility and love's perversion in the face of unfathomable reality."

—*The Jerusalem Post*

THE SIEGE OF TEL AVIV

A NOVEL

HESH KESTIN

DZANC
BOOKS

**DZANC
BOOKS**

5220 Dexter Ann Arbor Rd.
Ann Arbor, MI 48103
www.dzancbooks.org

Library of Congress Cataloging-in-Publication Data

Names: Kestin, Hesh, author.
Title: The siege of Tel Aviv : a novel / by Hesh Kestin.
Description: Ann Arbor, MI : Dzanc Books, 2018.
Identifiers: LCCN 2018051981 | ISBN 9781945814839
Subjects: | GSAFD: War stories | Fantasy fiction
Classification: LCC PS3611.E87 S53 2018 | DDC 813.6--dc23
LC record available at https://lccn.loc.gov/2018051981

First US edition: April 2019
Interior design by Michelle Dotter
Jacket design by Matthew Revert
Contact Hesh Kestin at heshkestin@gmail.com

Printed in the United States of America

10   9   8   7   6   5   4   3   2   1

for
STEPHEN KING

America's storyteller,
undaunted friend,
mensch

AUTHOR'S PREFACE

IN OCTOBER OF 1973, I flew to New York from my home in Israel to tell my parents their younger child, my twenty-six-year-old kid brother Lawrence, was dead. This was not something I could do by phone. Freshly married, Larry was an architect working for an Israeli government agency responsible for planning new Jewish settlements in what some called liberated Judea and Samaria and others called the Arab West Bank. Whatever you called it, on a dirt track near Jericho the car he was traveling in flew off the road and tumbled into a dry river bed. An Arab shepherd nearby heard the stuck horn and managed to flag down two Arabs in a pickup truck, who drove them to the nearest Arab hospital, in Ramallah, bypassing Jerusalem. Bad luck. The Arab doctors in Ramallah then sent my brother and his driver back to Jerusalem. Thus what was probably an act of Arab terrorism was balanced by the humane reaction of other Arabs to try to save their lives.

Following surgery at Hadassah Medical Center in Jerusalem, Larry's driver remained comatose for months, then came to. Larry died on the operating table, possibly the first casualty of the Yom Kippur War, which would break out in a matter of days. Any investigation into this mysterious single-car accident would be put off and then filed away. Israel had more urgent matters to attend to.

I was with my father in synagogue when I heard two men behind us whispering that war had broken out. We left immediately. I had to get home: my wife and then infant daughter Margalit were alone within rifle range of three Arab villages. But all commercial flights to Israel had been canceled.

I called the Israel consulate. Unimaginably on Yom Kippur, someone picked up the phone.

"Consulate of Israel, how may I help you?"

"I need to get to Israel immediately."

"I regret we are providing transportation only for Israeli citizens."

"I'm an Israeli citizen!"

"Then why are you speaking English?" she asked with that wonderful bureaucratic impatience that Israeli government functionaries have honed to an art form.

I switched to Hebrew. "Because, you—" Here I inserted a long list of biblical and more contemporary curses, some of them physiologically improbable— "you were speaking English! Now can you get me on a fucking plane?!"

"Be at Kennedy Airport at three," she said, and rung off.

The El Al flight was full of silent IDF reservists, but no one needed military expertise to know how bad it was. In the north, Syrian tanks were threatening Haifa; in the south, masses of Egyptian mechanized infantry were within artillery range of Tel Aviv. It was inconceivable that the few hundred of us on the plane could make a difference. The mood was somber until, over the Mediterranean, about a half hour's flying time from Ben-Gurion Airport, we picked up an escort of two Israeli Super-Mystère fighters. The entire cabin broke out in song. If the Israel Air Force could spare two of its twenty-four Mystères, perhaps things weren't so bad.

Alas, they were. Flushed with confidence from Israel's victory over the same enemies in the 1967 Six Day War, Israeli military intelligence had failed the nation. The IDF did not believe the Arabs were up to mounting a successful multi-front invasion.

Apparently, neither did the Arabs. Unaccustomed to victory, there were no plans to finish the job. Fearful of going forward without orders, the Arab armies stood in place. But the enemy's major blunder was timing: they chose the one day on the Jewish calendar where most of the IDF, especially the reservists who made up two-thirds of its manpower, were either at home or in synagogue. The roadways were deserted and thus wide open for soldiers to speed to their units' staging areas.

I found my way home to another kind of threat. My wife Leigh answered my knock at the door with a loaded shotgun pointed at my head. Later she told me she'd considered cutting the intruder down through the door; she couldn't imagine that I had managed to return home.

As for what ensued, at the price of 3500 Israeli fatalities, the IDF regrouped, counter-attacked, and repelled both Egyptian and Syrian invasions. But there was another price. Never again would Israelis take for granted that their country would be safe from Moslem conquest. Rarely discussed, this nightmare lives within the heart of the entire nation.

Could it happen? You've come to the right book.

—HK

THE SIEGE
OF TEL AVIV

1

ALEX LOVES SILK. IF she lived in a colder country she would love furs as well, to say nothing of black leather. She delights in high heels—hers this evening are knock-offs of an Italian pair she saw in *Vogue*, size twelve, made by a talented pair of Christian Arab brothers whose workshop is a hole in the wall in Jaffa, not a virtual hole in the wall but a real hole in a real wall—just as she loves nylons, and jewelry, and perfume, and her collection of wigs that scream *woman*. Were it not for Alex's profession, she wouldn't mind growing her hair out, but the Israel Air Force frowns on its fighter pilots wearing theirs long enough to catch in the complex wiring of an F-16 helmet or, worse, tangling in the hundreds of miles of cable exposed when a pilot blasts out of the cockpit in an emergency ejection. This is why female pilots in the IAF wear their hair cropped short. But Alex does not quite fall into that category.

As it happens, Alex is the IAF's leading ace, a pilot so skilled, her reflexes so honed that, simply in terms of physical abilities, the specific athletic attributes of a fighter pilot, he is the most perfect specimen the Israel Air Force has ever strapped into the seat of an F-16. Alex is as known for his leadership qualities as she is for her capacity to survive a 4-G power dive for three minutes without blacking out, and as admired for her guts as he is for her unique ability to choreograph and control a multiple jet fighter attack as though one brain were at the instruments of many aircraft.

She, he? His, hers? If this is confusing consider the effect two years earlier on General Motta Ben-Sheikh, commander of the IAF Fighter Academy, who happens one evening to be sitting with his wife in the lobby of the Tel Aviv Hilton entertaining relatives visiting from France, a yearly ritual that is never anything beyond familial obligation. General Ben-Sheikh's people, originally from Morocco, chose different places of refuge when it became clear after the establishment of the State of Israel in 1948 that the Jewish community of Fez had no future in a Muslim country: most fled to Israel, many finding careers in the armed forces and police. The wealthier, however, emigrated to France, where seemingly without exception they prospered in the manufacture of women's undergarments.

Whenever his Parisian cousins visit Israel Gen Al-Sheikh makes it a point to entertain them at the Hilton, a not so subtle indication that he in his way has done as well as they in theirs. And moreover that while the Al-Sheikhs of Paris, despite their wealth, will forever be outsiders in their adopted country, filthy Moroccans, second-class citizens in *la belle France*, the Al-Sheikhs of Tel Aviv are not second-class anything.

This particular evening, General Al-Sheikh finds himself looking past his garishly dressed *nouveaux-riches* relations to a woman seated at the bar with a group of equally young and stylish Israelis. From a distance he can just about make out their easy banter in colloquial Hebrew, and he tries to hear what this especially striking young woman is saying when he feels his wife kick him under the table. Hard.

"If you can take your eyes off that cheap bitch for a moment, I wouldn't be the only one having to carry on this stupid conversation with your vapid relatives," he hears her say in Hebrew, using a tone meant to suggest something on the order of *Darling, do you think we should order dinner now or have another round of drinks?* Which is precisely how she explains the veiled reprimand to her husband's non-Hebrew-speaking relations.

For answer, General Al-Sheikh excuses himself, walks over to the bar, and without so much as a pardon-me asks of the young lady, "Miss, do I know you? You seem awfully familiar."

In reply the young lady rises from her barstool, stands straight and elegant in her four-inch heels—and salutes.

"Captain Alex Shabbati, sir!" she barks. "You taught me everything I know about aerial combat, sir!"

The good general, who through three wars and countless hours in the sky thought he had seen it all, shakes his head with an uncommon briskness, as though shaking off a mosquito. "Clearly, captain, not everything."

Within forty-eight hours, the problem is bucked up to the head of Fighter Command, then to the commanding general of the IAF, then to the IDF chief of staff, then to the minister of defense, before it lands with an unwelcome thud on the desk of the prime minister herself, who runs her eyes over the single paragraph labeled *Issue* attached to Major Shabbati's military biography and security summary.

"Must I read the whole thing or can you spit it out?" she says with her usual impatience. Shula Amit can be charming, but rarely wastes this talent on subordinates.

The defense minister clears his throat. "Simply put, when not in uniform our ranking ace dresses as a woman."

The prime minister examines the photos in the file. "Quite fashionably too."

"Madam Prime Minister, the defense establishment does not find this to be a laughing matter."

"Who's laughing? This suit is classic Dior—probably a knock-off, but still…"

"Nor do I find it—"

"Though the purse is way too big. A delicate outfit like this…"

"Madam—"

"Then again, doubtless he carries his service pistol in it. Dior never had that problem." She offers a lethal smile that vanishes immediately. "Why is this on my desk? Can't you people deal with something so small? No, tiny. *Miniscule.* You *are* the defense minister, are you not?"

"There may be political ramifications, madam. Sacking the man would put us in a bad light. If he went to the press we'd never hear the end of it—"

"Gays are not barred from serving in the military. As you well know, one of our leading generals is as pink as a Mediterranean sunset."

"Major Shabbati isn't gay."

The PM lifts one of the photos. "With such a *tuchus*?"

"He's as straight as I am."

"I'll take that for what it's worth. Look, Duvvid, is there some reason he shouldn't serve? Has he suddenly forgotten how to—what was it the newspapers said about him?—knock an apple out of the sky at four hundred miles an hour? The man isn't thirty and he's a legend. If he is still—"

"The best, yes. No question."

"So?"

"He goes to bars this way, restaurants. Dances with foreigners. They could be spies."

"*I* dance with foreigners. Every one of us does. The head of the Navy sleeps with a Bulgarian with tits he is apparently ready to die for, though we both know she works for us. Incidentally, they're fake. What then is the problem?"

"The Air Force believes such behavior may be detrimental to morale."

"Whose?"

"The men under his command. Presumably."

"Presumably?" the prime minister asks. "You've taken a poll? Look, we're at the edge of an historic moment. In a matter of weeks, perhaps days, we may finally have a breakthrough with the cousins." As is common in Israel, she uses the Hebrew term for the entire Arab race, who as sons of Abraham are genetically related to the Jews. "Is it so important that one of our flyboys, even the best of them, dresses, shall we say, more elegantly than expected? He does his job. Why don't you and your subordinates in uniform simply do yours?"

"The brass wish to sack him. I think they're right."

"And I think that if we go around sacking people who in their non-working hours do odd things, then we might as well be Saudi Arabia. Put another way, you sack Major Shabbati and I will sack the entire Air Force command, and you with them. Now was there something else, or can I return to leading this country into a new era of continuing prosperity and, hopefully, peace?"

"I shall make your decision known to the Chief of Staff."

"Thank you," the prime minister says. "And if you can find out who is his dressmaker, I really would like to know."

2

AT THIRTY, DAMIAN SMITH has just negotiated a new and lucrative contract with CNN in Atlanta, where he can claim a fairly active though not exciting sex life—according to Smith, what the hell else does anyone do in Atlanta?—and has just had his teeth re-capped for high-definition television, the aesthetic standards of which demand nothing less than glaring perfection. On this particular Wednesday, Smith finds himself scheduled for a remote with Connie Blunt, the one person at the network he cannot abide: vain, overpaid, thin-skinned, shallow, under-educated, and pretty enough to get away with all of the above. Smith detests people like this, though it rarely takes more than two drinks for him to admit that he himself is people like this. If not worse.

On the screen behind him is a still of winds battering the Caribbean; the still will become video as soon as he goes live. In his earpiece, the segment director's voice counts steadily down to the end of the commercial break. "Three, two, one."

"*And* welcome back to Breaking News on CNN, as gale force winds batter coastal areas of the Dominican Republic," Smith reads from the teleprompter. "With hundreds of fatalities and property damage already estimated at three hundred million dollars, the US Weather Service is now issuing hurricane warnings for Florida and up the Eastern seaboard as far north as Maryland. Still officially designated a tropical storm, Lucille is expected to make landfall by tomorrow morning. The National Weather Center warns the storm may well grow into a hurricane as it mixes with cooler air moving east. Officials in both Florida and neighboring Georgia have called for coastal residents to evacuate, and the Red Cross has gone on high alert. More on Lucille as we receive updates. Meanwhile, in a surprisingly more peaceful situation..."

Behind him, the screen goes to a simplified map of the Middle East, zeroing in on Kuwait, then to a grand Arab-style building, then to the building's ornate Hall of Unity, where diplomats from member states of the Arab League raise their hands to vote.

"...In the Middle Eastern nation of Kuwait, member states of the Arab League voted unanimously today to pursue peace with Israel with no preconditions, an historical first. From Jerusalem, Connie Blunt. Connie, how is this news being received in Israel?"

Framed by Orthodox Jews dancing at the Western Wall, Blunt, thirty-five, a lot blonder and clearly female but otherwise a smudged carbon copy of the anchor in Atlanta, breaks into what passes for incisive reportage in American television news.

"Damian, news of the Arab League's sudden turnabout in its refusal to negotiate with Israel, which only two of its member nations recognize, hit the Jewish State with all the force of what one Israeli I spoke to called 'a big wet kiss.' Newspapers, television and radio here have been calling this, quote, 'the beginning of true peace in the Middle East.' Never has the Arab League agreed to sit down with Israel without the intervention of middlemen such as the US or the European Community, with—and this is the important part—no preconditions, no demands that Israel close down its settlements on the West Bank. Damian, this looks so much like the real thing..."

While Blunt continues in a voiceover, the screen goes to the floor of the Knesset, where Israeli parliamentarians applaud a just concluded statement by Shula Amit in her trademark pearls and Chanel suit. The prime minister, who leads a broad coalition that only a week before was on the verge of collapse, simply beams.

"...that the normally fractious Israeli parliament has become one big ear-to-ear grin, the prime minister roundly lauded as, and I quote, 'the prime minister of peace', a far cry from how the right-wing politician is usually portrayed and portrays herself. Observers here point out that it was far right Prime Minister Menahem Begin who in 1979 signed a peace treaty with Egypt. Regarding any new peace treaty, however, officially the government here is playing it close to the vest. A foreign ministry spokesman limited his remarks to saying, 'The State of Israel looks with favor upon recent developments in Kuwait.' But I've talked to cab drivers, schoolteachers, restaurant workers, and even soldiers, and all are clearly excited that the current united Arab initiative may finally bring peace to a Middle East battered by a hundred years of senseless bloodshed. Connie Blunt, Jerusalem, Israel."

Back to Atlanta, where despite his normal loathing for her, Damian Smith cannot help but feel Blunt is as much a television news pro as he is. The bitch. "Thank you, Connie. Stay with us for more on peace in the stormy Middle East, and regular updates on the northward march of what may soon become Hurricane Lucille. You're watching Breaking News on CNN. Stay...connected."

3

IN THE PRIVATE TOILET adjacent to her office, Shula Amit refreshes her makeup. This is one advantage men have over women in politics—that and not having a period, which at forty-seven Shula still has, in spades, ten bloody days a month. The extra-large breasts she developed at age thirteen are gone, however. As a child of privilege—her father's contracting firm built much of Haifa's seaport—Shula had them reduced immediately after serving her two years in the Israel Defense Forces, where despite custom-made restrictive bras she had to have her uniforms hand-tailored by her mother's dressmaker, and twice asked her father to intervene with the chief of staff when her superior officers went beyond leering. Even then, she had in the back of her mind the idea of a career in public service, and knew she would be judged not by her ability to make decisions or analyze policy, but by her tits. To Israeli men, anything over a B indicates bimbo. A male politician may possess a huge dick but—aside from that bizarre case involving an inane congressman in America—the public does not see it, but a woman's breasts, especially when so prominent, are the first part of her to enter a public space. Any public space. Even the Knesset plenum. Especially, she thinks, the Knesset plenum.

Back in her office, Shula takes the usual afternoon call from her mother, whose mission in life is to oversee the nanny who oversees her two grandchildren.

"She gives them watermelon for dessert."

"Ah, yes. Watermelon poisoning," Shula says while reviewing her notes for the cabinet meeting that will begin in minutes—why is a caterer on the list of attendees? "People do eat watermelon from time to time and survive."

"But the children stop eating lunch. Once she puts the watermelon on the table—"

"Mom, don't you read the papers, listen to the radio?"

"Peace, shmeace," her mother says. "In seventy-two years of my life, how many peace conferences have there been?" She pauses for a moment of fraudulent modesty, a family trait: her late husband carried a hard hat with him a full thirty years after he had mixed his last bag of cement. He asked to be buried with it. "But what do I know? You're the prime minister."

"I am indeed the prime minister, and just between you and me and the rest of the world, a happy one at the moment. Mama, this could be real." Shula will not say more. Not even to her mother. Considering her mother's inability to keep secrets, especially not to her mother.

"From your mouth to God's ear."

"Let's hope She has one," Shula says.

This passes over her mother's head. For years, the leading columnist at an opposition newspaper has signed off his column with, "And Shula speaketh to God, and God answereth, because Shula speaketh only to herself." Nevertheless, Shula has a talent for political jiu jitsu, taking criticism head on and using it against her political rivals. When accused of being a person of privilege, Shula countered that this gave her no reason to take bribes. Still, the last thing she needs is an opposition party at home.

"Mama, you're right to worry about the watermelon. Just make sure they do their homework."

"Why bother?" her mother answers. "They're like you. Five minutes after they return from school, it's done."

A caterer. The press would have a field day with that. SHULA'S LIFE IS A CABARET! or CUTS FOR THE POOR, CUTLETS FOR SHULA! A caterer in the cabinet room? Once that is known, the whole world will know negotiations have not simply begun, but have been concluded—with festivities. The secret will be out. As agreed all around, the US president is to have the honor of making the formal announcement, and—at least domestically—taking the credit in an election year. If he is cheated of that, there will be hell to pay.

A caterer, Shula thinks. *I will have someone's head.*

4

THE BUILDING MAJOR GENERAL Dareh Niroomad enters, calmly smoking a Havana—he favors the Rothschild Magnum, but cigars with Jewish names are out of favor in Tehran, so this one is a Montecristo which, the general knows, because of its last two syllables, might soon come under similar prohibition—is faced with huge painted banners of the mullahs who rule Iran. Whether protectively or threateningly, take your pick, they look down on a fleet of black Land Rovers carrying the raised-rifle logo of the Revolutionary Guard, the most politically reliable force in the Iranian military, and the institutionalized motto of the Guard: *Allahu Akbar*, God is Great.

For Niroomad, all this God stuff is something of a bad joke, but he long ago came to terms with the zaniness of the theological-political echelon. Like his father, who perished leading an infantry division in the Great War of Defense—what the West calls the Iran-Iraq War of 1980-88—he is prepared to die for his country, and to kill for it, but not to take seriously the sulfurous mouthings of the fools and brigands who run it. If the Shah manipulated Iranian nationalism to torture and imprison his own people, the mullahs manipulate religion to do the same. To Niroomad, it hardly matters: whether under a crown or a turban, the clowns decide and the military executes. That is all of it.

As the elevator descends, carrying the general and his staff—all of them wearing the sunglasses that have come to be as much part of the uniform as epaulets and insignia of rank—to a secret war room that even some of the ruling mullahs do not know exists, Niroomad feels the old excitement rising within him. The deeper they descend, the more intense his excitement. This is what he was trained for and what he has worked toward for almost a year. On the elevator wall, a panel of lights winks from white to coral to pink to red. Four stories underground, the elevator doors open to reveal the future of the Middle East.

5

IN THE MAIN SALON of a fifty-two-foot Hatteras yacht moored at the end of a long pier in the Tel Aviv marina, Misha Shulman wears what is in effect his professional uniform of too-tight black silk shirt, long sleeves in the Israeli style rolled up over arms rippling with muscle, his trousers shot through with silver thread, his shoes pointy-toed and Italian, around his neck a gold chain so heavy gravity keeps it from shifting as he moves. In Shulman's hand is a gold-plated CZ .40-caliber semiautomatic pistol whose extended double-stack custom magazine holds twenty-two rounds. This weapon he does not hold to the head of the man tied to the chair in the center of the yacht's salon so much as he gesticulates with it as though it is a laser pointer and he a teacher in a class of idiots, each articulation yet another threat.

The man tied to the chair is Alon Peri, at forty-five the same age as his captor, sweat pouring down his face like wind-driven rain so that in the harshly air-conditioned cabin he feels it turn almost to ice. Peri is a manufacturer of sophisticated technology, mostly under contract to the Defense Ministry. In size, his factory is tiny compared to the behemoths that make up Israel's arms sector, but he specializes in delicate yet stable fuses and remote triggering devices without which the giants of the industry could not survive. Lately he has developed a line of near-microscopic firing mechanisms for the newest generation of Israeli drones, which permits a reduction in weight, doubling their effective range.

While a dozen of Misha's fellow hoods come and go in the salon, where a smaller group of four is intent on watching a television musical on the high-definition screen, Misha engages Peri in a long, if one-sided, negotiation.

"Mr. Shulman," Peri says, sweating, "I have a board of directors. I just can't say yes or no. It's a corporation."

"Board, shmord—you sell, I buy. It's business."

"Can I be frank?"

"We're friends," Misha offers. "Certainly, we could be."

Peri continues to sweat, the runoff burning his eyes. "Your name can't be anywhere near the deal. Not even a whisper."

"Whispering I can't prevent. It's a small country. Everybody knows everything about everybody. You want to know my shoe size? Ask a taxi driver. When the prime minister gets her period, it's a national day of mourning."

"Mr. Shulman, your name just cannot be in it."

Misha turns to his colleagues, who, as if drawn by invisible strings, turn to him from the television. "Balls the man has. I give him that. Brains, it's an open question."

Eight eyes return to the flatscreen. In many variations, they have seen this before, both on the screen and on the yacht.

"Look, Alon—can I call you Alon?"

"Sure," says the man tied to the chair. "My friends call me Alon."

"I don't come to you like a leech, to draw blood. But as a partner." Misha smiles wide enough to reveal a gold mine in the rear of his mouth—the lowliest Russian dentist knows more about precious metals than any ten jewelers at Tiffany. "Alon, I want to make you money. I want to make us both money. There's nothing wrong with that. Nothing illegal."

The man tied to the chair tries another tack. "Arms have a way of announcing themselves, Mr. Shulman. Every time I want to sell to, let's say, a gray party, the government refers my request to committee. I'm not even sure there is such a committee. At bottom, it's Washington that decides. The Americans don't want to see our technology in the wrong hands."

"Hands they don't control."

"Exactly."

"What you're saying is, me they can't control."

"Exactly exactly."

"True enough. In Russia, they sent me to the gulag for seven years, and still they couldn't control Misha Shulman. From Siberia, I ran everything."

"If I deal with you, someone they've been trying to throw in jail for years, they'll shut me down."

Misha shakes his big head slowly. The heavy gold chain around his neck barely moves. "Whatever happened to capitalism?" he asks.

6

AT PRECISELY THE SAME time, at a Syrian Air Force base so secret even the intelligence arms of the various rebel groups fighting at the country's borders have not so much as a clue it exists, ground crews begin fixing air-to-ground missiles to the undercarriage of sixty-two SU-24 Sukhoi jet fighter-bombers diagonally lined up on the runway like dancers in some lethal corps de ballet.

Because the Sukhoi normally carries fuel for a range of 1700 miles and only some 120 miles round trip will be required for this mission, the Russian-made jets are modified to carry four extra missiles instead.

As the mechanics work, a general in a jeep passes down the line. He is nothing less than the Syrian Air Force chief of staff, thought to have been killed in a rebel suicide raid months earlier. Instead he has been working steadily in secret, totally focused on what he expects will be the capstone of his career. Compared to sending jets to strafe and bomb primitive rebel positions in the eastern hills, this will open for him the doors of paradise, where he will reside in eternal pleasure, to say nothing of assuring his place in the history of military aviation. Not bad for the third son of a grocer in Aleppo.

7

IN HIS STUDY IN a villa in Herzliya Pituach, a beachfront community just north of Tel Aviv that is home to Israel's old wealth—anything over five years qualifies—Yigal Lev, barefoot in pajamas, sits dictating to his secretary, who is nowhere to be seen. In only a few hours, she will transcribe these recordings into letters, emails, and faxes and send them out to Yigal's network of business associates. As he sits in his favorite leather chair, feeling the wetness of the sea air envelope him like a damp blanket, he is blissfully unaware not one of these letters, faxes, and emails will be sent.

Isracorp, which Yigal founded twelve years earlier to coordinate the array of properties he accumulated based on a hunch—that Israel's astoundingly successful high-tech sector would not merely generate fame for its originators but cash they would need to invest—is the country's largest single business. It controls two banks, a shipping company, Israel's second-largest airline, a phosphate mine at the Dead Sea, a boutique hotel chain, and the construction firm rebuilding the country's railroad into a high-speed link that ties together its four largest cities, a nice complement to Isracorp's chain of gas stations. "No bus company is for sale," he was quoted in *Globes*, the Israeli business daily. "Otherwise, we'd have three out of three." Outside the country, Isracorp mines gold in Zambia, grows pineapples in Sri Lanka, assembles cars in Brazil, tractors in Mexico, cell phones in Malaysia. To make this work, Yigal depends on a second hunch, which is that the same skills that created the technology providing key software for Microsoft, Apple, and Google can also provide the management talent for so many disparate companies. Both hunches proved correct.

At forty-six, Yigal Lev is a legend in Israeli business and a major player in the world economy. Unlike others of similar attainment, he prefers to live in the country of his birth, close to his boyhood friends, to the son serving as a young officer in the IDF, to the armored brigade he has commanded for the past ten years, men he loves and trusts, and who feel the same way about him. He has spent most of his military life with these men, starting as a young tank commander in the now obsolete British Centurion.

A model of that tank sits on the bookshelf opposite him the

way another man might have a model of the Ferrari in his garage. Another reminder sits within him: a jagged bit of steel that lodged in his spleen twenty years before when his tank was destroyed around him. After a medic patched him up, he refused to be evacuated to the rear and instead took command of an orphaned Mk I Chariot whose commander had been shot by a Syrian sniper when he got out to take a piss. Over his years in the armored corps, Yigal insisted that every one of his tanks carry sufficient empty canteens.

"Never leave your tin can," he likes to tell his men. "It's all you've got."

These tankists admire and respect him, not because of his career as a tank commander, but because once he briefs them he encourages them to fight as independent units, sometimes as a battalion, sometimes in platoons, and sometimes in individual tanks. Always he trusts the judgment and initiative of his officers, just as he trusts the judgment and initiative of his managers.

Until they fuck up. Then he moves quickly to replace them.

"Business and warfare are alike," he likes to tell his military colleagues, for that—in typical Israeli fashion—is the way he sees them. "Small, smart, and devoted always defeats big, stupid, and indifferent."

Now, unable to sleep, half-glasses perched on his nose as he peruses the emails he was unable to get to during the day, he dictates in a voice that is at once flat and declarative, like a man giving directions to a tourist in a rental car. From time to time, he glances at the wall to his left, opposite the bank of windows looking out at the Mediterranean, which is almost invisible on this moonless night.

"Marcantonio Feretti, Zamoni S.p. A., Milan. Dear Marco. While we have been considering restaurant chains for some time, organizing one in the US out of independent pizzerias strikes me as bold, which I like, potentially profitable, which my investors like, and strikingly perilous, which nobody can like. Yes, branding the neighborhood pizzeria could create a national, even international, chain out of a chaos of small businesses, but three problems must be overcome. One, how precisely to control quality in a business known for cutting corners; two, whether or not Americans or anyone else sees pizza as anything more than a commodity; and three, whether the current suppliers can easily be supplanted. As you know, I'm not above a fight, but I am concerned with whether a fight for control of such a business is worth the trouble. We're still interested in the concept of rolling up independent businesses into a single entity, but I prefer to choose another battleground. With all good wishes, et cetera."

Almost without missing a beat, Yigal goes on to the next.

"Yukio Nasaki, chairman, Doyo Heavy Industries, Tokyo. Esteemed Yuki-san. Thank you for your recent communication regarding a joint venture in the South American market. My colleagues and I see a great deal of merit in both economies of scale and cross marketing. However, Isracorp does not engage in joint ventures in the international business arena. May I suggest that either Doyo buy out Isracorp's investment or that we buy out your own? Considering that the impetus here comes from your side, we at Isracorp would be honored to consider an offer for our facilities in the area. Should that not come to fruition, we would be pleased to make a counteroffer for your own. With all good wishes for future success, et cetera.

"Lawrence K. Stanton, Bloomington Corp., Bloomington Indiana. Make this a fax, the man doesn't read emails. Larry, Isracorp is willing on condition as outlined. Let's meet in Geneva next week and settle it. Yigal. Suzanne, find me a time slot for an hour that's not dinner. The man likes to drink and the evening can go on forever.

"Next. Via email to Sir Charles Murray, chairman, Olnay's Bank, London. Dear Bunny, I share your hopes but not your optimism. Any deal with the Saudis remains dependent on the political outcome. For all we really know, the current noise is merely—"

He looks up. Judy is standing at the door in a pajama top and heels. Lately his wife has taken up the bikini wax, which confuses Yigal because for twenty-two years he has been happy with the look

God gave her. She does not seem to be the same woman.

"—the product of the hopeful imagination of yet another naïve American president. To quote Ronald Reagan, 'Respect them but suspect them.' Let's wait and see." He turns to his wife. "What?"

"My love, you must be the most cynical man in Israel. The whole country is celebrating."

"A bunch of Arabs declare peace? Every time they talk peace, we have a war."

"Wouldn't it be better if Cobi didn't have to be in uniform until he's forty-eight? If you don't?"

"I like being in uniform. Anyway, it's just two more years."

"Two more years of you disappearing and me never knowing if you'll come back. And now it's the same with Cobi."

They are speaking English now. His wife has been an Israeli for more than two decades, but will never be at home in Hebrew. Partially it is his fault, he knows, because his English is solid and always at the ready when she pauses to reach for a word. Often they converse in two languages, he in Hebrew, she in English. And sometimes in a third language. His wife taught him Pig Latin. He took to it immediately, especially in bed.

"Judy, we're not talking wishes. We're talking facts. These people want to kill Jews. They've changed their minds? Good. But you know what the Romans said. *Si vis pacem, para bellum.* If you wish peace..."

"I know, I know: prepare for war. But it's all over CNN. The Arabs are finally ready." She steps into the room. "Esidesbay ichwhay, Iway amway ootay,"[1] she says in Pig Latin, which she taught him early on when she was too shy to tell him what she wanted in English.

"Entay inutesmay. Ogay armway upway ethay edbay."[2]

She moves closer and sits in his lap as she used to do before they were married. "Owhay eedsnay away edbay?"[3]

---

1 "Besides which, I am too."
2 "Ten minutes. Go warm up the bed."
3 "Who needs a bed?"

8

IN A FIVE-STORY HOTEL on a dark side street in the Imbaba quarter of Cairo, far from Egyptian military headquarters and the Israeli operatives who, it is thought, permeate every square meter of the capital, a light flashes briefly from a high window.

Inside, in the war room of Second Division, Special Operations Branch, Lieutenant Colonel Jamil Anwar slaps the face of the young adjutant pulling back the edge of the blackout curtain to peek at the street below.

"Pitiful lump!" the colonel hisses. "Blackout means blackout. Everywhere are Jewish spies."

Though only a colonel, as head of field security for all ground forces of the Egyptian Army, Anwar is one of the most powerful men in Cairo. Modeled on the SS—indeed, founded in the 1950s by German veterans of that organization who had found shelter in the Middle East—the Field Security Office is one of unique prestige and privilege, with the power of immediate arrest and trial of all officers below the rank of major general, and even these may be arrested at any time and the charges against them forwarded to the Grand Military Council. The files of the Field Security Office hold dossiers on every serving officer, up to and including the commanding general.

Col. Anwar's brief is brutally simple: Monitor the activities of all enemies of the state who are in contact with Egyptian enlisted men and officers, all of whom are considered targets of opportunity for the Israeli, American, British, French, German, Chinese, Saudi, and Libyan spies who operate with impunity across Egypt. These are said to work incessantly to listen in on military communications frequencies, photograph military installations, and—most damaging—bribe its underpaid and thus inherently untrustworthy personnel.

Like any good security chief, Col. Anwar often exaggerates the threat of foreign subversion in order to gain leverage for his organization and for himself, but he also knows that the threat, however exaggerated, is real. That is why he set up a war room here, where no one would think to look, and where a curious adjutant peering through a crack in a blackout curtain deserves the back of his hand. If Col. Anwar had his way, the man would be shot, but his adjutant comes from a good family. Besides, the colonel is obese, and the adjutant has been trained to help him into his car, an olive-green 1978 Cadillac Coupe de Ville, without drawing attention to the strenuousness of his efforts.

9

ON THE WESTERN RIDGE overlooking a shallow muddy stream, two months before the winter rains will transform the Jordan for a short while into a rushing river, Lieutenant Cobi Lev, at twenty-one already a three-year veteran of the IDF, stands atop a very nice facsimile of an Israeli-made Chariot tank—the IDF is not about to waste a real tank at this symbolic post—peering through an Israeli-made starlight scope at the nighttime landscape on the opposite bank. The SLS presents a ghostly picture, a kind of X-ray in green and white, but so precise Cobi can make out an owl diving at thirty miles per hour to snatch a field mouse.

On the opposite bank, semi-trailers are lined up on the roadway leading to the Jordanian customs post guarding the approach to the Allenby Bridge—and to Israel, a former enemy state now something less than that, not yet an ally, merely a neighbor. This single-lane commercial link permits dozens of trucks to cross the rickety bridge carrying fruits and vegetables bound for Israel's open-air markets, along with manufactured items, mostly piece goods stitched together in Amman, for export to Europe and the United States through Israel's ports. Jordan has only one seaport, at Aqaba in the south, directly across from the Israeli vacation resort city of Eilat, but that port faces the wrong waterway. To reach Europe, the same goods would have to travel south down the Red Sea, whose mouth is infested with Eritre-an pirates, then north again through the Suez Canal, whose mouth is controlled by Egyptians comfortably ensconced in arguably the world's most expensive toll booth. At the end of this journey of five hundred miles, the shipment would be an hour's drive from the same Allenby Bridge. Through a careful arrangement, Jordan uses the Israeli ports of Haifa and Ashdod as though they are its own—and unless the goods are destined for Israeli consumers, there is no tax.

It is this example that the United States and its fellow peace bro-kers have utilized to convince the Arab League to exchange the bomb for the briefcase.

Cobi's cell phone chimes the opening notes from *Happy Birth-day*, the ringtone a present from his mother the month before.

"Mom," he says. "I told you never to call me at the office."

"I was thinking of you."

"It's four in the morning. You should be sleeping."

"Your father and I were talking. I can't wait until tomorrow to know you're well."

"Do we still have hot water?"

"Hot water?"

"Then I can't wait until tomorrow either. Look, Mom, I really—"

"And with all the good news..."

"What good news?"

"The peace."

"Yeah, well," Cobi says, a twenty-one-year-old trying his best to sound grown-up, which to him means cynical, world-weary—his fa-ther's son. "We'll still need an army."

"But no more war, darling. Think about it."

"Not my job, Mom."

"Stay safe," she tells him. "At the last minute, always at the last minute, boys die. If they don't decide to be heroes, if they can just wait on the sidelines..."

"Love to Dad," Cobi says. He has heard this before.

"I love you."

"I love you too," he says, clicking off. He turns to the radioman squatting next to him, smoking a joint. "I'm here nineteen days. I never saw this many trucks."

"I'm here nineteen months. Jordan Customs opens only six hours a day. They get backed up."

"Still, that's a lot of trucks." He considers letting it slide, then: "Get me HQ."

"We're reporting trucks?"

"Too many trucks."

"Your funeral," the radioman says, drawing in a long toke before he puts through the call.

10

IN THE PASSENGER SEAT of a white Volvo sedan speeding south to Tel Aviv from his home in Caesarea, the ancient port that was at one time the Latin-speaking capital of Roman-ruled Palestine, Lieutenant General Pinchas Harari listens carefully to what is being explained to him on the phone. Harari is one of those officers who refuses to delegate but hates being bothered by details, an impossible contradiction that wears him down and earns his staff sleepless nights. If he were the head of a corporation instead of an army, he would long ago have hired a psychologist to help him resolve this conflict, but as chief of staff of the IDF he has no such luxury. If a secret like that ever got out, it would end his career. His predecessor—the most capable officer of his generation, who liked a drink from time to time—was branded an alcoholic and lost his job as a result.

"Repeat."

General Harari listens even more carefully than before. "Coincidence is not conspiracy," he says. "But I'm on my way. Continue monitoring." To himself he mutters: "Sissies."

"Commander?"

General Harari turns to his driver. "Gingy, I said something to you?"

"I don't know, commander. I thought maybe—"

"How long have you driven for me?"

"Six years, sir. Almost seven."

"In that time, when I gave you an order, did you ever consider I was asking about your taste in ice cream?"

"No, sir."

"In simple Hebrew," the general said, pissed off that they awakened him to leave his soft bed and warm wife to fly on a fool's errand to Israel Defense Forces headquarters in Tel Aviv before four in the morning. He has no one to scold but his driver. "When I have something to tell you, you'll know it."

"I understand, commander."

"And stop calling me commander."

"Sorry, Pinky," the driver says. "Pinky, it's just when you're in a mood, it puts me on edge."

"How the hell do you think it makes me feel?" the general asks. "Interrupted sleep, it's part of my job." He laughs despite himself. "Yours too. Forgive me, Gingy. It seems in the entire IDF, bristling with communications devices and computers and who knows what more, no one has bothered to read the papers."

"The papers?"

"The papers. Everyone knows we're on the verge of peace."

"That's what they say, Pinky."

"That's what they say, Gingy. That's what they say."

11

AT A ROYAL JORDANIAN tank base only fifteen miles from the Israeli border, which has been quiet for decades, a military band plays Arab martial music, replete with bagpipes—the effect approximates dozens of cats being strangled by uniformed sadists—as Royal Jordanian Army Major General Tawfik Ali, standing in the rear of an open 1956 Rolls Royce Silver Wraith, takes the salute of his tank crews standing at attention before an endless row of Challengers. The rumbling of the powerful 1200-horsepower diesel engines mixes in the night air with the screeching of the military band to create a musical miasma, a symphonic swamp so murky that any hint of melody is lost in the noise.

General Ali feels at home with this noise. His family estate in the Scottish lowlands was itself awash in the sound of bagpipes, and this continued through his education at Sandhurst, where generations of British officers are trained in the art of warfare to the sound of pipes. There he was known as Twyford (Ticky) Oliver, second son of Baron Allmond of Cleave. As with many British noble families— Lord Allmond was born twenty-third in line of succession to the throne—the non-inheriting sons found careers in the foreign office, the clandestine services, or the military. It was Ticky Oliver's fate to be employed by all three. Simultaneously. Having gone out to the Hashemite Kingdom of Jordan to train and then build up the Royal Jordanian Armoured Corps, then Col. Oliver grew close to the late King Hussein, a tank buff of the first water. When the little king wasn't flying military jets, he was playing with his tanks as though they were toys in a sandbox.

One day during maneuvers, His Majesty made the young colonel an offer of no small consequence. Should the Scotsman convert to Islam, he would be given lifetime command of an armored force equal in vehicular strength to half the British tank corps, in effect becoming what he had been robbed of at home by an accident of birth: a baron, not of nobility but of firepower.

The young colonel begged leave to consult with Whitehall. The Foreign Office saw a nice opportunity to regain influence in the Middle East, to say nothing of huge armaments sales to the Hashemite Kingdom. Whitehall passed Col. Oliver to MI6. Ticky now had three masters, as a result of which, like anyone with three masters, he was his own man.

Now pushing seventy, Tawfik Ali is well prepared to unleash upon an unsuspecting enemy the full force of his devoted armored corps, whose Bedouin tank commanders are as loyal to the major general as to the king himself. But unlike the men under his command, who love him for having embraced Islam, he has never been comfortable with its ingrained hatred of the Jews, nor does he share the British nobility's disdain for the Hebrew race: his roommate and best friend at Sandhurst had in fact been one Puffy Bornshtain.

In truth, it hardly matters to Major General Tawfik Ali whether the opposing army is commanded by Jews, Iraqis, or Martians—only that there is a designated enemy, a military target marked for destruction. This is business.

12

IN A LONG DRAINAGE ditch within sight of hundreds of IDF jets on the tarmac of the military field adjacent to Ben-Gurion Airport, sixty Hamas commandos crouch and wait. Though Shia Iran's military planners see no future for Hamas, whose members are Sunni and Palestinian, and thus doubly irredeemable, these fighters will play a key role in the coming battle to liberate the holy land.

A day earlier, three trucks painted in IDF colors and bearing IDF license plates crossed beneath the sand dunes from Gaza, which Hamas controls, into Israel proper. The half mile of paved tunneling that permitted this took almost a year to construct. Working at night under the very eyes of the Israelis, Hamas removed tons of sand—a good deal of it in buckets—until they got earthmoving equipment into the tunnel to create a sub-rosa highway just big enough for Ford F-150 half-ton trucks. Though Iranian engineers planned and supervised the operation, there was no question in the eyes of the Hamas leadership that the terror organization would later be seen as key to the success of the entire war. They would be wrong. None of the states involved—Egypt, Syria, Jordan, nor Iran—turned out willing to see a Palestinian state emerge in what they were already calling "Former Israel." In every detail of post-war planning was embedded the unspoken message "Fuck the Palestinians."

But at this stage, the Palestinians are needed. No other fighting force can provide the Hebrew speakers necessary to get through a dozen roadblocks. Most members of this force are graduates of Israeli security prisons, some specially trained by diction coaches in the art of sounding like native-born Israelis (because there is no *p* in Arabic, the students are trained not to use words like *papa*, which would come out *baba*). Some have been trained to speak Hebrew with French or English or Russian accents, as would any group of IDF soldiers. A dozen, Circassians, are blond and blue-eyed. Their uniforms, down to the hand-painted slogans on their helmets and the mud on their brown paratrooper boots, are IDF issue, stolen by Bedouins from army bases in the Negev. For this one performance, they have been rehearsing six months, speaking only Hebrew. Should one unlucky commando fall out of a truck, he will not give the others away. Even the cigarettes in their placket pockets are Israeli. The bandages in their medics' pouches are marked MADE IN ISRAEL. The orders their commanders carry are beautifully forged IDF documents. They are perfect replicas of Israeli paratroopers moving in perfect replicas of Israeli military trucks through a very real and very vulnerable Israel.

Having taken up position in the drainage ditches surrounding this Israel Air Force facility, like similar infiltrating forces in place at four other airfields, they appear to be IDF infantry in protective posture, their backs to the F-16s arrayed in ready formation.

At precisely 3:55 a.m., the darkest moment of the night, they turn around and train their weapons on the planes. A phalanx of

TOW missiles sails through the air. At each airfield, the tarmac is a sheet of flames.

The Israel Air Force is no more.

13

IN HIS TEHRAN WAR room four stories underground, General Niroomad watches on the wall of screens as an orbiting Iranian satellite transmits real-time video of Israel's F-16s burning on the ground.

He turns to his operations officer and gives the command. "Launch air."

14

SIX SECONDS NORTHEAST OF Jerusalem, twenty-eight Sukhoi SU-24s fly low in broken formation to avoid Israeli radar. This close to target, it will hardly matter. Israeli countermeasures are already compromised. The Syrian and Iranian pilots own the skies. According to plan and confirmed by Iranian reconnaissance, the IDF ground-to-air shield is all but destroyed. Because the enemy planes fly low, what is left of Israel's heat-seeking rocket capability must arc *down* from 20,000 feet to as low as one thousand. Of this they are capable. But Syria's Russian military advisors, sitting safely in the Caucasus just over the Turkish border, have launched a miasma of heat-producing Yakovlev Pchela drones. As predicted by the theorists in the Nikolai Zhukovsky Air Force Engineering Academy, the Israeli missiles home in on the drones. The Russians call them flying hair dryers. All twenty-eight Sukhois penetrate Israeli air space as though it is undefended.

Which it is.

At this point radio silence is no longer necessary.

The mission's commander opens communication. "Chief to all Indians," he says, first in Arabic and then in Persian, which phrase he has memorized. "We have penetration. Combine to wing."

For answer, twenty-seven pilots press their speak buttons and howl like wolves. The pilots call their unit the Wolf Pack. The planes move off their random positions and reform behind the lead aircraft, a scattered flock of geese that becomes a series of straight lines and then a wing. And then a flying wedge.

"Chief to all Indians, home in on Buffalo."

As one, each of the pilots logs onto his GPS-based mission profile. Each device holds the coordinates for preselected targets. Except for Israel Police headquarters in Sheikh Jarrah, all are in West Jerusalem: the Knesset, the Prime Minister's Office, the Defense, Interior, Justice, and lesser ministries, Israel State Television and Radio, the headquarters of a number of specialized security services, secondary military installations on the perimeter, Jerusalem's Mahaneh Yehuda fruit and vegetable market, and certain symbolic sites, such as the Israel Museum, the Yad VaShem Holocaust Memorial, the Central Synagogue. The entirety of mostly Arab East Jerusalem, including the Old City, is spared, the Jewish and Armenian quarters to be dealt with later, along with the remaining Western Wall of the Holy Temple, Judaism's holiest site. To attack these targets from the air would risk damaging the Sacred Precinct, the tel upon which is built the Dome of the Rock and the Mosque of Omar, under which lie the ruins of the Holy Temple itself, which according to Islamicist propaganda never existed.

Wolf Pack's commander need hardly remind his pilots to limit their depredations to their designated targets. The Sukhois carry just enough destructive material to do the job. But he makes sure. "My Indians, avoid the railroad lines and bus station, and protect our holy places. Good hunting! God is great!"

15

DANCING WITH GAY MEN is not Alex's preference. But with women there was a problem. Alex had had a few girlfriends, but in man-short Israel—emigration and war tends to thin out the number of available males—even the most desperate women are not that desperate. Alex's sexual orientation simply does not correlate with his sartorial preferences. Neither is cavorting on the dance floor with straight men an option. What straight men seek Alex cannot supply. Nor can he take to the dance floor in lesbian bars. The bulge in his pants tends to give him away. Surprise: lesbians are not interested in straight men disguised as women. So when he wishes to dance as a woman he is all but compelled to dance with gay men, which is what he is doing at a beachfront bar called Ema, Hebrew for mother.

On this particular evening, the hunk Alex dances with follows her back to where she has left her drink and places a large hand around her waist where a bustier just covers her navel. With her own equally large hand, she brushes it away.

"You don't find me attractive?" the hunk asks. Clearly unaccustomed to resistance, even in Dutch-accented English his tone reveals equal parts disappointment, resentment, and shock.

"I'm sure you're a nice person," Alex answers, her voice dropping an octave. Sometimes this works.

The hunk persists.

"I don't think you get it," Alex says. "I'm not into men."

"It's a gay bar," the hunk says, not without reason.

"Anyway, I have to be in uniform in three hours."

The Dutchman's eyes light up. Apparently he likes uniforms. "You're military?"

One thing about hunks, Alex thinks: if they ever had brains, these early on atrophied from disuse. She is beginning to realize she may have to clock him. "Isn't everyone?"

The hunk leans forward but stops suddenly, as if pulled back on a string. In this he is no different from everyone else in the bar. The pulsating music, the lights, the movement all seem to pause.

Sirens at this hour can mean only one thing.

Within seconds, the bar is deserted as its customers scramble for the exits, find their vehicles, and take off to report to their units.

16

OUTSIDE ON THE PROMENADE, the dog walkers, prostitutes, elderly couples taking the cool evening air, lovers smoking grass and off-duty soldiers of both genders—in fact, everyone but the confused tourists, who have no idea what is happening around them—*to* them—disappear as if plucked by an invisible hand. But as the sirens continue their incessant bleating even the tourists get the message and hurry back to the shelter of their hotels, but here too there is no one to tell them what precisely is going on. Doormen, desk clerks, bartenders, chamber maids are all gone, vanished as if they never were. For fear of reprisals, even the Arab workers are gone.

17

IN THE MASTER BEDROOM of the White House, the president, a slick cracker who has spent his entire political career decrying the same "pointy-headed intellectuals" who, at Harvard and then Yale Law, taught him much of what he knows about the intricacies of the American election process (except how to get around it, which he learned as a congressman), stops doing what he is doing while the First Lady, her head all but shaved in order to accommodate the wigs she wears as a matter of course, keeps on doing it. The president's bed continues to creak as she works harder to convince him in the only way she knows to ignore the bedside phone with the unique ring: the Star Spangled Banner in blues tempo.

"Dwayne, honey, don't you dare answer that." It is half demand, half plea.

The leader of the free world rolls off. "Hon," he grunts. "This one I got to."

18

THE WHITE HOUSE SITUATION Room sits in a bunker whose thirty-inch thick ceiling is fifty feet underground. Guarded by a special detail of Secret Service personnel known as the Paleface Squad because they never see daylight, it is able to function for two weeks without outside power and is supplied with richly oxygenated air, highly filtered water, and sufficient vitamin-enriched food for thirty-six designated individuals whose idea of roughing it is a four-star, not a five-star, hotel.

No matter what hell is breaking loose above ground, if you are not on that list you do not get in. Among those on the list are Admiral Brent Staley, chairman of the Joint Chiefs of Staff, at sixty-five about to be retired; Prof. Felix St. George, the Hungarian-born foreign policy guru to four presidents, a seemingly ageless hard-head who—having studied under Henry Kissinger at Harvard—has never seen a stable dictator he doesn't like; and Flo Spier, the president's thirty-eight-year-old domestic policy advisor, a specialist in assessing the internal political implications of foreign policy decisions whose impact the generals and statesmen surrounding the president tend to ignore. As one political columnist famously put it: "Here's why the US will never go to war with Poland: Even if Prof. St. George thinks it's in the best strategic interests of the US and Admiral Staley gives it every chance for success, Flo Spier—upon careful consideration of the Polish-American vote in Chicago—will kill the idea as dead as a swatted housefly."

The president's face is expressionless as he walks in wearing a silk robe with the presidential seal over where most people have a heart. All stand. Admiral Staley salutes his commander in chief, never a tradition outside of ceremonial occasions but the kind of ass-kissing the president normally cannot get enough of. He returns the salute by touching his right forefinger to his brow. "Folks, I hope y'all are aware this is my date night. The First Lady and I get one a week. So I got to assume this is important?"

Admiral Staley takes the point, and the point position. He is a military man. "Mr. President, I do apologize for interrupting your—"

"Just get to it."

Staley removes his rimless glasses, which causes him to look younger, somewhat innocent, perhaps over his head. He was not the president's first choice for the job, and he knows it. The admiral has been playing catch-up ever since. "Sir, DIA is picking up unusual activity in the Sand Box. At the same time, other agencies..."

St. George runs his hand over his shaved scalp, perhaps a vestige of the time he had hair. "Central Intelligence, sir, has reason to believe locations critical to operations of the Revolutionary Guard—"

"Iran? We were just in the Sand Box."

"Indeed, sir," St. George says. "We've been monitoring transmissions between Tehran and Damascus, also Tehran-Cairo, Tehran-Amman, Tehran-Baghdad. In other words, Tehran and every major player, including Hezbollah in Lebanon and Hamas in Gaza."

"What are they saying, how's your mom? Get to it, Felix."

"Mr. President, as yet..."

The president's face is no longer expressionless. "You don't know what they've been saying and you got me out of bed?"

The guru persists. He is known for it. "Sir, we do know coded traffic has been rising over the last two months. This week it's intensified."

"Yes?"

"Yesterday it reached a crescendo, sir."

The president is not happy. These people never get to the point. "What does that mean, music? Guys, I get one early night a week."

At this point Felix St. George displays an impatience of his own. He knows he can get away with it. He learned that much from Kissinger: when dealing with the leader of the free world, show no fear. "Mr. President, all messaging has stopped. Total silence. At the same time, the general staffs of the Revolutionary Guard and the military leadership in Syria, Egypt, Iraq, and Jordan are not in their beds. Ditto Hamas and Hezbollah."

The president considers. "The Israelis?"

"Minutes ago, Israel station clocked IDF Chief of Staff leaving home. In a hurry."

"Mobilization?"

"Not yet," Admiral Staley breaks in. When it comes to military matters, he is not going to play second fiddle to some over-educated Hungarian who wore a uniform only when he was a child; in Admiral Staley's mind, the striped pajamas of Bergen-Belsen don't count, especially since when he came to the US St. George changed his name to suit his new religion. "But if they're seeing what we are, you can bet on it."

"Are they seeing what we are?"

"Impossible to say, Mr. President."

"Well, at the risk of asking the goddamn obvious, has anyone informed them?"

The silence that ensues seems to last minutes, but it is only a matter of seconds.

"Flo," the president says. "You hear that? In an election year."

"We can turn this around, Mr. President," Flo says in a voice as raspy as a nail file. "But not in a vacuum."

"I hear you, Flo," the president says. "I hear you loud and clear. Now, will someone get that Israeli bitch on the phone?"

19

THE PRIME MINISTER IS deeply asleep when the red phone on her night table rings with its special buzz of angry bees. It is only minutes since Israel's air force has been destroyed. She turns on the light to check her face in the hand mirror before picking up the receiver, thinking: *Good the man can't see me. I look like hell.* "Good evening, Mr. President," she says brightly, an acquired skill. After all, it is only 9 p.m. in Washington. "I must say this is an unexpected pleasure." *At 4 a.m. it would be*, she thinks. But it wouldn't be a precedent. When first in office, she got a call at 2 a.m. wishing her a happy Yom Kippur. What was she supposed to do, lecture the leader of the free world on the solemn significance of Judaism's principle day of mourning? *Was there no Jew on the White House staff aside from that horrid Flo Spier?*

"Madam Prime Minister, if this call is truly unexpected, it might not be a real big pleasure."

Absurdly she thinks, *It's not my birthday, is it?* She has just been awakened from a deep and peaceful sleep. She switches into what she thinks of as Amerispeak, a form of discourse that reflexively puts the spotlight on the other person, *his* life, *his* interests, *his* needs. "Mr. President," she says. "If there is anything my government can do, please let me know."

The president's voice takes on the dramatic timbre that got him elected, and may again. "Madam, according to our sources, still unconfirmed—"

A tremendous explosion rocks the building, then in rapid succession six more, the last of which blows in the windowpanes, fragments flying into the room like shrapnel. A two-inch shard slices into her arm. Shula rushes to the window. She is thinking of the children, upstairs with her mother. What she sees causes her heart to stop.

Lit by exploding bombs, a cloud of black-clad paratroopers fills the sky. Even on this moonless night, she has no trouble seeing them. The sky over Jerusalem is on fire.

With her heart now pumping so hard she can feel it, Shula picks up the white phone, which is attended twenty-fours a day by a security liaison in the basement. The system was established by her predecessor, who proudly showed it off when he walked her through the prime ministerial residence. In its weekly tests it always operates faultlessly, connecting her at once with the IDF chief of staff, the chief commissioner of the Israel Police, and the heads of the Mossad and Shabak, which correspond roughly to the CIA and the FBI respectively. In addition, there is an optional link to the head of the Israel Broadcast Authority, so that if need be she can address the nation from her bedroom or kitchen, or toilet. In every case, should the primary contact be unreachable, a connection is made immediately to his second in command. In test mode, the system never failed.

Now all she has is a mild and distant static.

She moves to her personal cell phone, where the same numbers are on autodial. Silence.

20

IN THE WHITE VOLVO flying south down the near empty coastal highway, the chief of staff reaches for his cellphone at the precise moment he sees the southeastern sky light up as though it is Independence Day. Later he will not be certain the phone rang at all. He may have picked it up to call headquarters. Or perhaps they were calling him.

"Skull Prime here. Report." He listens, then responds. "Code blue. Repeat: code blue." He turns to his driver. "Gingy, drive like your life depends on it."

The driver floors it.

"Because it does."

21

On his fifty-two-foot Hatteras in the marina at Tel Aviv, Misha Shulman is not happy. This Alon Peri is being stubborn. *I could pick up his family, his wife, his children,* Misha thinks. *Or bomb his factory. Or drug him and have pictures taken that would ruin his life.* None of these is appealing. Misha has given up this kind of thing, the way he has given up dealing in prostitutes. He sees himself these days as a legitimate businessman with the misfortune of having started out as a criminal. In Russia, what other choice did he have? He had no rich father—in fact, he had no father at all. His mother died when he was twelve. For three years he lived on the streets of Moscow like a feral dog, eating garbage, selling his body, dealing in drugs until he was able to buy himself shelter in an abandoned warehouse near the Promzona metro station, and then to acquire a car—a Moskvich: only sixty-eight horsepower, but not many seventeen-year-olds in Russia drove a car—all the while putting together a group of young thugs who like him had no place in the new Russia. In the old Russia, under the Communists, he would have been sent to an institute for wayward youth, forced to listen to endless lectures on the evils of capitalism, and in so doing at least avoided hunger. But the new Russia offered a different kind of education.

By the time he was twenty, Misha Shulman was known as Big Misha. He controlled dozens of street prostitutes and a handful of better-quality escorts who serviced the new capitalists of Moscow, along with diplomats and foreign visitors. He had connections with the Georgian mafia and the opium growers of Tashkent. In the power vacuum that was the new Russia, Misha Shulman was a power. Until the bureaucrats tracked him down and demanded a piece of the action.

When he refused, a smirking judge sent him to the same gulag that had existed since the time of the czars, a prison stockade in Siberia whose name was a number and whose infamy was legend. There, despite his reputation, or more properly because of it, the guards organized their favored trustees to teach him a lesson.

Instead Misha taught them. Within a month he was on top again, running the prison, and within a year was directing his Moscow operation via remote control, using the guards and their families to send and receive messages. In three years, through the influence of lawyers delivering bags of cash to the same bureaucrats who had imprisoned him, he was out.

On one condition. He would have to leave the country.

An unlikely Zionist, Misha found himself in a Tel Aviv that was not so different from Moscow. A million and a half Russians had emigrated to Israel during his years as Big Misha and his exile in Siberia. He did not know the names of these new Israelis, but they knew his.

"Alon Peri," Misha says. "How would you like if I break your legs?" Before Peri has a chance to consider this offer, Misha sighs dramatically. "Ah," he says. "That was the old Misha Shulman. Now and again he pops up and wants to beat the shit out of somebody."

"Mr. Shulman," Peri says from his chair. "You have no idea how—"

When silence becomes a noise it can be very loud. The TV music has stopped, the screen blank. The four musclemen watching it look abruptly to Misha, but he is looking to the TV, as if in anticipation. The television issues three long beeps.

The angst-ridden face of a familiar news reader comes on. "We interrupt our regularly scheduled programming for the following public service announcements." Then, reading from a list, he carefully enunciates: "Tired Toe; Blue Ears; Rusty Knees; White Eyes..."

Misha rises. "That's me."

One of his crew shakes his head. "Misha, it's just a drill."

"At 4 a.m.? They don't do drills when everyone is sleeping."

As the news reader continues to read code names for IDF units, a siren goes off.

"Ladies, go to your units." Deftly, almost magically, a knife replaces the gun in Misha's hand. He approaches the man tied in the chair. "Alon Peri, you too," he says as he slices through the ropes. "Looks like we're partners after all."

22

DETERMINED TO AVOID THE central strategic miscalculation of what the Jews call the Yom Kippur War and the Arabs call the Ramadan War, the planners in Iran early on discovered they must choose from two modes of attack. In 1973, the armies of Egypt, Syria, and Iraq, together with contingents from Saudi Arabia, Kuwait, Libya, Algeria, Tunisia, Pakistan, Sudan, Cuba, and North Korea, converged on Israel on the holiest day of the Jewish year, when all shops, offices, and businesses were closed, most of the population was fasting at home or in the synagogue, the country's well-organized bus system closed down, its trains sat in their marshaling yards and no vehicular traffic was on the roadways. On this day even Israeli Arabs made sure not to drive, at least not through Jewish neighborhoods. The IDF whittled itself down to a skeleton force as soldiers and reservists found their way to a day of fasting, prayer and reflection at home.

On any other day, the reservists who make up the bulk of Israel's armed forces would have been scattered and the roads so congested with traffic it would have taken hours for pilots to reach their planes, tank crews their tanks, sailors their vessels. Israel's telephone system would already have been at peak capacity. The extra usage as parents called their children, as officers and enlisted personnel called their units, would have turned the national communications grid into one long busy signal.

Instead, when the sirens went off on Yom Kippur, there was not a man, woman, or child in Israel who thought it might be a drill. Phone calls were put through immediately. Reservists drove on near-deserted roads at one hundred miles an hour to reach their bases. Tanks and military vehicles used the same wide-open roads to meet the enemy attack and hold it until the reserves arrived to back them up. Were it not for the strategic blunder of an attack on the least effective day of the year, Israel might well have been destroyed in 1973.

General Niroomad's planners spent months dissecting that day. They concluded that only two modes of approach were possible: a daylight attack that would have the Israel war machine tied up in traffic jams, or a nighttime attack benefiting from surprise. In the end the element of surprise, supported by fifth columnists to neutralize the Israel Air Force, won out. But the Iranians knew a night attack would find resistance from the Muslim armies: by tradition or preference or just fear of the dark, Arabs had never favored fighting at night. Even T.E. Lawrence could not convince his faithful Bedouins to attack before dawn.

Recognizing this lapse, during the British Mandate an officer in His Majesty's forces sympathetic to the Jewish cause organized the first Jewish commando since the days of the Maccabees. Major Orde Wingate knew what he was doing when he called his outfit the Special Night Squads. In Israel's War of Independence, IDF units became adept at taking back during the night what had been lost to overwhelming Arab forces during the day. But now the Iranians had a solution: the starlight scope, which sucks in available ambient light from even a moonless night and concentrates it to create a ghostly green-tinged image of what cannot be seen with the naked eye.

Armed with the SLS, not only Arab officers but entire units could proceed as though in daylight. SLS devices could be mounted in Egyptian, Iraqi, Syrian, and Jordanian tanks, on sniper rifles, on mobile artillery, even on trucks and armored personnel carriers. The question was: where could these instruments be obtained in massive numbers?

Though the West maintains constant satellite surveillance of the arms factories of the People's Republic of China, no Western nation bothers monitoring the center of optics manufacture at Wuhan in Hubei Province—who cares if the Chinese are suddenly a good deal more myopic? In return for the usual guarantees of access to Middle

East oil, China provided Iran, and through Iran the Arab armies, with a secret weapon that was hardly secret. SLS devices had been part of every armed conflict since the Vietnam War, but they had never been used strategically.

Now the Arabs are no longer afraid of the dark. What does it matter if the IDF is better trained, better organized, and more intensely motivated than any fighting force in history? Compared to his enemy, the Israeli soldier is blind.

23

THIS DISADVANTAGE IS NOT known to the IDF command as 200,000 Israelis, men and women up to the age of fifty-five, fathers and sons and mothers and daughters, are called to duty. There is no warning: the sirens go off in the cities at the same time as the population hears, sees, and feels the sound and fury of a military attack already in progress.

The primary target is Jerusalem, the seat of Israel's government, where the first assault is from the air. A second wave of bombing very quickly arrives at Haifa and Beersheba, the country's third and fourth most populous cities. Aside from carefully chosen targets—the IDF's headquarters at the Kirya, the Mossad's operations center in the northern suburbs, and the municipality building on Ibn-Gvirol Street—Tel Aviv is studiously ignored.

Because it is barely touched by aerial attack and has no tanks and infantry at its gates, Israel's first city responds by the book. Municipal buses make for designated staging areas where they will be filled with reservists to be delivered to their bases, from which they will move as units to the front; police are issued automatic weapons and take to the streets directing headlong traffic traveling without headlights on roads whose lighting is snuffed out; doctors and nurses not in the reserves make for emergency rooms at nearby hospitals, where generators are readied and marginal patients are sent home to make room for a flood of wounded; gas stations are reopened in the middle of the night; the population is warned via television, radio, and loudspeaker to enter the shelters below every apartment house or the hardened concrete rooms in every private residence, to black out all windows, and to make sure that everyone remembers to have his gas mask within reach.

While the rest of the country reels in confusion and shock, Tel Aviv is awake and responsive.

Right off the beach promenade at the gay nightclub called Ema, the strobe lights continue turning above the abandoned dance floor, drinks stand unfinished on tables, high-decibel recorded music pounds a room empty but for the odd cigarette burning down in an ashtray.

At the nearby marina, the fifty-two-foot Hatteras bobs peacefully at its mooring at the end of a long dock, its lights out, television silent. Boats of all kinds remain tied up, except for a few powerful vessels owned by visiting yachtsmen, who decide to take their chances on the seaway to Cyprus, 230 miles distant.

And in a villa in Herzlia Pituach, seven miles up the coast, a forty-six-year-old industrialist ceases making love to the wife whose passion for him has reignited now that their son is out of the house. As the sirens go off, Yigal Lev reaches for the television remote, sees the face of a somber newscaster before an image of the national flag, and moves immediately to pull his uniform from its special place in the closet. As he straps on his sidearm, he hears his wife whisper their son's name.

He takes her in his arms long enough to tell her, "Cobi will be fine." And then, like two hundred thousand other Israelis, Yigal Lev is gone into the night.

24

IN THE WAR ROOM of the Revolutionary Guard, an eerie silence pervades the subterranean space, a silence underscored by the cricket-like keystrokes of ninety intelligence officers bent over their computers before a display wall of coordinated monitors that can show a dozen scenes or be united to display a single image. Right now that image is Jerusalem, burning.

General Niroomad puffs on his second Montecristo. "Knesset," he says to his technical assistant, a captain trained at Caltech.

The giant image zooms down to show a building destroyed, smoke rising above it in a black column. Earmarked as a prime target, the Israeli parliament has been destroyed not because its legislators might be in the plenum at four in the morning, but because of its symbolic significance, both to the Muslim attackers and the Jews.

"Haifa."

Built along the sides of Mount Carmel as it flows liquid-like down to the enormous cranes of the container port at its base, the city is aflame. In the harbor, two dozen commercial ships list, some already half-sunk. Farther north, thirty-two IDF Navy missile boats burn in the harbor.

"Tel Aviv."

Here the picture is different. Because only a few specific sites have been targeted, the city appears as peaceful as it should be this early in the morning, though traffic—running without headlights—has begun to move in the darkened streets

"Airbases."

The single tiled-together screen devolves into twelve separate images, under which like subtitles in a foreign-language movie are the airbase names in Farsi. Except for these, each screen shows the same scene: IAF aircraft in flames, the tarmac beneath them itself a sea of fire. Here and there explosions erupt as fuel dumps ignite, making the screens go white, momentarily overwhelming the automated lighting adjustments of the satellite cameras.

General Niroomad carefully drops a half inch of ash into a crystal ashtray engraved with the seal of the Revolutionary Guard. So quietly only his adjutant can hear, he says what he has been longing to say for a year.

"Commence ground."

25

COBI'S RADIOMAN CLIMBS DOWN off the tank to take a leak. For fear of angering the tank gods, no armored corps soldier will ever piss off the top of a tank, even a dummy tank. The radioman may not be a gung-ho soldier but he knows enough not to do that. He leaves the radio with Cobi.

There are now lights on the other side of the Jordan.

From his position standing atop the tank, Cobi lets his SLS drop down from the strap around his neck, as though somehow what the instrument tells him is false and he must see it for himself, through his own eyes. The far bank is now so well lit he does not need the night-vision device. Before him, a giant operation is in process, one which will change his life and those of six million other Israelis.

And, eventually, alter the world balance of power.

As if they are all controlled by the same switch, the steel rear doors on a hundred tractor-trailers crank open. This takes all of thirty seconds, but to Cobi it seems like an hour, not least because he cannot figure out what he is seeing, or even that he is seeing it. The rear doors on a hundred tractor-trailers are not supposed to be opening simultaneously at four in the morning on the Jordanian side of the Allenby Bridge.

But they are.

They remain open long enough for the young lieutenant to realize that what he is seeing is not only real but unaccountable. He checks his watch so that when he gets to company headquarters later in the morning, he will be able to make a precise report before setting off on his way to three complete days of leave, starting with a shower so long and so hot the water in his home's solar boiler will begin running cold, and then a nice meal with his mother—he is partial to her macaroni and cheese, and she adores him for it, even if he does ruin the subtlety of her recipe with ketchup. Then he plans to go down to the beach, swim out a couple of hundred feet before returning to the sand to check out the girls. His father will be home by the time he rinses the sand off in the outdoor shower by the pool. His dad always comes home early when Cobi gets leave. The two will talk tanks for a while, which will almost certainly lead to his father asking him about the future: what does he really, really want to do? There is a certain inevitability in his going to work for his father's huge enterprise, but like all Israelis who are conscripted into the military upon graduation from high school, Cobi faces beginning university at twenty-one or twenty-two, with three years ahead of him just to get his bachelor's degree, and then maybe business school or law school or something he can't know now, some mysteriously hazy and possibly dreary profession. Or he could stay in the military and take his degree as an officer, with any luck reaching his father's reserve rank of major before he is thirty, and after that—

Abruptly this reverie is shattered. *Bats? Bats in trucks?* Then: *A thousand bats with buzzing motors?*

He sees them, but doesn't believe what he sees until one drone peels off, making straight for his tank, a dummy but a convincing one.

26

HEADING NORTH ON THE coastal road, traffic thickening around him as more reservists head for their units, Cobi's father shoots the BMW sedan to 130, then 140 miles per hour. As he drives, Yigal buttons his uniform shirt, then slips on his dog tag in its leather pouch, which most Israeli soldiers wear so that the metal won't reflect light.

His pistol is on the passenger seat. All of this he keeps prepared: his field uniform hanging in the closet, IDF identification card in the placket pocket over his heart, a ballpoint pen and a yellow map marker in the right-hand pocket, along with a tiny steel jar, not much bigger than a thimble, in which he keeps the present his own father gave him on his induction into the IDF. "In case you fall into captivity," his father told him. "They're not like us."

His father was a hospital orderly for forty years. One day during that time he must have liberated the pills in the steel container. Yigal never opened it. He is certain there is nothing left after so many decades in his pocket other than fine powder, and maybe even that has disappeared. He carries it for luck, and to remember. He taps the cellphone in his lap.

"Call Noam," he tells it.

Busy circuit, a series of short buzzes.

He taps the phone again, this time pressing down heavily.

"Call No-am!"

The circuits are still busy. They will be all day and into the night. He knows why. After all, Yigal does control the second largest of Israel's four cell phone companies, a gold mine really, but as with any gold mine, its proprietors—he is thinking of himself—are reluctant to invest when profits are easy, and equally reluctant when they seem like a distant goal. Why spend the profits when things are good? Why add to the losses when they are not? These are business decisions. But in times of emergency he is one of millions paying the price of his own investment strategy.

He presses his foot down on the accelerator pedal: 145, 150, 155. Beyond that, Yigal fears he will not be able to control this beast of a car. Should another automobile swerve into his lane it will be over for him in seconds. The brigade will be leaderless. He drops it down to 150. *One-fifty is good*, he thinks. *I can handle one-fifty.*

He turns off to the east before the exits for Haifa. Above the city already he can see the black smoke rising. The port is on fire, he thinks. No, he knows it. The car's speakers, tuned to IDF Radio, little different from a commercial station in time of peace, are still calling codes: Dry Fish. Hairy Leg. Broken Nose. Dark—

The speakers emit a sound that is the beginning of a boom, then silence.

Yigal has been in three wars. IDF Radio has never been down. He pushes the BMW to 160.

27

ON THE RIDGE OPPOSITE the Allenby Bridge, Cobi lies dazed on the ground, his dummy Chariot literally shot out from under him, burning. He has been thrown fifty feet. For a long moment he thinks he is dreaming, but as his eyes return to focus he can see the lights moving on the far side of the Jordan as the tractor-trailers, performing some sort of brutish ballet, move aside to create corridors. Through these appear hundreds of Jordanian Challenger tanks, which line up like dutiful children to begin crossing the rickety bridge.

He shouts for the radioman and then stops when he looks behind him. What is left of the kid is distributed over a wide arc of perhaps twenty feet. Immediately he scans the gut-spattered ground for the radio, but sees nothing. Then he recalls it was at the top of the tank. He gets to his feet, feels one of them collapse in pain—either his ankle is twisted or gone—and prepares to climb the burning ruin when he sees the radio, intact, about ten feet away. He hobbles to it.

Amazingly, it works. IDF radios are meant to survive the worst.

"Aleph-Bet to Skull, Aleph-Bet to Skull. Skull, we are under armored attack. Urgent request air support. Hundreds of Challengers crossing Allenby Bridge. Repeat, hundreds of Challengers crossing Allenby Bridge. Urgent request for air to knock out Allenby Bridge. Knock out Allenby Bridge! Over."

Three miles to the west, a radio in brigade headquarters barks out the message. But Jordanian jet fighters have already been here. There is nothing left but the smoking remains of a body-strewn headquarters tent, and Cobi's desperate metallic voice.

"Aleph-Bet to Skull. Repeat, we are under massive armored attack. Require immediate air support. Knock out Allenby Bridge! Knock out Al—"

Cobi hears a series of explosions through the radio, then silence.

28

OVER JERUSALEM, THE BOMBERS complete their runs and head north and west to secondary targets. Were the city built of anything other than stone, it would be one huge conflagration. As it is, only sporadic fires burn amid the destroyed government buildings. The Knesset is leveled, the Prime Minister's Office and the Defense, Justice, and Interior Ministries reduced to rubble, Israel Police headquarters adjoining the Sheikh Jarrah neighborhood on the border of Arab East Jerusalem a giant hole in the ground. Here and there the Jews of West Jerusalem step out into the streets to peer at the predawn sky, empty now of bombers, only to see waves of transport planes, Dakotas and C-130s, coming in with the gathering dawn.

Propeller-driven, they are announced by the noise of their engines, each wave delivering slow-falling bits of black soot which in a matter of seconds reveal themselves to be parachutes and then, in a heartbeat, black-garbed commandos.

Intensely trained for months, these Revolutionary Guard shock troops know the topography of Jerusalem better than many native Israelis. Though each flight also carries Hebrew-speaking graduates of the Iranian military's Jewish Thought Institute in Qom, every paratrooper has been schooled in Hebrew sufficient to the requirements of their mission: *Yadaim l'malah!* [Hands up!] *Al ha birkaim!*

[On your knees!] *Nashim v'yiladim smola!* [Women and children to the left!]. But that is for tomorrow. Today's imperative is to hunt down the Jewish leadership and, in the words of their mission statement, to "cut off the head of the rabid dog." This does not mean take them prisoner. According to the Iranian analysis of Nazi Germany's campaign to cleanse Europe of Jews, Hitler's singular mistake was to attempt to do it humanely.

The Revolutionary Guard parachutists expect to encounter strong resistance, but they meet little.

For thirty years, Israel maintained a policy of strict gun control. Civilians wishing to obtain a license for even a shotgun to be used in hunting or a small-caliber target pistol often gave up in the face of bureaucratic barriers. Even a speeding ticket could cause ineligibility. Israelis with gun licenses that were not renewed annually—even in cases where the license-holder was in the reserves or abroad on government business—lost them automatically. When they tried to renew, they found themselves disqualified because they had been found guilty of possessing an unlicensed firearm. In one infamous case, a ninety-two-year-old retired accountant lost his license when some zealous Interior Ministry bureaucrat discovered the old man had been convicted during the British Mandate of illegal possession of firearms when he was a gunsmith working for the Jewish resistance. Even worse, unlike the Swiss, whose reserve soldiers are required to keep their issued weapons at home, the IDF keeps theirs under lock and key in centralized depots throughout the country. Thus, when it comes to armed resistance by civilians, there is none. The tragedy of the Nazi era is now repeating itself: the Jewish population is unarmed.

Entering from Balfour Street, black uniformed Revolutionary Guards guided by officers following step-by-step instructions on preset GPS units rush past the Israel Police kiosk, where the bullet-riddled body of a single cop hangs lifeless, and kick down the door of the prime minister's residence. Making short work of two security men armed with Tavors and a cook wielding a meat cleaver, the attackers kill the nanny coming down the stairs, then the grandmother and the two children in their beds, before finding the prime minister in her bedroom screaming into a dead phone. Pursuant to orders, she is photographed first alive and then dead, the images transmitted instantaneously to Tehran. There the photos will be matched with file photos of Israel's leadership on a gruesome checklist where names are crossed off in a relentless tally.

Though rape will become common in the days ahead as less disciplined Arab armies swarm Jerusalem, these Revolutionary Guard commandos work by the book. In a few minutes, they are out the door and on their way to the next target. The Minister of Agriculture lives on the next street.

By the time it is light, the entire administrative structure of the State of Israel has been decapitated. The list is so thorough that even the director of the Israel Museum is wiped out.

29

Two miles from the Jordan, a column of two hundred Jordanian Challengers grinding up the winding road westward encounters its first resistance.

Six Israeli Chariots crest an embankment concealed by a turn in the road and, opening fire, destroy the first five Jordanian tanks, causing the column to stop dead. The IDF commander has chosen his spot well. The Challengers attempt to move off the road, but on one side there is a sheer stone wall and on the other a severe drop of several hundred feet. Dazed, a dozen Challenger commanders attempt to descend rather than remain sitting ducks. Their vehicles lose traction immediately on the loose stone and tumble down into the abyss.

The Chariots keep picking off Challengers until drones appear overhead. They dive. As the Chariots burn, the most forward of the Jordanian tanks bulldoze their own incapacitated armor off the road and proceed westward. There are no more Israeli tanks. Around the next turn, a sign in Hebrew, English, and Arabic reads JERUSALEM 5 KM.

All in all, the Islamic Liberation Force—so the Arab and Iranian invaders have styled themselves—will utilize no fewer than six thousand drones, their warheads constructed of depleted uranium from the nuclear reactors Iran convinced the world were limited to peaceful use.

The drones, a product of the People's Republic of China, whose need for oil is all but unlimited, are used on every front within the first hours of the war to wipe out Israel's first line of defense. Planners in the Iranian equivalent of the Pentagon studied Israel's defense profile from all angles and discovered what the Wehrmacht discovered in preparation for its invasion of Poland: only a thin line protected the interior of the target country. Once that line is shattered, any reserve units would not have a line to defend, and could then be picked off by conventional means, which in the case of armor means overwhelming force of numbers. Thus the Iranian planners demanded full commitment, not one drone held back, and made sure of it by concentrating control of the drone force in Iranian hands. In the twenty-first century, the blitzkrieg is reborn.

30

AT THE ISRAEL AIR Force base adjacent to Ben Gurion International Airport, bulldozers push aside the still-burning jets that litter the field, allowing three surviving IAF F-16s to take off in the direction of Northern Sinai in an attempt to head off a massive Egyptian mechanized infantry force headed to Tel Aviv.

From his bunker in what is left of IDF headquarters in the Kirya, the Chief of Staff orders the Air Force to stop the Egyptians at all costs.

"Jerusalem is lost," he tells the head of the Air Force. "We must save Tel Aviv. Throw everything you have at them."

The head of the Air Force, whose heart will give out within hours, victim of a cardiac condition he concealed for a decade, gives the order.

"Roger that," answers the wing commander as three planes break the sound barrier. His face is still adorned with traces of lipstick.

31

AT AN ARMORED CORPS base thirty miles from the Lebanese border, Misha Shulman finds most of his fellow tankists, the majority from northern Israel and thus closer to the base, in manic disarray. The headlights of his Mercedes reveal the same scene repeated at Armored Corps bases across Israel. Inside the reinforced concrete structure that holds the brigade's ninety-two tanks and six jeeps, all is ready. The vehicles are gassed up and loaded with ammunition, spare parts, medical equipment, and food rations for two weeks. Trickle-current has kept their battery banks charged. They are ready for action, but for one minor detail. The six-inch-thick sheet-steel gates of the bunkers are locked.

Through the kind of snafu that is common to all armies, even one so well organized as the IDF, the base's regular-army maintenance crews have been rushed to the front, and with them the keys.

Misha assesses the situation in an instant.

Before him, his fellow tankists attempt to pry open the locks with tire irons from their civilian vehicles, but the tire irons bend and the lock hasps remain rigidly in place. An officer attempts to shoot off a lock with his sidearm. It makes a big noise.

There is a certain absurdity built into the structure of the IDF that is not found in any other army. All armies but the IDF are organized in a top-down command structure in which the best trained, most capable personnel command and those less qualified carry out those commands. But Israel's defense system is dependent on reserve soldiers who may be corporals in the IDF but run huge businesses in their civilian lives. In order to concentrate on their civilian careers, many leaders of Israeli society avoid taking on the honor of high rank in the reserves because that honor carries the burden of extra months of training and maneuvers every year. The head of a company employing a thousand workers may thus find himself under the command of a schoolteacher whose leadership experience is confined to a classroom of fourth-graders or a farmer whose civilian responsibility is a herd of dairy cows. In times of peace, these differences are swept away in a kind of gentleman's agreement. But in times of war, leadership tends to occur organically.

To wit: Reserve Staff Sgt. Misha Shulman, whose formal education ended before high school, whose military training outside of ten years in the IDF reserves consists of five years on the streets of Moscow, seven years in the Siberian gulag, and twelve years running Israel's principal criminal organization.

"Get the fuck out of the way," he shouts to the lieutenants and captains attempting to pry open the locks.

In response, the lieutenants and captains who are in theory his commanding officers melt away from the gates.

Misha is already in his Mercedes: the heaviest model made, two tons of German automobile powered by a five-liter engine so over-engineered it will outlast the car itself. At speed he backs it up thirty feet, then throws the vehicle into drive, flooring it. The car hits the gates so hard the steel gives way with a sound like an enormous hammer pounding a reinforced concrete wall.

The gate remains on its hinges, but one of its doors is bent sufficient for the bright lights of the tank bunker to shine out into the early morning dim.

Misha backs up again, now to fifty feet.

This time, when the vehicle hits, the sound of metal on metal is accompanied by a hiss from the car's crushed radiator. Beyond the escaping steam is an opening wide enough for a man to slip through.

In a moment the man is in, and in another comes the sound of a Mk IV Chariot tank's enormous 1200cc diesel starting up. As the other reservists run to the side, Misha among them, the tank snaps open the steel gates of the bunker and pushes Misha's steaming Mercedes out of the way like a cheap toy.

Brigade 112 is off to war.

32

YIGAL SEES THE CLOUD of dust from half a mile away. The brigade is heading north at speed, probably hitting sixty-five miles per hour and tearing the roadway into a mulch of pulverized asphalt. In moments he catches up to the rearmost tank, whose commander spots him on his 360-degree video screen. Almost immediately, the entire column slows to a halt, moving off the roadway to give the red BMW a chance to reach the column leader, which is just behind the brigade's reconnaissance jeeps. When he gets there, Yigal dumps the car by the side of the road. The tank's hatch opens and Ephraim, his driver, pulls himself out.

Ephraim is one of six Ethiopians in the brigade: three drivers, one loader, one gunner, and one commander. For unknown reasons Ethiopians are drawn to the armored corps. These are the sons of immigrants whose lives in Africa centered on subsidence agriculture, whose most advanced technology is the ox-drawn wooden plow— the low-tech model is pulled by a man. These are people who in one generation have leaped from pre-history to computer-guided fire control. As a driver, Ephraim is responsible not only for maneuvering sixty-five tons of war machine but for keeping it operational. He is twenty-eight years old, and like most Israelis has mastered the art of aggressive understatement.

"Yigal," he says as the man from the red BMW clambers onto the tank, "you almost missed the party. We were going to start without you."

As is common in the IDF, officers are called by their first names or their nicknames. There is not a private in the IDF who would hesitate to call the chief of staff Pinky.

"Traffic," Yigal shouts as he settles in to the right of the driver. "Every time there's a war, it gets awful." He pulls on his helmet, adjusting the mic over his lips. "To all units, this is Roller One. I need status. Noam, come in. Over."

Through his earphones, he hears the voice of his operations officer four tanks to the rear, his voice tinny but clear, special filters canceling out the deep roar of the engines just in front of him. To protect the crew, which IDF doctrine holds as being more important than the tank itself, Chariots are the only main battle tank produced whose engine is forward of the crew compartment. This adds tons of steel between the crew and any missile coming head on. The Chariot is less well protected in the rear, but as General Israel Tal, its designer, is said to have explained, "The armored corps is not expected to retreat."

"Noam to Yigal, we're in shit. HQ reports two to three hundred cans now crossing Lebanon border at Adamit, invaders splitting, half to coast, the rest southeast to Safed. Ours to interdict coastal force. They're heading to Haifa. Over."

"Roger, Noam. Rendezvous Position 253. Repeat: Rendezvous 253. Proceeding to objective in three columns. Noam, stay with me on 79. Itzik, your guys break off on 541. Amir, your cans via 545. Resume forward movement at maximum speed. Confirm, over."

The battalion commanders report as the tanks start forward, each unit led by two recon jeeps, essentially the eyes and ears of any armored force. Even with 360-degree video, a main battle tank is an ungainly beast that must be led to battle and provided with real-time intelligence. This is especially true at night, when jeep reconnaissance is essential in revealing the enemy's order of battle. In Yigal's brigade, as opposed to the more centralized structure of the armored corps as a whole, each recon platoon, either two or three jeeps, reports directly to the commander of his battalion, not to the brigade commander, thus encouraging independent action on the battlefield.

"Amir here. Roger, Yigal. In twenty. Over."

"Noam confirms. Moving out. Over."

"Yigal, it's Misha. Arik probably still on his way. Can't get him on cell. I've taken command. Over."

"Roger that, Misha. Get yourself a gunner. You can't do both. Let's go kick Syrian ass. Over and out."

"Noam here. Yigal, kicking Persian ass. Over."

"Say again? Over."

"Element splitting to coastal road is Iranian Revolutionary Guard. Repeat: Iranian. Over."

"Impossible, Noam. HQ is paranoid. Over."

"I wish. ID positive. Updated T-72S. Revolutionary Guard. Over."

Yigal does not miss a beat. His men expect nothing less. To pause even for a moment would be to telegraph doubt. "Okay, we've seen the same tin cans before. Same Russian hardware we know and love. Aim forward and low. That's the sweet spot. Iranian. Amazing. Over."

"Bad news, Yigal. Per HQ, these are likely fitted with Russian Svirs. Laser guided, not heat. Over."

"Roger that, Noam. Revised instruction to all commanders. Stay within three hundred meters. Fire from cover. Lasers inoperable where obstructed. Repeat, obstacle defense. Party time. Over and out."

In two miles, at the appropriate intersection, Armored Brigade 512 splits off onto three separate roads to regroup at the rendezvous point above Highway 4, which hugs the Mediterranean from the Lebanese border to Haifa.

33

IN THE WAR ROOM of the Revolutionary Guard four stories underground in Teheran, General Niroomad sees something he doesn't like in the satellite image on the wall of tiled TV screens. "Closer on screen three, colonel." He likes this less. "What are they thinking? Colonel, get me the Syrian fool."

The adjutant transmits the order. "Syrian operations, sergeant."

Almost instantly the small screen in front of General Niroomad opens on the Syrian war room, where Field Marshal Al-Asadi can be seen smoking a cigarette in a long holder.

"Greetings, my brother," Al-Asadi says in English, smiling as he delivers a virtual slap in the face to Niroomad, whose Arabic is rudimentary despite three years of study. He is smiling.

"Blessings upon you, field marshal. I see all goes well."

"The fruit of careful planning, my brother."

"For which you and your magnificent staff are to be commended," General Niroomad says. "Only one small thing."

"Certainly, my brother."

"Regarding your descent from Lebanon..."

"On schedule," Al-Asadi says. "All proceeding as planned."

"Yes," General Niroomad says. "But I beg to bring to your attention a Jew tank brigade moving to intercept Revolutionary Guard armor moving south on the coastal road."

Al-Asadi flicks the ash off his cigarette in the holder. "This is not possible. Syrian Air Command has neutralized all Israeli armor across the north."

"Field marshal, I regret to inform your excellency that in this matter your intelligence is faulty."

A long silence ensues. "Do you offer criticism, my brother?"

"I offer advice. This is the same armored brigade that stopped your tanks in previous wars. And for the same reason: insufficient field intelligence which did not call in air support."

"Traitors were responsible," Al-Asadi says with studied coolness. "As you may know, we in Syria have a Shia problem. As a Shia, you yourself know they cannot be trusted."

"Sunni dog, if you cannot fight a war, at least fight your tongue."

"Dog? Your mother's cunt, Persian."

The screen goes black.

General Niroomad purses his lips. He knows the answer, but asks anyway. General Niroomad assumes nothing: it is his trademark. "Colonel, is there no line of communication with our unit heading south from Lebanon?"

"Only through Damascus, sir."

"Thank you, colonel."

"Sir, given twenty minutes perhaps I can revive communication via—"

"Optimistic, colonel, but not realistic. Here then are my orders. Should we receive a Syrian request for support in any action from this moment on, be sure to answer in the affirmative."

"Certainly, my general."

"Send nothing."

"No support, my general?"

"The Sunni dogs are sacrificing our 32nd Tank Division. Do you know who commands that division, colonel?"

"I do, my general."

"When we finish with the Jews, we will deal with the Sunni," General Niroomad says, his voice dry, his gaze on the wall of screens. "My son will be avenged."

34

IN THE WHITE HOUSE Situation Room, the president and his advisors are joined by Lieutenant General Arthur Hefty, a pragmatic and some would say troglodytically gung-ho Marine who retains the crew-cut he had upon graduation near the bottom of his class at the United States Naval Academy at Annapolis. Much decorated for his early service as a lieutenant in Marine Reconnaissance during the Vietnam War, and for his frontline abilities as he rose in the ranks in every American military engagement since, General Hefty is a Marine's Marine. But not necessarily a diplomat's.

"Arthur," the president tells him with neither greeting nor preface, "we have a hot request from IDF. What's available and how fast?"

"Mr. President, the time frame?"

"Seems to be yesterday," the president says. "Israel has got itself in a kosher pickle." He pauses for applause, a familiar tic on the stump, and one the American public will see a lot of: this is an election year. Here there is only silence. "Seems we never bothered to share certain intelligence."

Felix St. George will not let this pass, president or no president. "Sir, this is classic Pearl Harbor. How could we know? All we picked up was increased communication."

"About which you neglected to inform Jerusalem," Flo Spier says. She is thinking about the Jewish vote, the Jewish lobby, the Jewish wallet, which no presidential candidate can afford to ignore. And now of course there are the damn-fool Christian fundamentalists, pro-Israel to the core. The bible-thumpers can easily throw the electoral college votes in six Midwestern states and most of the South. Just when the Jews had spread themselves out across the country and thus adulterated their vote, the born-agains came along. All they think of is abortion and Israel.

The president has no time for this, not now. But it is fair to say it remains in the back of his mind; the leader of the free world knows how quickly he can be out of the job. "What can we accomplish, Arthur?"

"The Sixth Fleet is off Izmir, sir," General Hefty says with zero hesitation and a good deal of enthusiasm. "That's Turkey, Mr. President. Figure eight hours. But we've got three hundred carrier-based aircraft within two. I can punch in twelve hundred Marines in four. En route we can coordinate with IDF. They're good like that."

Felix St. George already has a laser pointer moving across the eastern Mediterranean on the illuminated world map on the wall. "Russian naval units off Syria, sir."

General Hefty turns to his commander in chief. "Mr. President?"

There is a mechanical buzz. St. George puts a phone to his ear.

"I'm not afraid of the Russkies," the president says. "They'll fight to the last A-rab."

St. George puts down his phone. "Mr. President, Riyadh just announced they're terminating oil production in support of their Muslim brothers."

"What?"

"The oil weapon, sir," Flo Spier says. "Tomorrow's price at the pump will double all over the world—Europe, Asia, every gas station in America, to say nothing of heating oil when winter hits. Mr. President, this is worse than a major war. It's a political catastrophe."

The president decides to be presidential. "No damned A-rab is going to tell the United States of America how to conduct its foreign policy."

General Hefty stands. "Is that a go, Mr. President?"

But not too presidential. "Arthur, order your leathernecks on stand by. And tell your Israeli opposite number over there that the American people are fully committed to the security of the State of Israel and to its eternal capital, Jerusalem."

Admiral Staley offers a dry cough. "Jerusalem seems to have fallen, sir."

A long moment of silence ensues, the kind of silence that greets the sudden death of a rich relative who has not left a will. All eyes are on the president. "That's…unfortunate," the president says.

General Hefty does not hesitate. "Mr. President, with respect, the US and Israel have treaty commitments—"

"We'll reconvene at breakfast," the president says, standing. "I'm sure the Jews will figure something out by then. They always do." He turns with one hand on the doorknob. "Let's just hope it's not nuclear."

35

IN THE COMMAND BUNKER three stories underground in the Kirya, the chief of staff of the IDF is way ahead of him.

On an interactive map that takes up one wall, real-time intelligence from Israel's five satellites paints a digitized image of the country, with green—signifying Muslim control—spreading over Israel's borders like an uncontrolled amoebic plague. From the south, Egyptian mechanized infantry has swallowed most of the Negev Desert and is moving in a two-pronged advance on the southern cities of Beersheba to the east and the Mediterranean port of Ashdod to the west. Jordanian ground forces are closing on Jerusalem, having already barreled through the Judean suburb of Ma'ale Adumim. From the northeast, Iraqi infantry has moved through the Jordan Valley heading to Tiberius on the Sea of Galilee.

In the north, another front has opened, with hundreds of tanks, presumably under Syrian control but now identified as Iranian, crossing the Lebanese border. In each case, thin blue lines representing Israeli defenders have either cracked or fallen back. Only in a handful of places are they moving forward to engage.

"Get me the prime minister."

"Pinky," his adjutant tells him in a voice so low it is barely more than a hoarse whisper, "all communication with the PM is down."

"With the ranking members of the cabinet, then."

"Nothing." The adjutant pauses, looking at the spreading green blight on the digitized map. "Intelligence reports kill squads of paratroops within Jerusalem, nationality still unspecified. Pinky…"

"Say it."

"They're all gone."

"Shit." He sits for a while, wishing he had not given up smoking. There is no smoking in government buildings, of course, but this is not any day. *This,* Pinky thinks, *is a day that will be remembered in Jewish history forever, if there is going to be Jewish history after today.* He sits, heavily, as though irredeemably weakened. *It's an easy decision, really,* he thinks. *And down to me, number twenty-seven on the list. Who would ever have thought that numbers one through twenty-six would be unavailable? It's more a political than a military decision. Not my area at all. But there it is. Of course we could wait. But what would that accomplish? Another hour and the opportunity will be lost.* "Itzik!"

The chief of staff's deputy for extraordinary operations is across the room, monitoring his own small screen.

Brigadier Itzik Arian is a small and intense man of fifty who came to the IDF fifteen years earlier by way of academia, an expert in his field who has never been in battle, never fired a shot outside of the shooting range where, like all IDF staff officers, he must qualify every month. That this former professor is required to be proficient in small arms has long been a kind of sick joke in those rarified quarters where Arian's name and responsibility are known: it is like demanding a Tyrannosaurus Rex be handy with a flyswatter. Now the little Tyrannosaurus walks stiffly, almost reluctantly, to his commander in chief. In any other case, with any other officer, the chief of staff would simply have barked an order across the room.

"General Arian," Pinky says with a formality that betrays the gravity of what he is about to say. "In line with Government Protocol 221, and in consideration that all others authorized to make this decision are not reachable, I formally command you to initialize Operation Samson."

"General Pinchas, as you are aware, it is necessary to affix to such an order certain code numbers."

The chief of staff recites the list of ten digits he committed to memory on his first day at the top of the IDF command pyramid, and which every Sabbath morning as he strolls to synagogue he recites again like an article of faith. Were it not for the fact that such an act would be blasphemous among a people who had been tattooed for other purposes, he would have had these numbers inked permanently on his forearm.

Brigadier Arian moves his lips as though he has just tasted something unpleasant. "General Pinchas," he recites with the rigid solemnity of a high priest, "your command has been received and will be executed immediately. Pending further orders, Operation Samson will in one hundred twenty seconds be armed and prepared for execution."

When these two minutes pass, Israel will be the first nation in the world since the destruction of Hiroshima and Nagasaki to be one terse command away from unleashing a nuclear holocaust.

Pinky stares at his digitized map and speaks to his adjutant without facing him. "Moshiko, get me air command." He sighs. "What's left of it."

36

AT THE RENDEZVOUS POINT, the 112th Armored Brigade's 1st Battalion comprising thirty Chariot tanks takes up position behind tall pines in a line overlooking the north-south coastal road, beyond which a thousand feet of empty beach stretches to the lapping sea. The 2nd Battalion's thirty-two Chariots are nested behind a sharp turn in the otherwise straight highway a mile to the south; thirty Chariots of the 3rd Battalion are tucked away two miles to the north, poised to close off the enemy's line of retreat.

Further north, a reconnaissance unit awaits the arrival of the Iranian force at the ambush point. This recon unit is composed of three-man jeeps that in every other unit of the Armored Corps have been replaced by large, powerful American-made Humvees. At Yigal's insistence, the 112th has retained its old-fashioned jeeps because they present a profile one quarter the size of Humvees. The argument over their retention went straight to the commander of the Armored Corps, General Ido Baram, who had trained with Yigal. Reluctantly Ido agreed. Though he had accepted replacing Corps jeeps with the larger vehicles, he too doubted the decision of the chief of staff; Humvees had not done particularly well either in Iraq or Afghanistan.

Aside from the recon jeeps watching the coastal road to the north of the ambush point, another three jeeps guard the rear of the 1st Battalion from surprise from the east, just outside the communal settlement called Lohamei HaGeta'ot, the Kibbutz of the Ghetto Warriors. The settlement is named in memory of the Jewish revolt in the Warsaw Ghetto when, in spring of 1943, several hundred Jews armed with pistols and rifles took on thousands of heavily armed Wehrmacht and SS troops. At the kibbutz it is even worse: with every able-bodied man and women called to their units, defense has been left in the hands of mothers, children, and old men armed with little more than the weaponry of the original Ghetto fighters—rifles, pistols, grenades, and a single light machine gun.

The decision to fight rather than flee is based on experience gained in previous wars, when Arab soldiers seized every opportunity to kill Jews. However, in this war, bloodlust has been sacrificed to the grand strategy developed by Iran. The Muslim tank force on its way south from Lebanon intends to bypass such minor outposts in its rush to a target of strategic importance, the port at Haifa, just as in the south Egyptian armor will circumnavigate the outlying settlements, including the city of Ashkelon, as they drive for the port of Ashdod just to the north. Iran's war planners are intent on cutting off resupply from the sea.

Standing atop the roof of his tank, Yigal sweeps the northern horizon with his field glasses. The coastal road is empty in the gathering dawn, the best time outside of dusk for an armored attack. In a matter of minutes the field of muted grays before him will explode into light, but just now, if the damned Iranians will hurry up, his tanks are all but invisible, just so many gray lumps. The road below is gray, the beach beyond is gray, the sea itself calm as an ironed gray tablecloth in a dimly lit room.

He switches on his radio and speaks into the mic suspended from his helmet. "Roller One to all units, Roller One to all units. Final briefing. Recon gives the first of our tourists three minutes. If you need a refresher: rise to ridge, acquire target, fire. If Svirs are in play, drop below ridgeline, wait for next missile to pass, rise to ridge, acquire target, fire. Enemy requires twelve seconds to reload. That's our window. Twelve seconds. Commanders: status. Over."

"Noam here. Awaiting tourists. All in order. Over."

"Amir reporting. Ready to rock, Yigal. Over."

"Nasdarovia, over."

"Identify yourself, over."

"Yigal, you know it's me, over."

"Misha, I will fucking relieve you of command. This is not Dizengoff Street. You will pretend to be an officer. Over."

"I'm a staff sergeant, over."

"Misha!"

His voiced laced with irony, Misha offers the vocal equivalent of an exaggerated salute. "Yes, sir! Sir, Sgt. Misha reporting. Sir, all primed and ready. Sir! Over."

"You've picked up a gunner, over?"

"As you ordered. Sir! Over."

"Misha, remind me to have you court-martialed after the war. Over."

"Gladly, over."

"To all personnel," Yigal says, his voice now official, cool, as devoid of emotion as a machine. "If any of your cans is in less than fighting order, report now. Over." He waits precisely five seconds on his wristwatch. "Beautiful. On my signal then, over."

He is lowering himself through the command hatch when his radio buzzes.

"Super Skull to Roller One 1-1-2. Over."

"Roller One here. How goes it, Ido? Over."

"Is it you, Yigal? Over."

"No, it's the Queen of Sheba. Ido, we're about to make boom-boom. I can't chat with you now. Over."

"Forget boom-boom. You are ordered to abort. Over."

"Abort? We're in position. Over."

The voice of General Ido Baram almost cracks. "Straight from the top. You are ordered to fall back immediately to Herzlia. Full speed. Over."

Yigal is half in the tank, his head and shoulders exposed. "There's a timeout? What is this, the World Cup? Over."

"Pinky is setting up a defensive perimeter: Herzlia-Ramle-Rishon. Over."

"You're telling me we're sacrificing Haifa, also Netanya and Rishon? Over."

"Yigal, the situation..."

"Fuck the situation. I have work to do."

"Yigal, fall back to Herzlia. *Now.* Over."

"Ido, we're the only thing between the Revolutionary Guard and Haifa. Over."

"Roger that, Yigal. Order stands. Confirm. Over."

"Why? Over."

There is a moment of deep silence on the other end of the line. "Jerusalem's fallen, over." This is met with an even deeper silence, as though communication has broken off. "Yigal?"

"I'm here, over."

"A broad defensive perimeter is being formed around Tel Aviv. It's all that's left. Abort and fall back. Repeat: confirm receipt of this order. Over."

Yigal does not need his field glasses to see what is approaching at speed on the coastal road from the north. He can hear it. The sound of four hundred tanks is no whisper. He lowers himself fully into the Chariot, pulling the hatch cover tight and securing it. The hatch cover seal will keep out dust, flames, and poison gas. But not reality. "Aborting in one hour," he says into his mic. "Over and out."

What Yigal now sees again through the 360-degree video screen in front of him is both mortally frightening and oddly comforting: four parade-straight columns of Iranian tanks shoulder to shoulder speeding south down the four lanes of the coastal road as though late for a wedding. "Or early for a funeral," Yigal says under his breath.

Ephraim the tank driver picks up the muttered phrase in his earphones. "Commander?"

"Good where we are, kid," Yigal says, then taps his headset. "Roller One to all units, Roller One to all units. You will be pleased to know our guests are bang on time. Try first to kill those babies closest to the beach so they block the rest from going to the sand. Each gunner work back by fours so the entire column is bottled up. Whoever taught these Persians tactical approach was probably named Ginsberg. Misha, bottle our tourists from the rear. Same instruction. Don't bother with prisoners. Repeat, I don't give a damn about enemy personnel. For all I care they can swim back to Lebanon. We are here to destroy these tanks. On my command."

37

IN THE FIRST LIGHT of dawn over the Negev Desert, three Israel Air Force F-16s fly south in broad formation at 1500 feet, just below the radar of one hundred twenty-two Egyptian F-16s closing at two thousand feet above. In the lead plane, Major Alex scans the horizon as he applies lipstick, a muted peach. It's daytime, after all. "Take it off, put it on," he says to no one in particular, his talk button un-depressed. "The story of my life." He absolutely hates applying lipstick without a mirror. *On the other hand*, he thinks, *who the fuck is going to see my corpse?*

Certainly not the two pilots on either wing three hundred feet behind him. He picked these men himself out of the hundred or so who showed up at the air base to find themselves riders without horses. Of these, twenty-three were detailed to pick up El Al and Arkia civilian aircraft at neighboring Ben-Gurion Airport, the passenger planes to be loaded with bombs meant for Egyptian infantry. These are fighter pilots flying buses, and there is little doubt in their minds they will be blown out of the sky by enemy air-to-air missiles. For the Egyptian F-16s, this will be like shooting cows in a pasture.

Alex slips the lipstick into the slit chest pocket of his drab-green flight suit, ostensibly a standard-issue but—thanks to a certain talented dressmaker—cut exceedingly well. He taps his headset.

"Guys, sandwich high and low. I'm head on. Anybody doesn't take out thirty of these mothers is a douchebag. Look at those innocents, flying so close. Fire well and you'll hit two with one rocket. Just one more small thing: nobody returns to base with unexpended ammo. Repeat: pouches empty, not one round. Happy hunting. Over and out."

His left and right wingmen peel off. All three planes go vertical, attacking from below.

38

IN THE JORDAN VALLEY, his clothes torn and bloody, Lieutenant Cobi stumbles to the edge of a grove of date palms planted in a precise geometric grid. He knows he must find cover. Whatever is happening, Cobi intends to survive long enough to get back to a tank unit, any tank unit, where he can be useful. Like almost every other Israeli, he has no idea of the extent of the debacle, nor of what will come next. Almost all military communication is crippled, if not neutralized entirely. All he knows is that he is alone in a landscape barren but for the date palms, whose neat rows offer shade and perhaps water if he can find the source of the irrigation system that keeps them alive. Above him are tons of dates, probably not ripe but possibly edible. He intends to try one and wait for the effect, which he hopes will not be the runs. But first he must find cover and try to sleep. There is no sense attempting to locate friendly forces during daylight. His only chance is to wait until nightfall and proceed west.

He kneels, exhausted, his weight on his short-barreled Tavor rifle. For the briefest possible moment he allows his eyes to close, then—even before he knows why—his lids raise as though on springs. He looks up at the unmistakable metallic sound of a weapon being cocked.

Before him, almost within reach, is a Bedouin silhouetted against the rising sun. The Bedouin holds a shotgun. It is pointed straight at his head.

39

SIXTY MILES TO THE southwest, a parachutist floats silently toward earth. Above him, he sees his plane smash into an enemy fighter, both aircraft exploding simultaneously. Kamikaze tactics are not taught at IAF Fighter Academy, but with a crippled engine and depleted ammunition, it was either eject or lock his jet onto an enemy plane and then eject. A difference of seconds. His port wingman does not have that choice. A squad of Egyptian F-16s brings him down early in the engagement. His starboard wing remains airborne, but the parachutist doubts the poor guy will survive. With little to no ammunition, it will be a fox hunt, a dozen Egyptian aircraft in pursuit armed with heat-seeking AIM Sidewinder missiles. As he descends, he can see above him the Egyptian F-16 and his own aircraft plunging to earth in pieces, the same planes really—though the IAF version carries electronic modifications by Israel Aircraft Industries, both aircraft were manufactured by Lockheed Martin at the same factory in Fort Worth. The pilot about to come to earth visited that factory, just as it is possible his Egyptian counterpart, now dead, did also. For some reason this causes Alex to grin as the ground comes up fast to greet him with a thud.

40

IN THE BATHROOM OF his suite thirty-one stories above the roiling streets below, where thousands of American Jews are flooding in to demonstrate outside the United Nations General Assembly, Shai Oren, ambassador to the UN of all that is left of the State of Israel, shaves himself carefully with a straight razor, as he does every morning.

The razor was his father's, a prosperous furrier in Dusseldorf who in 1939 brought it with him to what was then British-governed Palestine. The Nazis had closed his business two years before. It took every pfennig the old man could gather together to buy the family out—what little savings were left, his wife's jewelry, the proceeds from the sale on terrible terms of their country house, the sale on even worse terms of a small Courbet that had hung over the fireplace in their home in the Oberkassel.

The razor, with its bone handle and Solingen blade, both worn down, like the old man himself is a talisman, a touchstone, a memory in ivory and steel of the time before the Oren family, then Kiefer, came to Israel as refugees, carrying little more than the clothes on their backs, heavy woolens unsuited to Israel's climate, and a new German-Hebrew dictionary.

In 1939, Ambassador Oren's father was thirty, spoke no Hebrew, and his only knowledge was of furs, not a likely path to success in the Middle East. Like tens of thousands of other German-Jewish refugees, who insisted on wearing jackets in the Palestinian heat, and ties, and proper shoes, not sandals, Ambassador Oren's father was part of a lost generation, unintentional Zionists, a people cut off from their Central European roots.

Among the few who did succeed in the holy land were a small group of architects who immediately found work as Jewish willpower built up the land (and who later emigrated to the US when the building boom ended), along with those whose professions were portable: bankers, musicians, doctors, dentists, accountants. Lawyers either learned Hebrew and prospered or could not and didn't. The rest, like Ambassador Oren's father, whose optimistic first act in the holy land was to exchange the old family name, German for *pine*, to its Hebrew equivalent, were condemned to agriculture or modest commercial activities. Some sold cigarettes in the street. The old man had held out until little Shai was six before slitting his throat with the same razor his son now holds in his right hand.

He has shaved half his face, holding his chin in his left hand like an object unconnected to him, stretching the skin for a clean cut. "This is it," he thinks. "I have reached the same state as my father, hopeless and fatigued and no longer sure of who I am."

Ambassador Oren had always considered the old man a failure, gutless in the face of a wall of impossibilities. All his life, Ambassador Oren had never backed down in the face of calamity. As a veteran member of Knesset who had seen his party disintegrate into factions and then into separate parties, he had been compelled to make political deals that sickened him in order to keep his seat so that he would have the chance later to do for Israel what Israel had done for him. He had seen his boyhood friends, friends even from kindergarten, perish in war. He had buried his elder son at the military cemetery on Mt. Herzl in Jerusalem. He kept silent when the younger son emigrated to California to take a position at Stanford, raising his grandchildren to be what he thought of as "surfer Jews," ignorant of Israel, ignorant of the Holocaust, ignorant of everything outside the Pacific Coast hothouse in which they were raised. They speak no Hebrew outside a few choice curse words, of which they are inordinately proud, and the odd terms for food, sex, and micturition. On the few occasions each year they saw him, now most often via Skype, they called him Grandpa. Ambassador Oren had always expected to be called the Hebrew equivalent, *Saba*, but their Hebrew was not even up to that. He had lived through his wife's death by cancer, followed by a progression of good but inadequate women whose company brought him only momentary cheer and then unfathomable loneliness. Through all this, he marched on, ever fearful that he might take his father's course.

Now he examines himself in the mirror of the large bathroom of the ambassadorial suite. It is guarded by a team of rigorously trained young security men and downstairs by a detail of New York Police Department whose numbers had tripled since what happened happened. He never thinks of it in terms other than "what happened," or "the thing that happened," as if it were a freak storm or a flood or an electrical fire, and not the ongoing catastrophe and something even worse, far worse.

He puts the razor to his throat, pauses for just a moment, then continues shaving in fluid, practiced strokes, careful as ever to avoid even the smallest nick, the tiniest drop of blood. Whatever else might happen, he has work to do.

41

WHEN THEY MOVED INTO the White House, the president cautioned his wife that it is unlucky for a new occupant to make changes to the décor. Jacqueline Kennedy had gone on a spending binge to renew the old place, and her husband had paid the ultimate price; Nancy Reagan, who did not go that far, saw her husband survive an assassination attempt. Perhaps worse in the eyes of the president, the White House had been seriously redecorated by his predecessor, at great cost to her popularity, which played a small but significant role in her defeat for a second term.

"Hon," the president had told the first lady, "if they don't kill you, they vote you out—and I ain't about to lose a second term because of some gay son-bitch wielding a fine aesthetic and an unlimited expense account."

With a sure sense of the American electorate, the president hardly requires an opinion poll to know the great unwashed was disgusted by the Franz Kline abstract in the Lincoln Bedroom and the Jackson Pollack in the Oval Office. His predecessor allowed presidential power to go to her head and in the process badly misjudged the tastes of the American people. Even her Democratic base looked upon the redecoration as a form of desecration when opposite a full-length Gilbert Stewart portrait of George Washington was hung a mobile in primary colors by Alexander Calder. One Fox Television personality termed the result "Washington crosses the nursery," and spent a month—forever in air time—demanding the Calder be scrapped. Wall Street, the Hollywood elite, museum curators, writers, and gallery owners protested that removing the Calder (to say nothing of the Rothko, two de Koonings, and that very large Jackson Pollack) would be giving in to American mass culture, while the rest of America demanded that the White House continue looking like the White House. The president did not need more than a minute to weigh the issues. "Some of this stuff ain't to my taste," he announced at a press conference, making sure to sound down-home. "But I'm no expert. So I am appointing a commission to study this issue and make recommendations."

Regarding the emerging situation in the Middle East, the president will be similarly decisive. In Washington, the appearance of action is better than action itself. Appearance rarely involves consequence.

42

As Ambassador Oren takes the podium, the General Assembly empties until only a scattering of delegates remain: the US, the UK, Canada, France, Germany, Guatemala, Holland, Italy, Panama, and Paraguay. It is as if a plague has entered the chamber in the form of one man.

The plague seems not to care.

"Mr. Chairman, distinguished members," Ambassador Oren begins. "It is now one week since the sudden, bloody, and unprovoked attack on the State of Israel by four of its neighbors, Syria, Egypt, Jordan, and Iraq, and by one distant self-declared mortal enemy, Iran. Their forces now illegally and brutally occupy over eighty percent of the State of Israel, the same State of Israel whose borders were affirmed in 1949 by this very body.

"In Israel's ancient capital of Jerusalem, Jordanian and Iranian troops, through the widespread use of terror, including centrally organized mass rape and murder, have caused the greatest refugee crisis since the Roman expulsion of the Jews from their homeland two thousand years earlier. The political leadership of Israel has been wiped out, either assassinated or missing. This includes all but one member of Israel's parliament. Israel today is leaderless. In Jerusalem alone, eleven thousand civilians are dead. The principal occupation of the population of Israel's ancient capital is the digging of graves.

"Some four hundred synagogues have been destroyed, their holy scrolls burned in the streets. Not content with wiping out every trace of Jewish cultural life, the Muslim invaders also burned or desecrated at least sixty churches. Though some video has been smuggled out, the true scope of the carnage is as yet not known. As in other areas under control of the invading forces, hospitals are closed to Jews, including women in labor.

"Mass terror, organized, planned and executed, is the rule in every Israeli city but one. Tel Aviv has so far not felt the imprint of one Arab boot.

"For those of you who see in this some sudden burst of compassion, be not deceived. The Muslim master plan for Israel is now clear. Even as I speak, Jews from outlying areas are being herded into ghettos in the major centers of population. Haifa, once a city of 300,000, now holds a million Jews. Beersheba, a city of 150,000, now holds 400,000. Jerusalem, home to one million Jews, now contains two million. In every case, Jewish civilians have no access to water, food, or shelter. What they do have is access to transport.

"Fellow delegates, as I speak Israel's national railroad, now in the hands of the so-called Islamic Liberation Force, is being used to funnel all of Israel's Jews into what is being called Ghetto Tel Aviv. Here they are forced to live on the streets and the beaches, surviving on shrinking reserves of food. Some eat grass pulled from the ground in public parks. Since the invasion, no ships have been permitted to bring aid to the starving people of Tel Aviv. For two weeks, no milk, flour, fruit, or vegetables have entered the ghetto. Electricity is limited to two hours a day and is expected shortly to cease entirely as supplies of coal dwindle and simply run out. Tel Aviv's hospitals have no medicine, and soon will have no power. By the time all of Israel's Jews are concentrated within the borders of Ghetto Tel Aviv, some six million men, women, and children will be concentrated here to starve or die of disease. When the time comes, the Muslim invaders will doubtless wipe out these survivors house by house, their bodies burned on the beach.

"Fellow delegates, yet again six million Jews will be killed—infants, children, mothers, fathers, grandparents—to fulfill the hideous dream of Israel's conquerors, to make of the Jewish State little more than a dismal memory and its population a mountain of bleached bones.

"Fellow delegates, when Israel turned to you for support in defending against this brutal, cowardly, and unprovoked attack, you paused, considered, pontificated, invited cease fires, and called for peace conferences, but did little other than to make the sympathetic noises whose words will redound to the shame of the human race for centuries. You remain sitting on your hands trembling that the price of oil might rise one cent more, frozen in fear that the Saudis and their colleagues in OPEC might make your lives a bit less comfortable. Despite the solemn treaties, the lessons of history, and the certain knowledge that your own non-Muslim countries too will soon fall victim to the same brutal aggression, you let it happen.

"Fellow delegates, I ask you to come to the aid of the State of Israel, now a city-state of the hungry, the thirsty, the homeless, the hopeless, the dying and the dead. Send your ships. Bring us food. Drop it from airplanes, as you did during the Cold War to feed the people of West Berlin. Bring it by sea, as you did to support the people of the former Soviet Union in World War II."

The ambassador seems now short of breath, or perhaps hope. He pauses, searching the faces of the few diplomats in the hall.

"And then begin the sad but necessary evacuation of the surviving population, six million wretched refugees belonging to a people whose contribution to the world has never been exceeded by any other people, large or small. The people of the State of Israel are prepared to help build your nations, your societies, your homelands. Step forward now as you did not in the previous century, when six million Jews were murdered. Please, I beg you, help save these six million."

As if in relief that this accusatory monologue is over, a sprinkling of applause rises from the handful of people in the vast space. When he steps down from the podium, the members of 181 other delegations re-enter the hall.

The chairman of the General Assembly, a Norwegian diplomat who sees himself as an international civil servant, a genial friend to all, replaces him. "Thank you so much, distinguished representative of Israel," he says with zero emotion, his face illuminated with divine neutrality. "I now call the distinguished representative of Algeria, followed by the distinguished representatives of Malawi, Iraq, France, and the Kingdom of Saudi Arabia."

43

IN THE OFFICES OF Isracorp, now descended from the thirty-second floor of the Isracorp Tower to the fourth because electricity is not available to run the elevators, two men sit together watching the proceedings of the UN General Assembly on a jury-rigged electronic connection, one of the few means of contact with the outside world. They watch in silence as the picture dims, then goes dark, followed by the office lights. Electricity must be saved. Tel Aviv's power station is now burning little more than coal dust. Tomorrow even that will be gone.

Misha relights his cigar. "I'm not going anywhere. You?"

"Wait until you're so hungry you'll eat your shoes," Yigal says.

The gangster removes the stylish moccasin on his right foot, and with a theatrical flourish inhales its aroma. "Italian cuisine," he sighs. "My favorite."

"We've given up. You heard it. Done. Take us away. The end."

"There are worse things."

"Like what?"

"Like this being my last Cohiba Esplendido." Abruptly Misha changes his tone, his voice dropping an octave. "Yigal, no one will have us."

"Probably not."

"We shouldn't have fallen back."

"Still, we destroyed four hundred Iranian cans," Yigal says.

"Eight hundred more came the next day. We fell back. We didn't advance. I've never not advanced. Not in Russia, where they called me filthy yid. Not here, where they called me filthy Russian. In a tank, not ever. How could it happen?"

"Too many Muslims. Too few Jews."

"Too few? Close to six million are now in Tel Aviv, more shipped in like livestock every day. Quite a few Jews, Yigal."

"Armed with what, Misha? Anger? Desire? Teeth?"

"They don't want us to fight, our new leaders. They want to be taken in and fed, like dogs in the street."

"No tanks, no planes, no ammo, no fuel. I run a global business—well, I ran a global business. You know how? With a weapon called money. Without this weapon, for investment, research, trade, leverage, I couldn't have run a falafel stand. The Americans have declared themselves neutral. Ipso facto, we have no weapons."

"But you didn't start with weapons. I didn't either. We acquired them."

"Over time. Of which we have none. Look out these windows. People sitting like statues in the street, moving only to find shade. For water they're already drinking from the Yarkon, a river so poisonous you could die from falling into it. It's over."

Misha goes to the window, coated with the desert dust that swirls in from as far away as Saudi Arabia. The huge sheet of polarized glass has not been cleaned since the invasion. "Yigal," he says, looking out. "I'm not the one who can do it. I'm a good criminal, very organized, good contacts, not stupid. But I don't have your experience. You run the biggest company in Israel—"

"What I run is an office building with really nice furniture. Everything else is gone. Factories, banks, telecoms, software. *Finita la comedia.*"

The gangster turns so that in Yigal's view he is now little more than a silhouette against the sun. "You through feeling sorry for yourself?"

"I thought I'd give it a bit longer."

"Fuck, we don't have any longer. Yigal, nobody will follow me. They *will* follow you."

44

THE MAIN JERUSALEM OFFICES of Israel Discount Bank were looted on the first day of the war by optimistic Jordanian mechanized cavalry who had seized the center of the city and then, with resistance melting by the minute, moved to seize the cash assets of the bank. This was patently a waste of energy; by the next day, the Islamic

Liberation Force had declared the Israel shekel as dead a currency as the eroded Roman coinage Israeli children often found in gardens and excavations at building sites. Only one day before the invasion, the shekel had been trading at a strong three to the US dollar. The next afternoon it was empty of all value other than nostalgia. The Jordanian troopers did somewhat better with the bank's small supply of foreign currency—like most Israeli bank branches, it did a brisk business in foreign exchange to serve the tourist trade—but there wasn't that much: the branch's dollars and euros were transferred every night to Bank Discount's vaults in Tel Aviv. Frustrated, the Jordanians next blew the vault and pried open one by the one its several hundred safe deposit boxes. These yielded a small pile of jewelry and masses of documents and family memorabilia—photos, ancient passports, brittle papers which ascribed to their namesakes the rights of citizenship in Iraq, Austria, Germany, Poland, Romania, Algeria, Syria, Lebanon, and other countries that over the years had voided the same documents. These litter the floor of the bank's vault like yellowing snow.

In the bank's second floor conference room, the Coordinating Council of the Islamic Liberation Force is holding its weekly meeting, Iranian Major General Niroomad presiding. Around the table sit Syrian Field Marshal Al-Asadi, Egyptian Field Marshal Haloumi, Jordanian Major General Said. (The Iraqi commander continues to boycott these meetings because Jordan will not permit the Iraqi flag to fly in Jerusalem.)

At the far end, wearing civilian clothes and a studied look of committed amity, is Aleksei Tupikov, blond, chunky, and vigorous, the Jerusalem station chief of the GRU, Russia's military intelligence agency. Tupikov is in fact charged with enforcing Moscow's directives for the entirety of former Israel. In order to preserve the myth that Russia all along has not held the hand of the Iranians who coordinated the conquest, Tupikov is not addressed by his rank, which is major general. His staff of fifty controls an entire floor of the King

David Hotel, now bizarrely renamed the King Hotel. The Hashemite royal family thought at first to call it after the current monarch's father, but even decades in his grave King Hussein remains despised by the Egyptians, Syrians, and Iraqis for staying neutral in the Ramadan (Yom Kippur) War of 1973, thereby contributing to Israel's victory. Thus the King Hotel, at least for a time, the word *David* simply blacked out in its arched entranceway.

"If I may?" Tupikov says in impeccable Arabic.

"Please, Mr. Tupikov," General Niroomad says in his Arabic, which is clearly peccable. Though he takes daily lessons in the future tense of Arabic verbs, as far as the general is concerned the Arabs' only future is as vassals to Iran. "In Persia a guest is always welcome to speak."

General Said takes issue. "Is Jerusalem now Persian?"

"Dear distinguished general," Niroomad says, with the unctuous delicacy of a higher life form being exaggeratingly respectful of a barbarian, "all Islam celebrates in the cleansing of Jerusalem. Let us not quibble."

"Jerusalem is holy only to the Sunni," Said retorts. "To the Shia, it means little. Why are the Shia even here?"

Tupikov shifts sufficiently in his chair to call attention to himself. "Who shares an enemy shares a friend," he says. The Arab proverb carries within it an even more cynical truth: who ceases to share an enemy ceases to share a friend.

Field Marshal Haloumi, always pragmatic and very much aware that in numbers Egypt has provided the war effort with more soldiers and hardware than all the other countries combined, speaks quietly but with authority. His sweetly musical Egyptian Arabic is almost soothing. "My brothers, we have strayed from our topic: the precise delineation of zones of authority. War is chaos. Peace must be orderly."

General Al-Asadi, whose Syrian death squads have all but wiped out the Palestinian officer class of Hezbollah that Damascus and Tehran have subsidized for twenty years, becomes agitated. "To achieve such orderly peace, brother, how many Hamas have you killed in Gaza?"

"We have dealt with the Palestinian rabble in the south as you have in the north," General Haloumi replies calmly. "Unlike our Persian brothers, we of Egypt do not accept theocratic rule. The Palestinians are poisoned with godliness. In the name of their God—"

General Niroomad straightens his back. "*Their* God? Is Allah not God of all?" Though the good general does not have a pious bone in his body, the line from the political leadership in Homs, where the mullahs preside, is paramount: Muslim unity must be emphasized, never Arab unity, otherwise the desert rats will throw off the Persian leadership that united them in victory. As he is aware, Iranian dominance becomes more tenuous every day. "Let us hear from General Ali, who is inscribed for the floor." *Scheduled* is the word he would prefer, but he cannot quite recall it. The Arabic language, he thinks, is as difficult as its speakers.

General Said stands, a figure straight as the saber at his side. His uniform, perfectly pressed, is the best in the room, designed and fitted by the same firm of Savile Row tailors who have supplied the British general staff for decades. In matters sartorial, the Jordanian command class follows the lead of their king, a great fan of the film *Lawrence of Arabia*, in which the king's great-grandfather is portrayed by Alec Guinness, whose robes—on celluloid at least—are richly ornamented and spotless, spun of the most delicate English tropical wool.

"Brothers, I have the honor to bring you greetings from his royal highness the King of Jordan, who wishes only the blessings of most merciful Allah upon your heads and upon those of your children and your children's children."

General Niroomad is so tired of this. Must one hold a gun to an Arab's head to get him to come to the point? Besides, Russian military intelligence has already informed Niroomad of what Ali is about to say.

"By His Majesty's decree," General Said intones, "all of Tel Aviv and its dependencies rightfully now revert to Jordanian rule."

"Just at the moment," Niroomad says drily, "Tel Aviv has reverted to the stench of Jews."

General Said pretends not to recognize the Persian's tone. "This, matter," he says, "will be corrected soon enough."

General Niroomad offers a sigh worthy of a particularly untalented drama student. "Millions of Jews," he says, sick at the thought but relieved that someone else actually wishes to do this hateful work. "Even the great Hitler did not dream of snuffing out the lives of so many in one day."

45

POCKETS OF RESISTANCE REMAIN. But because the country is essentially *judenrein*, the few bands that form in the wake of the invasion, largely composed of IDF soldiers and escapees from the cities, can find no shelter among the indigenous population. Outside of Tel Aviv, there is none. But in the north, deep forests provide cover, as do the caves penetrating the cliffs of the Mediterranean coastline from Binyamina north to Mount Carmel. The south, being mostly flat if not outright desert, provides little natural cover—Bedouin bands seeking bounty would certainly pick off any Jews foolish enough to try this inhospitable terrain. To the east, in Judea and Samaria, the country is hilly, which offers possibilities for harassment and sabotage, but once this is achieved escape is difficult. Movement must be by foot or, in several instances in the cattle-grazed Golan Heights, on horseback. Non-military vehicles remain banned from the roads. Even should civilians—whether Israeli Arabs or Jews disguised as same—manage to seize the kind of transportation that can get by the ever-present roadblocks manned by Arab machine gunners, such as UN-marked buses or enemy jeeps, no gasoline is to be had outside of the Muslim military bases, which are of course former IDF bases with fresh signage.

Worst of all, like the anti-Nazi partisans in Eastern Europe, these makeshift bands find themselves working in isolation. Command and control does not exist for the same reason the units themselves cannot contact one another: the sophisticated and extensive IDF wireless network almost immediately fell into the hands of the Iranians, whose Hebrew-speaking intelligence officers monitor it for any sign of organized resistance. Israel's civilian phone companies, wired and cellular, no longer function. At best each group of holdouts eventually must find its way to Tel Aviv, there only to discover their own lack of capability mirrored in a leaderless, hungry, fearful, and dispirited population.

Though scattered small groups continue to move about with the intention of harassing the enemy, these have enough on their hands finding sufficient food to survive. Some bands stage attacks on Arab supply lines, but the weaponry they grab comes with little ammunition.

The last of the larger groups, close to one hundred men and women, mostly paratroopers whose unit lost its way in the initial fighting and then was bypassed by the enemy surge, manages to find a large cache of mortars, sten guns, and ammunition hidden in a cave on Mt. Carmel. In 1941, aware that then British-governed Palestine was the next target for Rommel's Afrika Korps, the Jewish leadership hid the weaponry for a last stand. Instead, Rommel was stopped in Egypt.

Though primitive by modern standards, the cache might have provided sufficient firepower for large-scale resistance. But the cave leaked rainwater for decades. The cosmolite-soaked rags that were meant to preserve these armaments remain in place, but the guns they embraced have long since rusted away.

Traveling by night in groups of ten, seventy of the Mt. Carmel partisans make it to Tel Aviv. The rest are never heard from.

46

AT THE WHITE HOUSE, the presidential press conference is packed with American and international correspondents, including a single reporter claiming to represent *Ha'aretz*, formerly the Israeli newspaper best known abroad, but now out of electricity, out of paper, out of business. A month earlier, Israel boasted a dozen daily papers; today there are none. As a matter of policy, the White House press office does not normally grant access to ghost correspondents from dead newspapers, but the White House gatekeepers examine only credentials. Though her newspaper is history, the Israeli correspondent's credentials look good.

The room is packed, and tense.

As is his wont, the president manages to be simultaneously folksy, curt, respectful, and evasive, recalling one of the chief executive's own heroes, Ronald Reagan, who like most dependable actors never strayed from the script.

"Now there's a real good point, Ted," the president pretends. "All I can tell y'all is we're meeting next week with my counterparts from Great Britain, France, Germany, Russia, China, and Jay-pan." As a graduate of Harvard, the president is well aware of how to pronounce the name of the country governed from Tokyo; he never spoke it that way at Harvard, or at Yale where he took his law degree, though admittedly second from the bottom of his class—the only graduate with a worse scholastic record is now one of the world's richest men. "With goodwill and persistence, the Jewish refugee problem will be solved." The president winks conspiratorially as he turns his broad smile to the other side of the room. "Rich, you look like you're about to have a cat."

"Thank you, Mr. President. Sir, there's been much speculation about Israel's use, or should I say non-use, of the nuclear option. Has the administration been restraining the Israelis from going nuclear?"

"Rich, I can't address that in detail, which I'm sure y'all appreciate. But I can say we have counseled patience to our Israelian friends. Elizabeth?"

"Mr. President, gas at the pump is now eight dollars a gallon and expected by some analysts to exceed ten dollars in a matter of days. Have you talked with the Saudis about restarting production?"

"Liz, no one feels the pain of the driving public more than myself. As a car collector and an amateur mechanic, which I guess most of you folks are aware of, seeing as how many of you have visited with the first lady and myself at the farm, there's nothing I like better than pure, unadulterated horsepower, which I hasten to add has been, is, and I expect will be for a good long time the pleasant pastime of many Americans. So the answer is yes, talks with our friends the Saudis are ongoing, and I hope to have good news soon for the American driving public when the king of that country and I meet in several days. Let me say this: there will not come a time while I am in office that one yellow school bus anywhere in America will not deliver our young'uns to school for lack of gas. Lance?"

"Mr. President, recent opinion polls show little enthusiasm for absorbing millions of immigrants. With so many Americans jobless, do you see political implications for the administration in an election year if, as some in Congress have suggested, some six million Israelis are to be admitted to the US?"

His smile narrowing only a little while his chin seems to jut out like the prow of a ship, his head raised as though seeking guidance from above, the leader of the free world nods the presidential head with a mixture of moral rigor, statesmanlike certitude, and religious faith. "Lance, if there's one thing I can tell the American people, it's this: our administration will do the right thing, both by the American people and by the Israelians who have fallen on such hard times. God bless America. Y'all have a nice—"

Before he can complete the sentence that customarily concludes his every public statement, a svelte woman in a red pantsuit stands and, in a voice at once professional and desperate, addresses the chief executive directly, her mild accent cutting through the manufactured ambiance, as the president would describe it later, like a hot knife through ice cream.

"Mr. President, I am Ornit Peck from *Ha'aretz* Israel daily newspaper. Can you please tell us if you have a plan to bring aid, specifically food, water and medicines to the refugees now in Tel Aviv who—"

Don Beadle, the president's press secretary, finds his feet, and as well an opportunity to prove that he is more than a mere mouthpiece. "Madam, I can understand your need to express yourself, but in fact the president has already concluded today's briefing. If you'd like, you can present any question you might have in writing and I'm sure—"

The president raises his hand. "Miz Beck, is it?"

"Peck. I—"

"Miz Peck, then. First and foremost, I want to state that I and every member of this administration, and I speak as well for my friends in the legislative branch on both sides of the aisle, that every American feels your pain and the pain of the Jewish people. I assure you that this administration will do everything in its earthly power to find a solution to what is certainly a disastrous situation, a solution that is amenable to all parties in the conflict, so help me God. We are working on it. Now, y'all do have nice day."

By the end of which nice day Miz Ornit Peck, ghost correspondent of the major ghost newspaper of what is barely more than a ghost nation, is informed via email that her White House press credentials are no longer valid, but that should she reapply under the auspices of a functioning media organization the White House press office will be pleased to consider issuing fresh credentials. This last flourish, uncharacteristically generous from a press office known to be hostile to the press, is the result of a comment by the president to Don Beadle on their way out of the hall: "Got to hand it to the little

lady. Jewess got her more balls than our en-tire Su-preme Court."
Absent that comment, Beadle would have had Ornit Peck or Beck or
whatever declared persona non grata for life. Or until the president
leaves office, which if the cost of gasoline at the pump does not drop
might be a matter of months.

Either way, Beadle's own future is assured. He receives fresh job
offers every day. At the moment. he is leaning in the direction of
a position as communications director of Shell, with a salary that
causes him to become hard as a teenage boy on his first date. Of
course, if by some miracle the president is able to resolve the oil crisis
and is elected to a second term, there is every reason to hang on as
press secretary for another year, not least to share in the triumph.
Shell will wait. They'll all wait. Whatever happens to the president,
whatever happens to Ornit Peck, whatever happens to those poor
kikes in Tel Aviv, Don Beadle's future is bright.

47

EVER FAITHFUL, JUDY DOES not object that Yigal is using her body
to forget at least momentarily how otherwise impotent he feels. She
knows that his thrusting is not even remotely personal, and though
this is probably the worst form of marital intimacy—two people en-
gaging their individual loneliness—she is not averse to being used
if it means being useful. Perhaps, she thinks, this will take his mind
off Cobi, who has not been heard from since the first day of the war.
It doesn't work, of course. Certainly not for her. She is so far from
arousal tonight's lovemaking might as well be a form of consensual
rape. She lies there as he continues to pound her, poor dear Yigal,
and thinks for the first time in a long time whether she should simply
fake an orgasm. Does Yigal require that as well? She doesn't know,
and then the problem is solved.

"I'm so sorry," he whispers. "I just can't."

She kisses the closest part of him, the base of his neck. "Me neither."

"I'm sure he's alive," Yigal says. "He's a survivor, that one."

"Like you."

He rolls off her, both of them stretched out and looking at the white ceiling, gray now in the night. In one corner it is lit by a projected beam of red light from a clock on the table on Yigal's side, one of those silly gadgets her husband likes to bring back from his travels abroad. The kitschy German cuckoo clock she would not hang in their home. She gave the foot massager to their maid, who probably sold it, along with the selection of miniature perfumes from the south of France. She prefers one scent, has for years, because Yigal likes it. Why change? But the time-projecting American clock, this found a home, though if she had her way she would have relegated it to Cobi's room—time passes entirely too quickly as it is. She is on her way to fifty. And now Cobi. And the war, though hardly anyone calls it that anymore because it is over. The defeat. The disaster. The holocaust. No, that one is taken. The end. Yes, that is available.

Last night she dreamed Cobi returned. A knock at the door. A stranger, and another stranger behind him. And then he was back, hugging her. But Yigal was not there. And then Cobi was Yigal. And she woke. The clock projected in red light on the ceiling reads 23:01—military time, as Yigal prefers, though she always has to work out the real time after 1200 hours.

She touches his thigh. It is cool, too cool. "Tell me Cobi is alive. That he's a prisoner somewhere. That he'll return. And we'll start again, somewhere, anywhere, from the beginning. Tell me that, my love."

"Cobi is alive," he says, almost whispering as though it is a secret that must be kept between them. "Cobi is alive and we will start again, our little family."

"We'll start again. With Cobi."

"With Cobi," he says, this time not whispering, almost too loudly for the distance between them. "We will start again."

"We'll go to the States. Miami. You have an American wife, remember. I'm the most valuable asset that exists in Tel Aviv, an American passport."

"I have a wonderful American wife," he says, drawing her close. "And we will build a new life." His voice drops an octave. "But not in Miami."

"Darling, there's nothing here."

"Not at the moment," he says.

48

In a shallow cave in a west-facing slope in the Judean hills, Cobi lies on his back half asleep. The cave is little more than an indentation in the rocks. Clearly Bedouin shepherds used it recently; there is enough dry sheep dung for a fire. This hardly matters. Even had he anything to cook, his father had not brought up an idiot. On the narrow roadway below, Syrian mounted infantry patrol like clockwork day and night, poor military practice because it is predictable, but less predictably helicopters of the Royal Jordanian Air Force—he still has his binoculars, though one lens is shattered—circle overhead from time to time, looking for just such a sign of Israeli stragglers.

Cobi considers there must be small groups of young conscripts like himself who were effectively passed by in the initial onslaught, or farmers, or settlers. One evening, from the mouth of the cave, he sees jeeps enter the settlement on the hill opposite, then hears gunfire: Kalashnikovs, the Russian-manufactured semi-automatic rifles that are coin of the realm in the Arab world. This is not, he knows, the gunfire of battle. There is no returned fire. He sees little, a grove of olive trees covering part of the view, the settlers pre-fab houses and trailers blocking the rest, but he knows what he cannot see. This was the sound of firing squads, a dozen rifles going off at once. The Syrians depart soon after, their vehicles loaded with household goods, pillows, televisions and microwaves, while behind and above them the settlement burns, the smoke of many fires rising in the still air like white pillars stretching to a moon so full it might be not be real. *What,* he asks himself, *is?*

He is thinking of that, half-thinking, half-dreaming, and then he hears something move close by, too close. He grabs his rifle and instantly is on one knee, the rifle at his shoulder: At the entrance to the cave, a silhouette.

"Cobi," the silhouette says in the dulcet Hebrew of a rural Arab. "By all that is holy, kindly endeavor not to kill your friend. It is bad manners. And it causes discomfort in my bladder."

"Fuck, man. Bang two rocks together four times. How hard is that to remember?"

"You were sleeping."

"I haven't slept for a long time."

The Bedouin enters the cave so that now Cobi can see his face, dark, unshaven, smiling. He drops a plastic-string bag on the cave floor.

"But you eat well."

"Thanks to you."

Abed watches the young man tear into the food, homemade pita, white sheep's milk cheese, onion, tomatoes, and olives. Wrapped in grape leaves, a sticky clump of ripe dates. Those in the palms above them are still green.

From the time the Bedouin found him, unconscious in the grove of palms that had been planted by the settlers from the hill opposite, Abed showed up every day with food and two full plastic liter bottles of water. He brought aspirin, and alcohol to clean Cobi's wounds. The wounds are superficial, but under present conditions might easily become infected.

When he first came to, the young soldier thought the Bedouin intended to kill him—for his gun, or his boots, or his watch—or turn him over to the enemy for bounty.

The Bedu chuckled at this. "You are my guest," he said. "And thus your life is my responsibility. I am obligated to protect you."

Very quickly Abed revealed more. For twenty years he was a tracker in the IDF, officially still is, but he burned his sergeant's uniform and buried his military ID when he saw how the wind was blowing. Should they discover he was not merely another Bedouin shepherd, the Syrians who held this area would rape his wife and kill his children before his own eyes, and then torture him to death with not even so much as a pause to think about it. Syrian hatred for the Bedouins was never a secret, and for those who joined forces with the Zionist enemy there could be no mercy. If Abed is glad of anything it is that his father is no longer among the living. The old man preceded him as an IDF scout, and the entire modus operandi of his life was to find a way to die gloriously. He fought in three wars, the old man, with the decorations to prove it, was wounded twice, almost willfully seeking a glorious death. His father alive would have got them all killed.

Abed considers himself a modern man. He can wait to die. His job is to stay alive in order to protect his family and small clan.

"My father, may he enjoy the fruits of paradise, was pure Bedu," Abed told his guest in the cave in the first days. "But I am compromised. I have responsibilities."

"Then you're foolish to risk your life for a stranger."

"You are not a stranger. You were, then not."

That was ten days ago. Sometimes Abed did not show up for extended periods, waiting until it was safe, difficult hours for Cobi as he recuperated from blood loss, shock, fear, and the gnawing perception that it is criminal for a soldier not to be in battle, though where that battle is he does not know. Maybe something happened to Abed, or his protector changed his mind. He knows that as a people the Bedouin are, as a reflection of necessity, not the most consistent of personalities. Perhaps a greater responsibility had presented itself, and Abed chose to protect his family and clan by turning him in. Cobi could understand that. Abed has six children. He loves his wife so much he has not taken another. If it comes to a choice, Cobi will understand. But always Abed returns, twice during the day with a herd of sheep as cover, though mostly by night.

Cobi finishes the bread, vegetables, and cheese and turns to the dates. "Abed," he says as he chews the sweet fruit he learned in school was the original honey of this land, his land, flowing with the milk of sheep and goats and the honey of dates. "I can't stay here forever. It's dangerous for both of us. And I have to get back to my unit." He pauses. "Any unit."

"A poor Bedu you'd make. Do you not know patience is a principal virtue of the Bedu?" He grins. "Maybe the only one."

"What's it like out there?"

"What is it like? Fucking Syrians steal everything. Last night a patrol took four lambs. *Inshallah,* to be again in uniform. Some believe we Bedu enlist for money. Cobi, no one can buy the Bedu. For the first time since the prophet, my tribe is not spat upon by Arabs. Why? Because we wear the uniform of the IDF. Why do we do this, work with the Jews? In twenty years no Jew, officer or enlisted, looked down upon me. It is disgusting what has happened."

"What has happened? Does anyone really know?"

"We will see soon enough. I must get you to Tel Aviv. That is your only chance."

"And how will you accomplish that? How do we do that if it's as you say—that the enemy is all over the land. Under every rock. In the shade of every tree. Your words."

"Fuck words," Abed says. He pulls from beneath his robes a worn, dusty suit of Bedouin garb, replete with headgear and a pair of battered sandals.

"Fuck words is right," Cobi says, examining among the robes spread before him a *kaffiyeh* and the *agal,* the loop of woolen rope that keeps it on one's head. "Abed, my Arabic consists of *surrender, hands up, bread,* and *your mother's cunt.* I wouldn't want to have to engage in an extended conversation on Sharia law."

"Dress then in these and keep your mouth tightly shut," the Bedouin says. "It will make for a pleasant change."

49

THOUGH TEL AVIV IS spared mass destruction, IDF headquarters in the Kirya in the very center of the city is a leveled field, bombed intensely on the first day of the attack, and though the war rooms in hardened levels deep underground remain intact, there is no longer any communications infrastructure to connect the military leadership with units in the field. In point of fact, there are no units in the field.

The air force is wiped out. IAF pilots and navigators are now relegated to sitting around the lobby of a hotel on the beach that has neither electricity nor running water. These mission-oriented men and women of action find themselves with no mission and no action. A good many busy themselves playing poker and gin rummy, the most adept amassing thousands of shekels in play money that can buy nothing. Few have sufficient energy for beach volleyball or swimming, or even enough to argue politics, once the national pastime of a people who had not been permitted to govern themselves for over two thousand years. But of politics, like food and water, there is now none.

In the fishing port of Jaffa to the south of Tel Aviv, which had almost immediately been abandoned by its largely Arab population on strenuous warnings from the Islamic Liberation Force, whose aircraft snowed leaflets over the town, a division of infantry was cobbled together. But with little weaponry, less ammunition, and entirely no transport, its fighting men spend their time fishing. It is a useless pastime: Because every third resident of Tel Aviv tries his hand at angling for some sort of aquatic protein, the waters close to shore are quickly fished out. Many soldiers play chess or dominos or shesh-besh, a variety of backgammon. One enterprising platoon, having discovered the epicurean delights of seaweed, manages to harvest sufficient for a handful for almost every man and woman in the division. After several days, there is no more.

The navy is gone, sunk in port or destroyed by Egyptian gunships after running out of fuel at sea. A few fortunate sailors swim to shore, the shark-ravaged bodies of the rest eventually joining them, skeletal remains wrapped in shredded tan cloth.

Only an expanded brigade of some 160 tanks remains capable of action, but these and their support vehicles are strung out in a Maginot Line of dubious efficacy on the eastern edge of the city. With low reserves of fuel, this armor, once the mailed fist of an IDF capable of lightning offensive strength and tremendous maneuverability, now function as a static, if not simply symbolic, line of defense. Fixed in place like artillery, their commanders' only hope is to discourage the approach of the first enemy tank. Once the next vehicles break through, there is nothing to stop them from entering the city. It will be over.

With little to command and no communications with which to do it, the chief of staff is reduced to traveling by jeep from group to group in a vain attempt to instill hope and a sense of military structure. An early attempt to restart training fails for lack of fuel, not merely for the armored corps but for its personnel. With next to nothing to eat, no one has the energy. Even basic morning calisthenics are abandoned, just as their chief of staff has abandoned all hope on his daily visits to the Hilton, where former low-level government functionaries go through the motions of pretending to administer a city-state of the damned. They have nothing to offer him in the way of resources, and he has nothing to offer them in the way of defense.

He is at the Hilton now, barely a mile away, when a column of civilian cars led by a red BMW pulls up to what is now IDF headquarters, a collection of camouflaged tents that fills the once-pleasant park lining the south side of the Yarkon River from Ibn-Givrol to Dizengoff Street, in the recent past Israel's thoroughfare of the young, the hip, the cool. Its bars and restaurants, broken into, now offer shelter from the sun to thousands of refugees. Pinky makes his visit to the Hilton every day at the same hour. It is no accident that the driver of the red BMW leading the column of civilian cars chose the same hour to visit what passes for military HQ.

Assembling his personnel, a collection of gangsters, miscreants, and triggermen from all over the country, Misha steps away from Yigal to speak his marching orders in terms that are as brief as they are chilling.

"Whatever happens," he says, "we don't kill our own."

A Druze drug dealer in the front rank, whose people in the northern village of Daliyat-al-Carmel were wiped out by the invaders, man, woman, and child, for collaboration with the Jews, utters a quiet, "God forbid." The Druze, an offshoot of Islam, have fought in the IDF for decades.

"Unless," Misha says, "absolutely necessary."

50

THE HEADS OF SIX Jewish organizations are seated like diplomats with the president and Flo Spier in the Oval Office, having first been treated to a group tour of the White House and then each photographed with the president, a print of which will no doubt take its place on an office wall full of similar souvenirs. All have been here before, guests of earlier presidents. Like earlier presidential advisors, Flo Spier counts them as necessary to electoral victory as the caciques of the Cuban exile community in Florida, the light-complexioned leaders of a dozen black organizations, the delegations of Hollywood stars lobbying for intervention in Africa, to say nothing of federal protection for the blue whale, support for the Dalai Lama, encouragement of wind power, and constitutional recognition of gay marriage. The president is already on good terms with almost every Pentecostal group; like the Jews, these too must be stroked. As must every other puzzle piece in America's fractious demographic jigsaw: Mexican-American leaders pushing for immigration reform, delegations from Wall Street and Silicon Valley looking for tax breaks, politically powerful Roman Catholic bishops in states where many people still insist on eating fish on Friday. Though today's delegation of grandees is aware that the Jewish vote is no longer concentrated in the northeast, Jewish money will be a factor in American politics for a long time. Fortunately, that money is now evenly divided in support for both parties. This offers leverage.

The president is not unaware. His guests have twenty minutes to make their case, or to feel they are making it. Egos are involved.

"Mr. President, Israel is an ally of the United States, a beacon of democracy in the Middle East." This from the doyen of American rabbis, a tennis-playing Reform cleric, hatless, beardless and—according to his more traditional colleagues—shameless.

"Well, Rabbi Joe," the president says. "I could be cynical here and say Israel is now not much of an ally of anyone. It's the incredible shrinking country. Of course, under our treaty we *will* come to her defense should Israel be subject to nuclear attack."

The representative of B'nai Brith, secular and centrist, has seen this coming. "But Mr. President, that's not the problem. The problem is Iran so far has not had to use nuclear—"

"Warren, below nuclear my hands are tied. My predecessors tried to get involved with improving the situation in other places in the Middle East, which I'm sure you know, and it cost this country a fortune in the lives of our brave young soldiers, to say nothing of vast reserves of treasure that have left the US economy in a state from which it has yet to fully recover. Y'all are not looking at a man who believes America should entangle itself in the affairs of every nation around the globe, noble and sympathetic as that nation may be. As for democracy, the Israelian parliament—what they call it, Flo?"

"The Knesset, Mr. President."

"The Key-Ness-Et. Been dissolved."

"Mr. President," the B'nai B'rith chairman blurts out. "By assassination!"

The leader of the free world checks his watch. "Gentlemen, let me be frank." One of the visitors will later suggest to his wife that this is pretty much an admission that otherwise the president has been less than that. "I've always had a soft spot in my heart for the Jewish people. My Harvard roomie was half-Hebrew, Benny Berman—everybody used to call him Berman the Vermin. All in fun, of course. I do admire you folks, no question, always have, always will. But there's more at stake here than what I call matters of the heart. My heart *is* with you, one hundred percent. But the national temper, that's a whole 'nother ballgame. Poll after poll, including our own unpublicized research, shows pretty damn clearly—excuse me, gentlemen, for my language, but I'm leveling with y'all—shows conclusively that if our Jewish citizens try to distort the national agenda to get us involved in another Middle East war to support Israel, what's left of it, then mark my words the American people will react on the parallel matter of immigration, a prospect I deplore, but won't be able to do much to prevent. We got us millions of refugees with no place to go but the bottom of the sea. That's the A-one, double-distilled, gold-plated problem before us, and it requires the acquiescence of the American people. Flo, what's that phrase these folks use?"

"*Shalom bayit,* sir. Peace at home."

"Exactly. Peace at home, my friends. We need things to work out here at home before we can go ahead and take care of your coreligionists over there in Tel Aviv. I don't have to tell you the first step in that process. It's solving the worst energy crisis this country has every faced. We got to get people filling their tanks with gas at prices they can live with. End of the day, those are the kind of tanks that are going to save your people, not the kind with guns attached. *Shalom bayeet.* I love the sound of that. It means with goodwill and a flexible foreign policy we can get the job done. Now let me thank each and every one of you folks for visiting with us. I'm advised you can pick up your autographed photographic records of this historic visit on your way out. I've always maintained an open door policy for the American Jewish community, and as Christ is my witness this President of the United States of America ain't going to let that change. Thank you for y'all's support."

51

YIGAL AND MISHA FIND Major General Ido Baram sleeping on a camp cot in the shade of a eucalyptus outside the headquarters tent. It is clear this is headquarters because a small hand-lettered cardboard sign so designates it. Otherwise, zip: there is no sentry outside, no adjutant hovering just within to make sure military procedure is followed to the letter. It appears military procedure has ceased to exist. Aside from the fact that the men and women sitting around in the shade as though on vacation are in uniform, or some parts of uniform, Camp Yarkon, as it is called, could be any low-rent holiday retreat in any park on the bank of any polluted river in any starving city anywhere.

"Ido," Yigal says quietly. "What the fuck?"

The general opens an eye. "Yigal?"

"Get up, man. We have to talk."

"Talk, then. Me, I haven't eaten since yesterday morning. I couldn't tell you what it was but I ate it." He struggles to sit up. Once an icon of physical fitness in the Armored Corps, said to go to war with a set of barbells in his tank, Ido Baram is now little more than a bag of bones covered in loose skin, his uniform flapping around his torso like so much torn wrapping paper. When he lifts his head, it can be seen that his holstered pistol acted as a pillow. He straps it on. Even this, a compact Beretta 9 mm, seems far too big for him. Once ruddy, his face is pale with a curious yellow underlay that is reflected in the whites of his eyes, whose ochre cast is unmistakable, a sure sign of jaundice. Slowly, he stands.

"See that? On my feet like a proper general officer." He peers past Yigal to Misha and the troop of big men in too-gaudy civilian clothes who keep looking around as if they expect to be arrested at any moment. "I can offer you water," he says. "Just you, unfortunately. We rigged a solar still. Not Niagara Falls, but we get by." He looks again at Misha's crew. "Friends of yours?"

"I didn't come for water," Yigal says. "Can we come inside?"

"Sure," Ido says, lifting a flap for them to enter. "But we'll have to speak quietly so as not to disturb headquarters staff, who are diligently planning the counterattack. To your left is operations, field intelligence to the right, over there manpower, logistics, and supply, engineering at the rear. Liaison is in the far corner and of course next to that communications."

The tent is empty.

"Oh, I forgot to mention medical. Just outside." Ido laughs, a kind of burp of self-derision. "We're not exactly staffed to the max, of course, because we have no tanks, no equipment, no ammunition, no planning, no personnel capable of fighting, much less walking around, no food and little water. Did I mention no air force or navy? Also no medical supplies, in case you're here in search of an aspirin." He pauses, as though unable to continue. Even to Ido, the joke becomes less funny the longer it continues. "Yigal, you haven't introduced your friend."

Misha offers his hand.

Ido pointedly ignores it, replying with a mock salute. "Misha Shulman, staff sergeant. I know you well. In fact, I tried to have you removed from the Armored Corps."

"I knew someone did. I didn't know it was you. What, afraid I'd steal a tank?"

"More like introducing hard drugs, selling military secrets, that kind of thing. Yigal, this is your friend?"

"You're both my friends."

"Yigal Lev," Ido says, "As always, a man of many parts. Can we get to the point? I find standing for more than a minute wastes too much energy."

Yigal squats on the ground. "Gentlemen, please be seated."

The two look at each other, then squat as well.

"Actually," Ido says, turning to Yigal. "You shouldn't even be here. Him even less. This is a closed military area. You're neither in uniform nor called up. In fact, if I remember properly, Yigal, I personally dissolved your brigade. In consonance with the rest of the IDF, it no longer exists. Also, if I recall correctly, Pinky wanted you court-martialed for disobeying a direct order on the battlefield. But as it happens he's been busy."

"Busy ordering a retreat," Misha says.

"Does he have to be here?"

Yigal nods. "Yes, Reserve Staff Sgt. Misha Shulman does have to be here. And I suggest you treat Misha with a modicum of respect, not only because he is my friend but because if you keep at him he is likely to shoot you in the head."

"I was thinking of the balls."

"Yeah, well, stop thinking of fighting amongst ourselves. I'm here because I prefer fighting the enemy."

"Over there," Ido says, waving airily to the east. "About six kilometers. You can't miss them. Arabs mostly, with a nice overlay of Iranians. Intelligence, when we had intelligence, also noted a Pakistani unit—imagine that, Pakistan—and a nasty group of rapists from Chechnya, of all places. What do you want me to do, Yigal, conjure up an army? You were sent home. Stay there."

"Ido," Yigal says. "I'm taking back my tanks."

"What?"

"I'm taking back my tanks. That's why we're here."

"Yours?" Ido says. "What did you do, buy them?"

"I don't have to buy them. They were taken from me without reason."

"Yours? Oh, I see. I thought for a moment you were sober. Very good. If I live through this I'll tell my grandchildren. It's like those *an Englishman, a Frenchman, and a Pole walk into a bar* jokes. A capitalist and a gangster walk into command headquarters and the capitalist says—"

"The capitalist says he wants his tanks. Why is that funny? You're not using them, are you?"

"Talk to the chief of staff. Pinky will be amused. He could use a good laugh."

"You talk to Pinky," Yigal says. "We're reactivating the 112th."

"That brigade *is* activated, Yigal. It's just blended into something else, which you have no part of. Pinky took the map with him. When he comes back you can ask him to explain our disposition of forces, including your former tanks, all well dug-in in defensive positions."

"Look, Ido. I don't want this to be unfriendly. We're taking our tanks."

"You were relieved of command. The gangster too. You can't just walk in and take tanks."

Misha has had enough. It does not take much. He reaches behind him and removes the gold-plated .40-cal CZ pistol from his belt and levels it at Ido's head. Firing at this range will leave nothing of it: torso, shoulders, neck—check. Head? None. "I changed my mind about aiming for the balls, Yigal. This piece of shit has none."

"Oh, now I understand," Ido says, showing no fear, a natural consequence of either hopelessness or constant hunger, perhaps both. Doubtless the jaundice does not help. "You're going to *steal* the tanks."

"You're going to stop us?" Misha says, holding the pistol so level a ball bearing would not roll off.

"Just like that? No permission? No authority?"

"Misha, put down the gun. This is not a matter for guns. Ido, listen carefully. You've got a defensive perimeter as effective as a line of clothes hanging in the sun. Fewer than two hundred tanks, most of them immobile, covering a line a hundred kilometers long. On the other side there are a couple thousand enemy cans, maybe double that, maybe triple. To know exactly we'd need a satellite, and I doubt we're in contact with those. The way we're disposed, the enemy can break through at any point. You and I could do it with three tanks. We don't have a defensive perimeter. We have an illusion."

"We have the best we can do."

Misha is still pointing the gun at Ido's head, but now it wavers, perhaps from doubt, perhaps because it weighs almost four pounds. Even a hard guy like Misha cannot hold a weight like that steady forever. "Yigal, let me just put him out of our misery."

"Misha, put away the gun. It's an order. Ido is a military professional. He understands."

"He understands this," Misha mutters. But like a child deprived of a favored toy, Misha tips up his pistol, then places it in his lap.

"Very good. Ido, I'm taking my brigade back. But I need more. I need control of all the armor you command."

"What is this, a coup d'état? We're what now, Haiti? Liberia?"

"Yigal," Misha says. "We're running out of time. And I'm running out of patience."

"Do you agree, Ido, that this defensive perimeter is a joke? I'm asking for your trust."

"You're asking for the keys to half the surviving tanks in the State of Israel."

"I'm asking for all of them. Look, Ido, we served together over twenty years. There wasn't a moment in that time, from officer's training onward, that I didn't trust you and you didn't trust me. Comrades in arms to the end, right? Well, my friend, we have reached the end. The State of Israel barely exists, but with your help it will."

"Yigal," Misha says. "Let me just shoot the fucker."

The look on Yigal's face is no longer one of friendly persuasion. "Sergeant, shut the fuck up. When I agreed to this, it was on one condition. What was it?"

Misha makes a face. "That you command."

"Exactly." He turns to the general. "Ido, what is IDF doctrine when we are surrounded, outnumbered, outflanked, and down to our last ammunition and fuel?"

Ido laughs. "Attack!"

"*Nu, mon general?*"

Mon General sighs, then offers a wan smile. "It's treason, you know. Pinky can have me shot."

"I know."

Major General Ido Baram glances up, now to Misha, then to Yigal. "Tell me what I need to do."

52

THAT NIGHT, SOMEWHERE IN the Negev desert—she is unsure precisely where, having dropped down out of the sky in an all but featureless landscape that might as well be the moon—Alex sits in a dry riverbed by the side of a paved road. She has already changed into female garb, her pilot's uniform stuffed into the bag that had held her makeup, dress, and high heels. The road is doubtless marked at some point, but all she can tell is that it runs north-south. Her compass is functioning, as is her mind, which seems to go into overdrive under critical conditions. As a pilot, she felt confident in her competence during training flights, or when delivering a plane, but once in combat she is always ramped up, super-capable, her reflexes so quick they operate without her knowledge, eye-to-hand controls moving seamlessly without routing through the conscious brain. In the more quiet moments of her life, and this is certainly one of them, she wonders if her wandering gender identities are in some way connected to the peculiar duality of her abilities as a pilot.

For hours, a dozen lappet-faced vultures have been circling above, even now in the moonlight. These respect neither rank nor politics, gender nor nationality. As far as the vultures are concerned, Alex is just another lone animal that soon, without water, will be weak, delirious, defenseless. The morticians of the animal world, they normally wait respectfully for their meals to die. But unconscious living flesh is the same as dead. Their eyesight is as sharp as that of the local Bedouin, whose appetite for prey is no less refined.

These Negev tribesmen are capable of spotting a lit cigarette a mile off. Alex knows enough about the clans hereabout to know how much danger she is in. In fact, though Israel Air Force doctrine focuses on saving aircraft as well as pilot, in case of an emergency over the Negev a forced landing is never advised. Let the plane crash elsewhere, miles from where your parachute falls. Landing the plane successfully means the pilot will be found in a matter of minutes, because there is no way to distance oneself sufficiently from the aircraft before it will be spotted by enemy reconnaissance from above, enemy ground forces nearby, or by camel-mounted Bedouin tribesman eager for bounty. In this three-dimensional game of chess, it is better to remain a live pawn than a trapped queen.

But this queen does not feel trapped.

Alex is already on the offensive, planning her next moves. First priority: wheels.

Just as she finishes applying her lipstick, a kind of crimson this evening (she prefers earth tones for daytime), a convoy of Egyptian infantry, some twenty trucks, comes into view. There is sufficient moonlight for her to identify the unit number painted on the sides, but of course no one to report it to, and no radio to report it with. Anyway, trucks full of infantry are not what she needs. Within a few minutes, there it is: a '70s-era Cadillac sedan painted olive green and flying the red, white, and black standard of the Egyptian high command.

She scrambles out of the wadi, no easy matter in four-inch heels, and flags the Cadillac down, showing a bit of leg in the process. As though magnetized, the staff car pulls to a halt, then backs up.

While she stands in the moonlight, the young adjutant driving leaps out to open the rear door. She cannot see inside but hopes there is no more than one passenger. Waving her left hand gaily she approaches the car with the other behind her back until she is close enough: one passenger, struggling to get out of the car. So far, so good. But she is still too distant for certainty. As she closes the gap, the single passenger, an obese colonel, manages with the aid of his adjutant to exit the car. He is grinning.

She takes the adjutant out first, one shot to the head. He is still crumpling when she shifts the barrel of her 9mm Israel Military Industries pistol and drops the obese colonel with two shots. In motion immediately, she kicks off her heels and gets to the car. The colonel is still moving. All that fat. There is less fat around his skull. A third shot does the job.

She knows she has mere minutes before more Egyptian traffic appears, every one of their vehicles running with full headlights, sign enough that for the Egyptian Army the war is over, the area secure. She leaves her pistol by the car, not the best thing but she needs both hands and her dress affords nothing to tuck it into. The fat colonel's uniform will do her no good, but after cutting through his trousers with a small, sharp IAF-issue emergency blade, she relieves him of his huge boxer shorts—a white flag may come in handy later. After rolling the huge corpse into the wadi, she turns to the adjutant. In a moment she is out of her clothes and into his, not a bad fit at all, though she will have to adjust the pistol belt holding up his, no longer her, pants. The adjutant's Colt Commander, a .45, looks so new she wonders if it has ever been fired.

"Shit," she says aloud. She should have done this before.

Climbing down into the wadi, she removes the colonel's brass insignia of rank and his pistol, another Colt, but this one gold-plated. She climbs back to the road, wraps her heels in her dress, tosses the adjutant's shoes into the front of the Cadillac, and takes off, leaving the bodies of the adjutant and Lieutenant Colonel Anwar, head of Egyptian Special Operations Branch, for the lappet-faced vultures.

In this there is the irony of rough justice. Col. Anwar has just come from setting up a "relocation camp" for the Hamas leadership of Gaza. Allied to the Muslim Brotherhood that for decades has been a thorn in the side of Egypt's secular leadership, Hamas has long been at the top of the Egyptian army's hit list.

Relocation is of course a euphemism. Just outside of Beersheba, Col. Anwar personally supervised the mass burial of twelve hundred Palestinians identified as Hamas, many of them accurately. Though Col. Anwar would have preferred to spend a bit more time on each one of these enemies of Egypt, this is hardly practical: wholesale torture in a war zone might leak out of even the most hermetically sealed area. The only choice was machine gunning them into mass graves and then bulldozing tons of sand to cover the bodies deep enough so that the ever-present vultures, whole flocks of which had migrated to feast on the victims of this war, would not spread their bones across the desert floor to become a diplomatic embarrassment and then, later on, a problem for tourists. For tourists, there can be nothing worse that coming across a pile of human bones before lunch.

Col. Anwar's engineers had identified a spring close to the burial spot, which is why it was chosen. In a matter of weeks, Egyptian peasants are to be brought in to plant date palms over the mass graves, whose decomposing bodies will provide excellent fertilizer and the spring adequate water. A meticulous planner, Col. Anwar early on filed a claim for the site, together with a thousand acres surrounding it, more than sufficient for a village. Given a bit of luck and special investment from Cairo, one fine day the village might become a city. Upon maturity, the palms alone will provide an annual profit sufficient to ensure a wealth stream to generations of Anwars, to say nothing of rents from the village, and then—Allah willing—the city into which it might grow. According to the Egyptian proverb: *Plant today, feast tomorrow.*

But according to another Egyptian proverb: *Because we feared the snake, we missed the scorpion.*

In her adjutant's uniform, adorned with Col. Anwar's rank insignia, Alex reaches the first of what will be many Egyptian checkpoints. Half a dozen vehicles are lined up. Alex drives the Cadillac briskly around them, taps the horn, and takes the salute of the four infantrymen standing guard. Having removed her makeup and blond wig, Alex returns the salute with the casual ennui of a staff officer and drives on through, barely slowing down as the barrier is lifted.

53

THE NEXT MORNING, BARELY a hundred miles distant, two dozen Chariot tanks with the markings of the 112th armored brigade roll south down the Tel Aviv beachfront, passing the startled residents of the tent city that runs almost the entire length of Tel Aviv's once pristine seafront. These are not tents precisely, but mere shelters strung together from sheets and blankets over whatever wood or metal could be scavenged from the beachfront hotels. Hotel mattresses provide the beds, each laboriously carried down dozens of narrow flights of stairs and then dragged to the beach. In a mélange of pragmatism and desiccated whimsy, most of these tent neighborhoods are marked with signage liberated from the hotels. In this way, one can say he now lives in the Herzl Suite near where Frishman Street meets the beach, or in the Presidential Ballroom at the end of Dizengoff Street. At the encampment marked King Solomon Conference Room, the tanks, led by a convoy of ten jeeps, turn east into the heart of the white city, rattle across a now brown public park, and come to a stop before the Tel Aviv Hilton. Compared to the massive armor the luxury hotel seems now blurry, faded, shrunken.

Its lobby is empty of furniture but not of people. These are not reading the *Jerusalem Post* and drinking espresso, signaling waiters for another round or meeting business associates. Instead the cavernous hall is full of children squatting on the now-filthy carpeting in jury-rigged classrooms whose walls are the box springs that until recently supported the mattresses moved to the beach. In the classic manner of educators everywhere, the volunteer teachers attempt to hold the attention of their students through a combination of charm and discipline. They use blackboards of all sizes and shapes, some merely framed prints from the guest rooms painted over in matt black. The children sit on the floor, some rapt, most allowing their gaze to widen at the entrance of Yigal and Misha followed by forty men, half of them in uniform, the rest in the telltale mufti of muscle shirts and gold chains. All are armed.

Yigal is surprised there is a clerk at the long front desk, quite as if there could possibly be paying guests now that almost all foreign nationals have been evacuated via special flights from Ben Gurion International Airport—now Yasser Arafat International, though no one in Tel Aviv can bear to utter the name.

The receptionist is not a Hilton employee but a dedicated civil servant, working of course without pay, because there is no one to pay him, and even if there would be, the money he receives will be worthless. A hand-printed sign is propped on the desk:

Government of Israel
RECEPTION
Unauthorized Entry Prohibited

Misha tips over the flimsy cardboard with the barrel of his gun. "Where do you keep the government?"

The clerk is not about to argue. He points in the direction of a sign that has not yet been taken down to become the name of a tent neighborhood. Misha motions to four of his men to remain in the lobby.

The others follow their leaders through the makeshift school, some making funny faces at the children in the way of adults who never had a proper childhood themselves. The kids laugh, any break in the school day a delight.

In a moment, the armed men come to a conference room whose double doors are open for ventilation—all exterior windows in the Hilton's public rooms are sealed. The entire ground floor is one big hothouse.

Around a long table covered in red cloth sit twelve men and women, their aides making up a second row so that altogether about forty are in the room. At midpoint around the table, his back to the entry, sits a sixty-year old bureaucrat named Uri Ben-Dov, who is so intent on his words, which are being inscribed for posterity by a stenographer—the hotel hasn't the electric power to run a voice recorder—that he is unaware Yigal and Misha have entered behind him.

"Any ideas, then?" Ben-Dov is saying. He notices the eyes of the others are fixed over his right shoulder.

"I got one," Misha says quietly. "Who's in charge here?"

Like any politician, Ben-Dov is not pleased at the interruption, nor by Misha's tone. "I am acting prime minister."

"Not a very convincing act," Misha says. "You're Ben-Dov, then?"

The acting prime minister looks beyond his two guests to the men in the corridor. "And who precisely are you?"

"What's important is who this is." Misha nods in the direction of Yigal.

"I know who Yigal Lev is. Mr. Lev, we met some time ago at a conference. In Caesaria?" Ben-Dov realizes he is not exactly displaying authority. He alters his tone. "Regrettably, this is not an open meeting, Mr. Lev. It is in fact closed to the public. A sign to that effect is posted downstairs at the—"

"Mr. Ben-Dov," Yigal says. "We're not the public. We're the interim government. You're being replaced."

Ben-Dov stands, looking around him for affirmation from the seated group, then back to Yigal. "I am the single surviving member of the Knesset. As such I am authorized by the Basic Law of the State of Israel, which stipulates that in case of emergency the senior—"

"The Knesset doesn't exist."

"Israel is still a democracy, Mr. Lev."

"Israel barely exists. Her only chance is to put herself in the hands of people who know what they're doing. You don't."

"I vehemently protest."

"Noted," Yigal says, with a nod to the stenographer. "Let the record show that the former deputy minister for culture and sport protests." He smiles at the woman, whose face seems at once to reflect confusion and relief. "You have that?"

"This is outrageous," Ben-Dov says, his voice rising an octave. "In this room is the legitimate government of the State of Israel."

Misha pulls out his gun. "In this room is a lot of bullshit."

Ben-Dov suddenly recognizes him. "I've seen your face in the papers."

"Misha Shulman, at your service."

"The gangster. I will say this once and once only. Please leave. You have no place here. Not you, Mr. Shulman, nor you, Mr. Lev. The State of Israel has problems enough without—"

"You know who fought to the last man in the Warsaw Ghetto?" Misha asks conversationally, cocking his pistol. "Jewish gangsters." The silence in the room is absolute. "Commander?"

"Okay," Yigal says quietly, addressing the room at large. "In a moment, papers will be distributed to each person here. They are formal letters of resignation. Those who sign will be free to go."

Ben-Dov's voice goes up another octave. "And if we choose not to sign?"

"You don't want to know," Yigal says.

54

US MARINE AVIATION FORWARD Attack Base Wildcat does not appear on any publically issued list of American military facilities, officially because it is a temporary base leased from the Principality of Oman for the purpose of search and rescue. This is disingenuity of the highest order, but it permits Oman's rulers to appear independent of the West and pure of desert heart should it be discovered that even so little as this twelve-plane squadron of F/A-18 Super Hornets exists, tucked as it is into an especially empty quarter of an empty sheikdom. The principality thus attempts to stay on the good side of groups such as ISIS and Al Qaeda, which have declared war on the royal families of Arabia, among other Middle Eastern leaders, for allowing non-Muslim fighting men (and women!) to set foot on the Arabian peninsula, upon which northeastern Oman sits like a sandy carbuncle. Though remarkably there is in Arabic no single word for Arabia, the very land upon which these feudal kingdoms sit is broadly considered to be holy unto itself: the Arabian peninsula is the home of Mecca and Medina; Arabia was the first conquest of the Prophet. To radical Islamists, that this first jewel in the crown of Islam should be occupied by the infidel forces of the Great Satan defies the deathbed injunction of Mohammed himself: "Let there not be two religions in Arabia."

Thus the Pentagon and the Omani leadership came to an accommodation: Marine Corps Aviation is just passing through, and as a guest in the desert its personnel must be welcomed and the baggage of its caravan protected, especially since its official mission is humanitarian in keeping with the hadiths: "Protect the innocent, ransom the enslaved, save the lost."

The base's unofficial mission is somewhat different: USMA Forward Attack Squadron Wildcat is deployed to protect the oil-rich Emirates from Iranian invasion.

Because its personnel serve six-month tours punctuated by month-long rotations back to their home base at Beaufort, South Carolina, the installation, which is totally isolated from any contact with the indigenous population, must supply its own entertainment. Thus it maintains extensive sports facilities, including two indoor basketball courts and a sixty-foot swimming pool, access to some 300,000 books and videos via the Department of the Navy's Online Library, and—aside from CNN—the full panoply of US television stations serving coastal South Carolina. There is not a burglary in the city of Beaufort that is not hometown news at Marine Air Forward Attack Squadron Wildcat.

Perched overlooking Iran's western flank, the base's pilots tend to watch CNN with interest. Their hearts may be in Beaufort, but their minds are alert to any change in the regional political situation: if things are heating up in the Persian Gulf, these airmen want to know about it.

In the duty room, three pilots watch with fascination as anchor Damian Smith narrates a special report called *Hell in Tel Aviv*. Once part of the international press's anti-Israel front, like most other news outlets CNN now finds itself in the unfamiliar position of rooting for the Israeli underdog in an update of the original David-and-Goliath story, except this time David lies mortally wounded on the Mediterranean coast.

The special report is little more than a visual dirge narrated by the normally upbeat Smith. "Thousands of Jewish refugees continue to stream into Israeli-controlled Tel Aviv," Smith reads as footage from Al-Jazeera shows rivers of refugees filling the highway past a sign that says TEL AVIV 30 KMS, then footage of former Israel Railways carriages, now crudely stenciled over in Arabic and English ISLAM RAIL, with Jews packed tightly within and riding between the cars and on top.

"Meanwhile, in Jerusalem, the Islamic Liberation Force has confirmed the destruction of the Western or Wailing Wall, the single remnant of the Holy Temple, said to be, to have been, the single most sacred spot for Jews everywhere." Grainy images show the massive stones of the Wall tumbling down in a cloud of ancient dust as Arab soldiers dance in celebration, then footage of weeping Orthodox Jews in New York rending their garments in mourning. "In London, when the destruction of the Wall was announced, Britain's chief rabbi, con-

sidered by many Jews to have inherited a mantle of authority from
the chief rabbinate of Israel, now defunct, called on Jews around the
world to begin a week of fasting, prayer, and repentance. Destruction
of the Wall was met by harsh criticism from most Western leaders,
including the president, who termed it 'an act of violence against
Jews, Christians, and peace-loving Muslims everywhere.'

"In Tel Aviv, widespread looting is reported to have broken out
as an estimated six million Jews search desperately for food and water. Arab control of Israeli airspace and access from the sea has cut off
the city and, some say, sealed its doom. From nearby Cyprus, Connie
Blunt in the port of Limassol."

Perky as ever, Blunt does a stand-up against the background
of fishing boats lined up romantically at Limassol harbor, a classic
Mediterranean view that could just as well have been painted on. Her
attire is vaguely nautical and clearly not inexpensive. Unlike earlier
generations of female correspondents, who felt they must prove to
be as tough as their male colleagues, Blunt does not travel light. As
well, CNN is contractually bound to pay for her on-screen wardrobe.
"Damian, from reports by Israelis who've escaped from what is being
called Ghetto Tel Aviv, mostly in small boats, a few in private planes,
the rump state of Israel has only weeks, perhaps days, before its population starves to death. Think of Manhattan Island, quadruple its
population, cut it off from food, and you can imagine the mounting
fear and very real chaos in the once-thriving metropolis, known as
the White City for its unique 1930s Bauhaus architecture and lit-up
nightlife. It used to be said of Israel's three major urban areas that
Haifa works, Jerusalem prays, and Tel Aviv plays. Now both Haifa
and Jerusalem are ghost towns, and in Tel Aviv, nobody is playing.
The people of Israel are dying, and the State of Israel with them."

"Connie, a moment ago you compared Tel Aviv to Manhattan.
We should point out that Manhattan is an island, surrounded by
fresh water. Sources in Washington tell us that water is in extremely
short supply in Tel Aviv. Can you confirm that?"

"Yes, Damian. I can. With me here in Cyprus is Dr. Heinz Wortzel, head of emergency relief for the International Committee of the Red Cross, who tells me the water situation is very bad indeed and becoming worse, not least because Israel's National Water Carrier, the pipeline system which supplies drinking water from the north of the country, has been disrupted. Dr. Wortzel, isn't this an act that some would term genocide on the part of the Arab conquerors of Israel?"

Blunt's cameraman pulls back so that the television screen in the ready room of Marine Aviation Forward Attack Squadron Wildcat shows her standing with a tall, thin man in rimless glasses, a light-colored suit and tie. He speaks with a Swiss-German accent at once dour and surprisingly musical. "In my professional capacity, I regret that I can neither confirm nor deny that the lack of potable water in the city of Tel Aviv is caused by purposeful tampering or redirection of the National Water Carrier. Such a speculation is not within my purview. Also it appears that the city of Tel Aviv is without electricity, as coal to power its generators is now terminated. This alone could be a factor of significance—water must be pumped, you see. However, it is a fact that the population of Tel Aviv is not in a good condition, which becomes worse every day."

"Dr. Wortzel," Connie asks, "what can be done to relieve the city and bring in needed supplies to avert a humanitarian disaster?"

"Since three weeks we have been in daily contact with the Red Crescents of the Arab nations concerned to find a way round many complex logistical and political obstacles."

Blunt becomes aggressive. "And how is that working out, doctor?"

"Under the circumstances, we are doing our best. These efforts will, of course, continue."

"Has the Red Cross been permitted to visit Israeli prisoners of war who are said to be—"

"Because of the many armies and political entities involved, we have not yet succeeded in this."

"I'm told over four hundred thousand Israeli POWs are being held in overcrowded camps, with no shade, little to no food or water, and no medical care at all for the sick and wounded."

"Having not visited these facilities, I am not in a position to comment. In coming days my colleagues and I hope to—"

James Boatwright, the pilot they call Jimbo, cuts off the sound with the remote control. That it is in his hand is a measure of his status among his fellow airmen. He is one of the few black graduates of Annapolis in Marine Aviation. These few spots are limited to those in the top ten percent of each class. Jimbo graduated third overall, first in English, Spanish, and French. However, despite his unerring linguistic abilities, when among his fellow pilots Jimbo prefers to affect the down-home accent that reflects his early childhood in Atlanta rather than his later education at Choate, the New England prep school that specializes in supplying wealthy white boys to the Ivy League. When it comes to his identification as a Marine, Jimbo is a reverse snob. A Marine, he likes to say, ought to talk like a Marine, and a Marine don't talk like they mouths is wired shut.

"You be all right, Stanny?"

A captain like the others, Stanley Field, whose father (born Greenfeld) was a decorated Marine helicopter pilot in Vietnam, grew up dreaming of Marine Aviation. "Why the hell shouldn't I be?"

"You don't look awright is why," the third pilot says. This is Christian Thurston, a Houstonian who seems perpetually to engage Jimbo in a competition to see who can talk more down home. He normally wins—with Thurston, the accent is not an affectation.

"*Would* you be lookin' awright?" Jimbo says. "I mean, seeing as how, you know, considerin'."

"Considering what?" Stan says.

"Might be you should have a word with the padre," Chris says. "He's the closest thing to a rabbi we got."

"I don't need a rabbi, or the padre."

"Stanny, we don't like this business no better than you do," Jimbo says. "It's just we don't want to be surprised by no six o'clock developments. If'n you get my drift." By this he means too late a warning that enemy aircraft are coming up from below.

Chris picks up the theme as though the two Southern boys have rehearsed it, which they have. "Stan ma man, we don't want you to go all vigilante on us."

"I don't know what you pricks are talking about."

"Just sayin'," Jimbo says, looking up for a moment at the mute TV screen. "Sometimes people gets all hot and bothered about certain things. Like one day when I's a kid I hit another kid for something someone tol' me he was sayin', and it weren't even not somethin' me and the other black kids might be sayin', on account we said nigger every third word, but it kind of got to me, from the white kid's mouth I mean. So I hauled off and done broke his jaw. Later I heard he weren't even the one sayin' it, was some other shit-faced—"

"Look, as a Jew it's true I may have certain feelings—"

"Hey, man, you don't have to be a Jew to have them kind of feelings," Jimbo says. "I mean, those things on CNN, man, they not right."

"Hell, this here matter ain't no Jew thing," Chris says. "Anyhow, I never even so much as knowingly *viewed* a Jew before I set eyes on your ugly face. First time we met I was all wondering how you fit them horns under your flight helmet. Ain't no Jew thing."

"I file them down every night."

"I mean to say, Stanny, not only Jews got feelings for the holy land is all. Or for a buddy." Suddenly Chris seems to find a bit of interesting lint on his flight suit. "I mean, just sayin'."

"Yeah?" Stan says. "Just what the fuck are you saying? You think I'm a Jew before I'm an American, is that it? Because if that's what you two-bit shit-kickers think—"

Jimbo cuts in. "Just, you know, lets us toss this around a little bit before we go and cowboy up." He turns on the TV sound.

"Meanwhile," Damian Smith is saying, once again hauling out the same predictable connective without which television news would be mute, "here at home, many churches have declared Sunday a national day of prayer for Israel. Rev. Gerry Stallwell, pastor of Nashville's Christ the King Family Mega-Church, leads a group calling itself Christ 4 Israel. Rev. Stallwell, your group has chartered two ships to bring aid to Tel Aviv. Is that true?"

The pastor's moonlike visage fills the screen. Middle-aged, his hair so elaborately styled, straightened, and oiled that it vies for attention with the huge gold medallion he wears on a gold chain high on his chest: a cross superimposed on a blue Star of David. "Damian, that's now six ships," he says with evident pride. "Seems like the plight of our poor Hebrew brethren in the holy land is worsening fast. We've got people over in Europe buying up food, water, and medicine. Folks sometimes forget that right in the middle of Jesus Christ there's the letters *U* and *S* plain as day, and that stands for the name of this great believing nation, which is to say, *us*. You might say every one of *us* here in the *US* is part and parcel of Christ our Lord. Which translates out to a simple message: sometimes the Good Lord can use a bit of help."

"Rev. Stallwell, are you aware the Islamic Liberation Force has announced it will open fire on any ship trying to break its blockade of Tel Aviv?"

"Son, as aware as Daniel in the lion's den, but we believe on the people of Israel as God's chosen. Don't forget Jesus of Nazareth was a humble rabbi, his stepdad a regular old Hebrew carpenter. Far as scripture is concerned, we're doing the Lord's work, and if those Muslimites blow us out of the water we'll just keep on a-doing it."

"There's been some criticism of these efforts, Rev. Stallwell, on the grounds that your group is actually creating and implementing an independent US foreign policy. Have you had any consultations on this with Washington, pastor? The White House?"

"Don't have to. You know why? These Friday people, today they're coming after the Saturday people. Know who's next? The Sunday people. Just like the Constitution gives every citizen the right to bear arms, so it gives us freedom of assembly. We are assembling a Christian effort to save the besieged Israelites, and in so doing we are defending our own Christian selves sure as we might with firearms. These people over there that invaded and are despoiling the holy land got a simple agenda: destroy the Jews, then annihilate the Christians. You know what, they got no use for Hindus and Buddhists neither. We people of faith got to hang together or we going to hang separately."

"So you see this as a religious conflict?"

"Damian, if it isn't, why are these fanatics knocking down churches all over the holy land along with the synagogues? Chew on that one for a while. Trouble is, the president of these United States won't lift a finger to help. He's afraid he may not get reelected if the price of oil keeps going up. Well, I got a message for our president, the Lord bless him and keep him: this county don't get off its heinie and save our Israelites, then the wrath of the Almighty is going to descend upon our elected leader for failing to do God's will and then for sure he won't be re-elected. Son, I got folks in my church vowing to vote for a dead skunk just to see the president punished for what you and I know, and every God-fearing Christian in America knows, is a sin that makes Sodom and Gomorrah look like a three-legged race at a county fair on the Fourth of July."

Damian is getting signals from his control room: get this crank off the air before he starts talking assassination. "And thank you, Rev. Gerry Stallwell, pastor of—"

Accustomed as he is to talking directly with the Almighty, the good reverend is not about to be shut up. "You folks at home. Visit with us right now at *christ4israel.org*. Reach down in your pockets. Time's a-running out. Save the Israelites!"

The control room goes immediately to station break, with no bridge from Smith, no teaser about what's coming up next.

Again Jimbo cuts off the sound. "Y'all heard the man. Tick tock. Time's a runnin' out."

"A-rabs gonna blow them Christian ships right out the water," Chris says.

"I ain't just sayin'," Jimbo says.

"We ain't just sayin'," Chris echoes. "Not no more."

Stan looks from one to the other. He has never felt so un-alone in his life.

55

DESPITE THE WORLD'S CONTEMPORARY dependence on technology, not all communication requires electric current. This is evident in any prison, where within hours, sometimes minutes, news can be transmitted via relay, either through voice or agreed signals. The prison that is Ghetto Tel Aviv is no different. That the State of Israel has come under new management becomes known in every part of the crowded city so quickly that it is difficult to believe this is the same Israel once dependent for information on radio broadcasts and newspaper reports amplified by a network of cell phones that kept every citizen in a constantly refreshed loop of fact, rumor, innuendo and, inevitably, falsehood. A photo of any prewar Israeli street would show a cell phone pressed to the ear of every pedestrian; it was not uncommon for Israelis to be seen strolling down Dizengoff Street, Tel Aviv's main drag, with a cell phone at either ear. Such a nation of communicators can hardly stop communicating despite no electricity, no radio, no Internet, no mobile telephony. The chief of staff learns of Yigal's coup in an hour.

Twenty minutes later, Pinky and twelve of his most senior officers—minus Major General Ido Baram, who is under guard in a tent at Camp Yarkon—pull up to the office tower that headquarters Isracorp, formerly the nation's most successful corporation, now just a brass plate outside a bank of elevators stalled in their shafts.

The lobby desk holds a familiar sign, with one alteration:

Government of Israel
RECEPTION
Unauthorized Entry Prohibited

The desk is manned by a white-bearded old-timer in a skullcap reading Psalms—the study and discussion of biblical texts has become a common pasttime in a city with no newspapers or magazines, even among the secular, many of whom now crowd Tel Aviv's once underused synagogues. "Peace be unto you," the receptionist says. Now in wide use, the once casual greeting has taken on a kind of bottomless urgency.

The chief of staff's adjutant, a colonel, has no interest in pleasantries. "Where's Yigal Lev?"

"Has the distinguished officer an appointment, sir?"

"This is the chief of staff, you fool. Tell us where Yigal Lev is or I'll shake it out of you."

Before he can grind out another threat, the very compelling sound of multiple guns being cocked echoes in the two-story lobby.

As one, the officers look up and around them. From doorways on the same floor and from the circular balcony above, a collection of Misha's gangsters point their firearms like accusing fingers.

The man at the desk stifles a bemused smile. "Please allow me to try the prime minister's secretary." He picks up a pink battery powered walkie-talkie bearing the insignia *My Little Pony.* "Alona? Mendel downstairs. The Chief of Staff is here. Shall I...?"

In the silent lobby, the voice on the other end is tinny and laden with static. "Yigal has been expecting him. Please send him up."

The receptionist turns to the visitors. "For the moment, our elevators are in a state of rest. Fourth floor. Kindly leave your firearms in the basket."

Pinky raises his hand to his officers, then places his Tavor, Israel's standard-issue rifle, into the large straw basket to his left. One by one, the officers follow suit.

"Please, gentlemen," the receptionist says. "Side arms as well."

Moments later, the group exits four floors of emergency stairs onto an office floor buzzing with people on computers. Alona Yarden, Yigal's longtime secretary, whose husband may or may not be a prisoner of war in one of the victorious army's detention camps, greets them. Like the families of some 400,000 IDF personnel not heard from since war broke out, she has no idea whether her husband is a prisoner or dead. "General, so nice of you to stop by. The prime minister will see you immediately. Let me show you to the cabinet room."

Pinky gives her a look of exasperation, but follows, his staff in tow. Their entrance to the floor causes some to look up, but otherwise the room continues its work. Alona opens a door to a conference room where a dozen men and women sit around a table strewn with papers. She stops. "Your officers will wait outside."

The chief of staff nods, enters.

Yigal stands. "Pinky! I knew you'd come. Let me introduce you to my—"

"Yigal, what the fuck is going on?"

"Well, right at the moment we are allocating electricity for the next ten days, by which time hopefully we can get some coal delivered to Reading 4—the turbines? We scrounged up some coal dust."

"I know what Reading 4 is. You have electricity and the army doesn't?"

"Put in a request. Pinky, this is Rochele, minister of power. We're looking for a minister of defense. So far it's fallen to me. Rochele, Pinky used to be the world's best tank commander. Now...it's hard to say."

"Yigal," the chief of staff blurts out. "Who made you prime minister?"

"I did. Winston Churchill was not available."

Pinky is now staring at the man to Yigal's right, who is also on his feet. "Do I know you?"

"Misha Shulman, staff sergeant, IDF reserves. You fired me along with Yigal and Noam here." He points to a thin man of thirty wearing a single gold earring. "Funny how things work out. One day this bastard is operations officer in a tank brigade. Now he's head of the Mossad."

Pinky's eyes roll. It has finally dawned on him. "You're Misha Shulman!"

"I told you that."

"The hoodlum!"

"Currently minister of police."

Misha is having too much fun to quit. "In Hebrew, everything's backwards. Other places the police become crooks. Here crooks become the police."

Yigal has let this go on too long. "Pinky, have a seat." As space is made, the new prime minister works his way around the table, introducing his staff. "Most of the people in this room have worked with me for a while, so I know them and trust them. Roberto here got our computers running. Only he knows how. Something to do with car batteries. Limited access to the outside world, but that only means the outside world can't tap our lines. Pinky, Sharona—minister for food. We don't have any yet, but we're working on it. The children have no milk."

"Tonight we're sending out our first patrol to bring some back," Sharona says. "Tell your boys not to shoot us."

"You're sending people behind the lines to steal milk?"

"Milk?" Sharona says, as though talking to an imbecile. "We're bringing back cows."

"You've got six million people. How many cows can you steal?"

"With all due respect," Sharona says, "they're our fucking cows. We've got 2,300 children between newborn and eighteen months. They need milk. About half the mothers are just dry."

"How do you know how many children?"

"We counted," Yigal says. "We're also starting a program for mothers with sufficient milk to suckle a second child whose mother is not so fortunate." He points. "This guy with the glasses, Tzvi, is minister for logistics. Somehow he knows how many of everything we have, including pistols, rifles, and shotguns."

Tzvi seems shy. Eventually he begins. "Tw-tw-twenty-s-s-seven thousand, six h-h-hundred and t-two." He smiles in relief. "As of y-yesterday."

"Ronny is our minister of health. Used to be my cardiologist."

Cardiologists everywhere come in two formats: excessively fit and trim, and soft and overweight. Herzberg is the latter becoming the former. He likes to say the population of Israel has lost more cumulative weight in the past several weeks than the total tonnage of the population of Rhode Island, a fact no one questions but which, in a moment of medical bravado, he made up. "Outside of the military, three thousand doctors, twelve thousand nurses. We're reopening Assuta Hospital tomorrow."

"You want to know how much antibiotics?" Yigal asks. "Ronny can tell you. For three days, we've been inventorying every possible medical asset."

The chief of staff is confused. "Why?"

"So we can move to phase two."

"Which is?"

Yigal laughs. "Counterattack."

"Counterattack? With what?"

"The short answer, Pinky, is with everything we've got." Abruptly Yigal's tone becomes formal. "General Pinchas Harari, as prime minister I am authorized to give you sixty seconds to swear allegiance to the interim government."

"Or...?"

"Be relieved of command."

"Command of what? I need planes and tanks. And ammunition. And fuel. What do the Americans say?"

"You know how they say 'fuck you' in Washington?" Yigal says. "'Trust me.'" He pauses. "Pinky, I'm giving the order to go nuclear. You need it in writing?"

The chief of staff is silent for a while, then simply lets go a long sigh. "I don't need a signature. I need capability."

"Surely we must have one plane?"

"Mr. Prime Minister, that's the least of it. We don't have one bomb."

"Pinky, you have my full attention."

"They're hidden safely underground. That's the good news."

"I can't wait," Yigal says.

"The bad news is they're a hundred meters under the Dimona garbage dump in what is now Egyptian-controlled territory. No one expected Israel would be reduced to just Tel Aviv. The order you want to give, I gave it."

"We have 182 nuclear bombs and no access to them?"

"176," Pinky says. "Wait a minute. Who told you 182?"

"Wikipedia," Yigal says. "Every taxi driver in the country used to be able to tell you that. Usually they'd swear you to secrecy. Eight are missing?"

"Six months ago, I sent two submarines, each carrying four nuclear missiles, into Iranian waters. It was one of those orders you give you don't even know why. Just having them cruising between Haifa and Marseilles didn't make sense. Your predecessor—the real one, the elected one—put up a stink. *Pinky, this could be construed as an act of war.* You could say she torpedoed the idea."

"And."

"And so I was compelled to deploy the subs on my own authority. My responsibility was—is—the security of the State of Israel. No fucking politician was going to screw that up."

Yigal nods. "So you understand why—"

The chief of staff cuts in. "I understand exactly why you committed treason—it is treason, you know—in replacing the legally sanctioned government of the state. Actually, I should have done it myself, but to tell you the truth, and I'm not really proud of this, all I could think of was my fighting men, my tanks, doing my job."

"Don't give it a second thought, Pinky. So we do have nuclear capability."

"In theory."

"What is theoretical about eight nuclear warheads pointed at Iran?"

"The subs are deep," Pinky says. "We'll have no contact until they surface."

"Which is when?"

"Six days."

"So," Yigal says. "Six days to win a war."

The chief of staff allows himself a wry smile. "It's not like we haven't done it before."

56

THE SAME DAY, THE president of the United States, having arrived in a convoy of presidential 707s—two are decoys carrying sufficient Marine firepower to secure a square mile on the ground—is seated in one of the Saudi king's twelve royal palaces on one of two facing gold armchairs. The armchairs are not painted gold. They *are* gold. As to the twelve palaces, these function much the same as the presidential air convoy. Should yet another attempt be made to separate the royal head from the royal body, the attackers can never be sure where to strike.

For his accommodation with America, ISIS and Al Qaeda have made the Saudi king Islamist target number one. The king may be Islamism's chief benefactor and a supporter of jihad-crazed Muslims from Nigeria to Pakistan, but the sin of his longstanding American alliance overrides all: it is unforgiveable. Consequently, the monarch never sleeps in the same palace longer than one night. Moreover, four royal lookalikes are shifted from palace to palace like roving players, each with his own retinue of advisors, all of them imposters, and wives, also imposters, though these are regularly made available to the replacement monarchs. Even the royal family is not privy to the king's location. Wisely—internecine bloodletting is an Arabian tradition predating Mohammed.

Seated behind the two rulers are *their* respective retinues, one of them in a burqa. A feminist to the core—though considering the administration she works for, never outspoken about it—Flo Spier finds the getup oddly suitable to her position as the president's chief political operative. Hidden in plain sight, able to watch, listen, and learn but not required to speak unless absolutely necessary, she is able to parse the political landscape with a certain curtained-off detachment, a Wizardess of Oz in Islamic drag.

Though the king's command of English is more than adequate, two translators hover nearby, the one to correct the other, a common practice when the royal head inclines to the West. Like competing viziers, each translator is quick to point out any error, especially of nuance, coming from the mouth of his rival. But when the king speaks for himself in English, neither risks challenging so much as a wayward gerund.

"Please, my dear honored guest," the ruler says with a kind of dainty generosity, quashing the English syllables like so many delicate Muscat grapes. For emphasis he raises his right hand, palm out. "Even before you speak, your dignity must know that every wish of your heart shall be honored."

"Well, your highness," the president rejoins. "That's mighty white of you. The American people appreciate your goodwill."

"Then it shall be according to your desire. We shall restart production of the oil." The king is a master of timing. "There exists, however, a small related matter."

"King, one hand washes the other."

The monarch sighs. He has seen *The Godfather, Part II* eleven times. He speaks slowly, Marlon Brando as an old sheikh. "The Arabs are a forgiving people. We do not wish to treat the Jews harshly. They are, as you no doubt know, a protected people. As are all Christians. Both are people of the book. Thus the House of Saud will pay for as many ships as needed, without limitation, to bring these Jews to new homes among their Christian brothers, so that they may prosper and multiply."

Flo Spier leans forward to whisper in the president's ear.

"Your highness," the president intones. "That's wonderful, truly in line with the Islamo-Christian tradition of turning the other cheek. But six million folks is one big demographic. They may have to stay where they are a bit longer, until myself and my co-heads of state in the West can work out how many go here, how many there."

"Delay, my dear Mr. President, could carry with it a resolution less than desirable. We have a proverb: 'Unwatered, the camel may travel great distance, but not forever.' As you are aware, these Jews illegitimately occupy Muslim land. Under such circumstances, it may be difficult to restrain other Islamic leaders from dealing, ah, less gently with this, as you call it, demographic."

"Well, your kingship, if you don't mind I guess it's time to deal with the press." The president has what he came for. As for the Israelis, that can wait.

Photographers move in to snap the two rulers shaking hands, again and again and again. Though the president would have liked to make the announcement in a joint press conference, the House of Saud scotched this from the get-go. The press conference is not an Islamic tradition. Arab democracy must be developed slowly and carefully. Perhaps in a hundred years.

57

IN THE READY ROOM of USMA Forward Attack Squadron Wildcat, the three pilots watch as Damian Smith announces what has just been agreed in the president's meeting with the Saudi monarch. "According to White House sources," Smith reads from a teleprompter, "gasoline prices at the pump are expected to fall slowly but steadily, possibly to pre-Mideast war prices, as existing more expensive oil stocks are depleted. In related news, the six-ship aid flotilla chartered by an American church group to bring humanitarian aid to the population of cut-off Tel Aviv continues to steam toward that beleaguered city."

The screen goes to an aerial shot of an old freighter leading five smaller ships in a long line moving across the Mediterranean, then to a stand-up of a blond woman costumed by Dolce & Gabbana as a French sailor—espadrilles, white linen culottes cut above the knee, horizontally striped blouse, and, just to bring it all home, a sailor hat topped with a red pompom. Past her at the taffrail, the other vessels bob in and out of view.

"CNN's Connie Blunt, looking very nautical indeed, is on the lead freighter. Connie, what's it like on board?"

Blunt takes Smith's tease as a compliment. "Damian, spirits remain high here on board the CV *Star of Bethlehem*, a former Greek vessel registered in Liberia. That's CV for Christian Vessel, though I have discovered a surprising fact: Christians are not the only religion represented aboard this vessel of mercy."

The camera falls back to reveal a group of four individuals arrayed against the rail.

"Hi there!" She offers her mic to a red-haired twenty-five-year-old, who is obviously thrilled with the chance to be on television. "What's your name, sailor?"

"Taylor C. Briggs, ma'am."

"And where are you from, Taylor?"

"Kansas City, ma'am. Just outside."

"Taylor, you may have heard this before, but you're not in Kansas anymore, are you? Care to tell us why you're here?"

"Well, ma'am, in church my pastor called out to volunteers for a Christian mission. I'm a diesel mechanic back home, tractors mostly. This here's a diesel ship. I got chose."

"Very good. And you, madam?"

The woman is about fifty and wearing a flowered kerchief against the wind, which she immediately removes. "Mary Beth Shostak— with a K? Lovelock, Nevada. A lot of people never heard of it."

"I can't say I have, Mary Beth. Where about is Lovelock, near Las Vegas?"

"Oh, my, no. That would be the other side of the state. We're just about seventy miles due southwest of Winnemucca."

"I see. Now tell us, Mary Beth, how it is that you're here, so far from Lovelock and, uh, Winnemucca."

"Well, I've been an ER nurse for twenty years. I guess that's why I'm aboard. Kind of a just-in-case thing. Never been out of the US ever. We don't get too many big ships in Nevada."

"Well, Mary Beth, let's hope your services are not required. And you, young man. I can see you're not a churchgoer."

In the studio, unseen, Damian Smith cringes.

"You mean because of this little thing on my head? Yeah, there's a large Jewish contingent, more on the other ships. William J. Hurwitz. Billy. I'm a student at Jewish Theological Seminary in New York. Can I give a shoutout?"

"Fire away, Billy."

Billy waves, only his fingers moving. "Just want to say hi to my mom and dad in Albuquerque, my baby sister Simone, and all the crew at JTS, especially my Talmud teacher, Rabbi Wolfe, and my girlfriend, Ruthie. Mom and Dad, this may come as a shock, but before I signed on I...Ruthie said yes!"

Applause and whoops rise from the larger group behind him, which the camera pans.

"Anything else?"

"Ruthie, I love you!"

More applause. Someone lets out a two-finger whistle.

"And why are you here, Billy?"

The young man seems momentarily at a loss. "I guess if you were Jewish, you wouldn't have to ask." He suppresses the urge to tear up, then looks around. "Or Christian. Which reminds me. Don't worry, Mom, Dad—Ruthie's one hundred percent kosher!"

"Congrats, Billy—and Ruthie. Or should I say *mazel tov?* Which brings us to a young man you wouldn't normally think would be on this ship going to the aid of Tel Aviv. Young fella, what's your name?"

"Mohammed Said. Mo. I'm from Detroit. Dearborn, actually. And I'm here representing the Palestinian community of Michigan, to protest the mistreatment of the Palestinian people by the Arab and Iranian invaders."

"Fascinating, Mohammed."

"Mo."

"Mo it is. I see you've got something prepared."

The kid raises a hand-written sheet, which he holds in front of him with difficulty as the wind pushes it back. "Seventy years after losing our land to the Jewish State, my people has again lost its land, this time to fellow Muslims. As usual the world ignores the suffering of the Palestinian people." He looks up to see how much he can get away with. "Just another few words?"

"Go ahead, Mo."

"On behalf of the Palestinian community of Michigan, I have joined this humanitarian effort in hope the Palestinian and Israeli peoples can work together to defeat the foreign invaders so that our two nations can live together in peace."

He is so relieved to have delivered the message he lets go the paper. It flies up, then back, rising over the bridge, and disappears.

"Wow. Mo, that was impressive. Is there anything you'd like to add?"

"Well, as everybody knows, tomorrow the University of Michigan plays Texas A&M in the Gator Bowl."

"Yes?" Blunt says.

Mo opens his jacket to reveal a U of M t-shirt.

"Go Wolverines!"

Her cameraman closes tight on Blunt. "En route to Tel Aviv aboard the CV *Star of Bethlehem*, where spirits are high, I'm Connie Blunt."

58

ON A MOUNTAIN ROAD in Syrian-occupied territory outside of Jerusalem, an olive-green Cadillac flying the pennant of the Egyptian headquarters staff passes two Bedouin flying little more than donkey stink. If the young colonel driving the staff car could see their faces, which he cannot because he too is going west, he might note their eyes turn suddenly down and their chins tuck into their kaffiyehs as they urge their donkeys further off the road.

Alex checks the gas gauge the way every driver running out of gas does, hoping that somehow the needle will point up. The needle has its own opinion. About five kilometers back, the warning light came on. Since then he passed two Syrian bases, which no doubt have petrol pumps, but the same general staff insignia that permits him to sail through roadblocks would no doubt get him invited to coffee or even lunch with the Syrian base commander. Alex's Arabic is properly inflected, but unfortunately he has the vocabulary of a ten-year-old, his age when his Egyptian-born mother, who raised him speaking Arabic, died. He is considering trying his luck at a Syrian base when a small gas station comes up on the right.

A young Arab mechanic is working on a car when he pulls up. The teenager wipes his hands on his trousers and comes out with a big smile. "Welcome, general."

"Premium, please," Alex says with great relief. "Fill it up. And if you have a jerry can, I'll have that full of gas as well."

"Regrettably we have no premium, excellency."

"Regular, then."

"Nor that, general. We expect a delivery at any moment."

"And how long have you been expecting a delivery at any moment?"

"Oh, several weeks, excellency," the kid says. He points to the east with a grease-darkened finger. "You must go back one kilometer, then left at the church. At the next building, ask for Abu-Yunis. He may have a small amount."

59

IN THE CNN NEWSROOM, Damian Smith runs methodically through today's top stories, none of them happy. In TV news, everyone else's tragedy is meat and potatoes. On the big screen behind him is a long shot of a red rescue helicopter hovering alongside a snow-covered mountain. "Meanwhile," Damian reads, "The search for those missing climbers has been called off as fog continues to close in on Mt. McKinley. Efforts are expected to resume as weather permits." He adjusts his earphone, leaning forward slightly in the atavistic gesture all networks train their anchors to stifle. The effort is futile. When humans don't hear well, we lean in. "In breaking news, warships of the Egyptian Navy are reportedly moving to intercept that Christian aid flotilla en route to Tel Aviv. Andrew Lagonis is live at the Pentagon. Andy?"

Lagonis, a sixty-five-year-old leftover from the glory days of network news, is doing a hasty stand-up in a Pentagon corridor while behind him uniformed officers cross hurriedly back and forth. Lagonis is breathless with the scoop.

"Damian, that's right. I've just gotten word an Egyptian naval taskforce is indeed moving to head off those six aid ships, many of whose passengers and crew are American. Sources here say US initiatives to convince the Egyptians to turn back have been unsuccessful. So far we don't know if Egypt aims to intercept the ships or, in the worst case, fire upon them. One thing is certain: the aid flotilla is on a collision course with the biggest guns in the Egyptian Navy."

60

IN THE MASSAGE CABIN of Air Force One, a navy corpsman works on the president's back while the leader of the free world, prone on the padded table, becomes increasingly more tense.

"Well, what the fuck does the damn press expect us to do? Go to war with the entire Middle East?"

Flo Spier, out of the burqa and into a red jogging outfit, stands to the side with Felix George, who wears a three-piece suit and his usual look of disdain. "They are American citizens, sir."

"They're damn fool American citizens mixing themselves up where they got no beeswax."

"Mr. President, the simple takeaway is American citizens on a humanitarian mission are about to be attacked. It's not going to play well on TV. They're flying the American flag."

"Illegally on non-US vessels," St. George says.

"I'm talking optics, Mr. President," Spier counters.

The president is having none of it. "And I'm talking pissed off. You mean to tell me the US of A is got to send in the Marines every time some lunatic bible-thumper inserts his dick in a foreign war? Isn't there some law, Felix?"

"Neutrality Act of 1935, Mr. President."

"Remind me again how that goes."

"In essence, American citizens on warring ships travel at their own risk."

"Sir, these are not warring ships."

"Neutrality Act of 1937," St. George says. "US ships are forbidden from transporting passengers or articles to belligerents in a foreign war."

"You just said these are not US ships," Spier tells him—and the president.

Felix St. George loves to play poker when he has all the cards. "Good one! That specific loophole was closed by the Neutrality Act of 1939. American citizens and ships are barred from entering a war-zone."

The president grunts as the corpsman leans hard on a nerve. "Flo, I think that's pretty clear."

"Mr. President, the American people—"

"Flo, the American people don't want to keep on spending ten bucks a gallon for regular," the president says. "Case closed."

61

IN NUMBER FOUR HANGAR at US Marine Aviation Forward Attack Squadron Wildcat, the installation's top non-commissioned officer, a sergeant major who in civilian life may have a proper name but here is known only as Sergeant Major, laconically supervises the base's cook, known only as Cooky, and five fascinated messmen. A Marine hoses fuel into a fifty-gallon drum heating perilously over a propane stove.

"Enough juice," Sergeant Major announces. "Now johnwayne them cans. All of them." He refers to the flat, hinged can openers used by the military since World War II—until the nineteen eighties the P-38, since then the larger P-51—though no one is certain why the actor, who never saw combat other than on celluloid, was so honored. By extension, to johnwayne something is to open it.

"Sergeant Major," the cook cautions, "we ain't gonna have no tomato sauce or ketchup for two months. When the colonel gets back, she ain't gonna like it."

"Boo fuckin' hoo. Until she comes back, the responsibility's mine."

Having filed notice of this potential problem, for which Cooky will have to pay when base personnel find themselves facing weeks of ketchup-less French fries, to say nothing of unadorned cheeseburgers, Cooky affirms his commitment to the command structure. "Aye, Sergeant Major!" Nobody, including the pilots who outrank him, fucks with Sergeant Major. Cooky shouts to the messmen, "Sergeant Major has spoken!"

After they pour gallon cans of tomato puree and ketchup into the oil drum, the master gunnery sergeant demonstrates the kind of expertise that only a grizzled twenty-year veteran Marine can boast. "Now secret ingredient numero uno."

The messmen dump in powdered milk and stir. The concoction turns an admirable Pepto-Bismol pink.

Sergeant Major's craggy face develops the rictus that passes, among Marine non-commissioned officers, for a smile. "Secret ingredient numero dos. Three volunteers. You, you, and you. One step forward, unholster them guns the good Lord give you, and fire at will."

"In the soup?" Cooky asks. He is not questioning Sergeant Major's authority, only his recipe. Even for Marine Aviation, this may be over the top.

Sergeant Major allows the rictus again to flash over his face. "Cooky, don't call it soup. It's paint, is all."

The three volunteers piss into the drum.

62

WITH ONE EYE ON the gas gauge and one eye on the road, Alex turns back in the direction from which he came, in doing so nearly hitting the same two Bedouin he passed only moments before. After he just about grazes them, he sees in his rearview mirror that they have stopped to bow. He thinks: if I really were an Egyptian officer, I would check them out.

At the turnoff he parks in front of a neat whitewashed stucco church, marked modestly with a cross over the door but boasting no steeple. Since the eighth century, when Islam swept across the Middle East, Christian Arabs have been careful to moderate public displays of their faith. Even under Israeli rule, when Christians no longer feared government persecution, it remained wise not to affront their Muslim neighbors. But however modest Arab churches appear from without, inside they are decorated like jewelry bazaars.

Alex steps into the smaller building to the right of the church.

It is a barber shop. Immediately, two customers waiting their turn beneath the cross that dominates the room quietly leave. An Egyptian officer is not to be made to wait. The territory once known as Israel, where every bastard felt himself a king, has returned to being part of the Middle East, where every king, no matter how small, lords over his bastards without limitation.

The barber is forty, bald, fat, and in need of a shave, practically the official uniform of the Middle East chapter of the barbers' guild. He nods to Alex as he holds a mirror to the gleaming, freshly shaved head of the customer in the single chair, who takes one look at Alex's uniform and gathers his things.

"Abu-Yunis welcomes you, excellency," the barber says in Arabic. "As it happens, you are next. Shave?"

"I was informed there might be petrol," Alex says in Arabic.

"But surely first a shave?"

Alex feels his face. An Egyptian staff officer would always be clean-shaven. "Why not?"

"Hair as well, Excellency? You will be satisfied. Abu-Yunis works clean."

Alex glances in the large mirror opposite to see the last customer's bald pate move out the door. "Just the shave, thank you." He takes a seat in the chair and immediately his face is covered with a hot towel. The sensation is at the same time one of luxury and paranoia—it feels so very good, but he cannot see.

"You drive west, excellency?"

"Ow mff jmmd o?"

The towel is removed.

"How did you know?"

Abu-Yunis spreads lather over Alex's face with a brush so soft it might be a caress. "Excellency, here Abu-Yunis is barber, gas station, grocer, also building supplies. Therefore he must know everything."

"I'm glad someone does."

The barber begins shaving Alex's cheek. His touch is light. The straight razor seems barely to graze his face.

"His excellency passed several Syrian bases, then. There is gas available there, or did the colonel not know? Excellency is a colonel?"

"I must have missed the bases. Colonel, yes."

"Colonel, I am Abu-Yunis. Please hold still—my blade is sharp. You travel to Tel Aviv?"

"To the front. That is correct."

Abu-Yunis pauses, the razor poised at Alex's throat. "To Tel Aviv?"

"For the final attack, yes."

Suddenly the barber is no longer speaking Arabic. "Why would an Egyptian officer in need of gas pass such military bases?"

"Is that Hebrew?" Alex returns in Arabic. "Regretfully, I do not speak it."

Nevertheless Abu-Yunis continues the same way. "If the colonel is an Egyptian, then Abu-Yunis is just a barber." He moves the razor slowly over Alex's throat.

Alex has no choice. "You're not just a barber?" he replies in Hebrew.

"Until one month ago, Abu-Yunis was a proud citizen of Israel. He voted. He had freedom of speech and movement. His children studied in good schools. He could not be arrested without just cause. Neither as an Arab nor a Christian did harm come to him."

"And?"

The barber shrugs. "From time to time Abu-Yunis assisted his government." He has finished the shave. With the still-warm towel, he carefully wipes the rest of the lather from Alex's face.

"What do I owe you, Abu-Yunis? Aside from my life?"

"To get to Tel-Aviv as quickly as possible. To tell your people that when the time comes the Christian citizens of this area will cut the invaders' throats as I have not cut yours." He laughs. "Also, next time to send a spy whose Egyptian accent is more…practiced."

"My mother grew up in Alexandria. She taught me."

"Just so. This is why we call it mother tongue. In speech the child emulates her who gave him life."

Alex cannot suppress the smile. "Sometimes not only in speech."

The barber smiles as well. "I can spare five gallons."

63

ON THE SCREEN BEHIND Damian Smith, Muslims and Jews clash at UN Plaza, a wedge of mounted New York police forcing them apart as the newscaster reads from his teleprompter. "Earlier today, a march down New York's Fifth Avenue to the UN by pro-Israel demonstrators culminated in violence with a counter-demonstration by Muslims and their sympathizers. Police reported seven injured before order was restored."

The screen goes to Connie Blunt aboard CV *Star of Bethlehem* with a tall sixty-year-old in a khaki officer's hat, black t-shirt, and jeans. He is smoking a cigar.

"Meanwhile, some five thousand miles away, Connie Blunt joins us aboard the Christian Vessel *Star of Bethlehem*, en route to Tel Aviv and possible interception by the Egyptian Navy. Connie, tell us what morale is like aboard the flotilla."

The sound of "Amazing Grace" rises and then is reduced by the control room so that Blunt can be heard.

"Damian, moments ago spontaneous hymn singing broke out here aboard the CV *Star of Bethlehem*, and I'm told it's spread to the other ships. It's hard to believe the Egyptian Navy will make good on its threats, but there's no knowing. The crew has been doing lifeboat drills since we left Marseilles."

"Connie, how long before you enter Israeli waters—or Islamic waters, as they're now called?"

"Damian, that's a very good question. Here with me on the *Star of Bethlehem* is its captain, retired US Navy Commander Franklin D. Levine, known aboard as Captain Frank. Captain Frank, are we sailing into danger?"

"Well, Connie," the captain says in a voice heavy with command gravel. "Your people probably know more than we do about that. All I do know is that we've been told the Egyptian Navy has warned they'll fire on us if we enter Israeli waters."

"I believe they're calling it Islamic waters now."

"They can call it dog (bleep) for all I care," the captain says. "We're on course for Israel, not some other place."

"Are you questioning the outcome of the war, captain? It seems to be well accepted, at least among the diplomatic commu—"

"You know the story of Abe Lincoln and the farmer?"

"Abe Lincoln?"

"Yeah, used to be president, and a better one than we got now. Abe asks the farmer, 'How many legs has a cow?' The farmer says, 'Why, four.' Abe says, 'Well, if we call her tail a leg, then how many?' The farmer says, 'Five.' 'No, sir,' Ol' Abe says. 'Just calling the tail a leg don't make it one.' This ship and the five in our wake are bound for Tel Aviv, *Israel.* Far as I can see, the Arabs can shove any other name for the Jewish State up their (bleep)."

"Be that as it may, captain, the Egyptian Navy seems to disagree. Will they fire on us, do you think?"

Captain Frank is not doing a very good job of concealing his impatience. His tanned face creases unpleasantly. "That's not known at this time."

"Captain, when will we know?"

The creases deepen. "When will we know if the Egyptian Navy

is going to fire on us?"

"Yes, when?"

Captain Frank looks up to the cloudless sky, as if seeking divine aid in dealing with this idiot. "About a second after they do."

Blunt is oblivious. "And when do you suppose we'll be crossing from international waters into formerly Israeli, now Islamic, waters?"

"Miss, you see that green stuff?"

Blunt shades her eyes to follow his finger.

"The *wet* stuff," Captain Frank says.

"The ocean?"

"Yeah, the Mediterranean Sea. Do you happen to see any lines out there, with markers and flags? Any buoys?"

"No."

"That's because there aren't any."

"Captain, I'm not sure I understand."

"When the shooting starts—that's when we crossed the line. That's when we know."

"Yes, but can you—"

"From our position and from what I'm informed of theirs, and assuming they're making twenty knots, two hours."

"Thank you, Captain Franklin D. Levine, commander of the six vessels that make up this aid flotilla on course for Tel Aviv. This is Connie Blunt, aboard the Christian Vessel *Star of Bethlehem*, somewhere in the Mediterranean."

"Thank you, Connie. And this is as good a time as any to tell our viewers CNN offered to evacuate Connie, producer Terry Santiago, and cameraman Buddy Walsh by helicopter. Each refused. Stay safe, gang!"

64

IN THE READY ROOM of US Marine Aviation Forward Attack Squadron Wildcat, the three pilots turn to each other as Jimbo, who as ranking pilot has charge of the remote, clicks off the TV. They are all in regulation flight suits that allow pilots of supersonic planes to withstand up to nine G's without passing out. The tight-fitting trousers prevent blood from pooling in the lower body, thus preventing it from draining from the brain. Unless they are about to fly, no pilot will wear them. The discomfort is considerable. Each suit weighs fourteen pounds.

Chris has an aeronautical map in front of him. "Two hours."

"Guys," Stan says. "You don't have to do this."

"Shee-it, everybody knows you Jews got no sense of direction. You people done wandered in the desert forty years. We wouldn't want you to get lost out there all on your own, would we now?" Chris folds the map.

"Hell, no," Jimbo says. "We sure as hell wouldn't want that."

65

ON A MOUNTAIN PATH west of Jerusalem, the two donkeys descend steadily. The shortcut takes their riders, both dressed in soiled Bedouin robes, from the secondary road where they were passed twice by an olive-green Cadillac flying the pennant of Egyptian headquarters staff to this narrow trail enfiladed by thick-trunked olive trees that bore fruit before the time of Jesus.

"Abed," Cobi says, "my *tuchis* is about to fall off."

"Why not let the donkey ride you?"

"Is this your idea of transportation, man? It's the twenty-first century."

"As it happens," Abed says, "I possess a Ford pickup, four-wheel drive, AC. Beautiful machine. Despite Hollywood movies, the Bedouin is no enemy of the internal combustion engine."

"So why in hell do we have to—"

"Because that vehicle is too big to negotiate this pathway. On better roads, we would be stopped, and questioned, and perhaps the Ford would be requisitioned. The Syrian sons of whores at the bottom, hidden in the foliage, they won't bother stealing two donkeys."

Cobi shades his eyes. "I don't see any Syrians."

Abed points to the rocky trail before them. "We've been following their tracks for two kilometers. Army officer, eh? Don't they teach you anything?"

66

GHETTO TEL AVIV COVERS fourteen square miles. Far larger than the municipal boundaries of Tel Aviv proper, this takes in Bat Yam to the south, parts of Herzlia to the north, and to the east is bounded by the Geha Road, whose six empty lanes prove as much a natural barrier as any river. To the west is the Mediterranean Sea. The area contains six hundred schools, three universities, and so many eating places—from falafel stands to sidewalk cafés to elegant restaurants— that even the municipal licensing authorities, when they functioned, were unsure of the precise number. At any given time, eight hundred buses ran on its streets, not including several hundred *sheroot* jitneys that followed bus routes and were authorized to stop anywhere along the way to pick up and discharge passengers.

Tel Aviv's luxury hotels lined the beach, each with hundreds of rooms, most of them booked year-round. Almost every commercial street corner held a kiosk selling everything from the nation's two dozen newspapers to snacks and, in some neighborhoods, tiny bags of locally grown marijuana and more costly Lebanese hash, a world standard since the time of Abraham. Banks and post offices punctuated every avenue, along with supermarkets and tiny owner-run groceries in the side streets. Most service businesses operated from early morning to late in the evening, perhaps a hundred never closing, remaining open 364 days a year—Yom Kippur being the exception—and for the privilege paying a municipal fine every week for keeping open on the Sabbath, just a cost of doing business.

Once a buzzing maze of heavily trafficked streets, boulevards, and highways, Tel Aviv was a walker's city, its ambiance a meld of New York, Paris, Nice, and Warsaw, with just enough of every other city in the world to make living there at once fascinating, complicatedly pleasant, and maddening. Half planned, half chaotic, it was a city of Bauhaus architecture, shortcuts, secret destinations, tiny parks, and favorite cafés. All it lacked was public toilets, but with so many cafés, no one complained.

Now Tel Aviv is one big public toilet. The cafés are closed, the offices empty but for squatters, and the only traffic on the streets is pedestrian, filling the roadways in search of food, drinking water, and news. Rumors fly the ghetto's twelve-mile length in less than an hour, all propelled by fear, hope, and desperation.

In the six days since Yigal Lev took over as prime minister, much of this changed. There are still no commercial establishments in operation, though every street corner is an ad hoc market where jewelry and watches are bartered for tiny plastic bags of moldy flour. No buses or jitneys run, and bicycle traffic is light, largely because Tel Avivians never really took up bicycles as a mode of transportation—most apartments are too small to store them. But in those first few days, a change came across the face of the ghetto: the ratio of fear to hope was altered. There is now just a bit more of the latter than the former. Not much more, but enough to make a difference.

Yigal's people managed to open the schools (which of course are flooded with the entire country's students, so that classes normally overcrowded with forty pupils now hold a hundred, each school running at least two shifts—why not, all the nation's teachers are available). The new government has re-established rudimentary policing, with former cops and former gangsters working together. That neither group has uniforms—the regular police early on got rid of theirs to avoid arrest, or worse, by the conquering armies—is not much of an obstacle: armbands with the large Hebrew letter *mem*, for *mishtara* (police), suffice. Most cops had kept their side arms; the hoodlums had their own. Public latrines are dug in parks, the stinking piles of human waste buried. Each block is compelled to establish its own voluntary workforce under the authority of street captains designated by the new government, most of these newly appointed officials functioning well enough, especially when they are female. It appears Jewish men are historically accustomed to being bossed around by females; even the most surly remains disinclined to sock a woman.

Almost immediately a sense of civic responsibility takes hold, aided in good part by the knowledge that there is no one else to do the work, that the next street already looks like humans live there, and that there is precious little else to do.

Yigal's choice of Misha Shulman as chief of police (or chief enforcer, as he likes to think of himself) goes a long way to make this happen. Just as the Arab invaders borrowed the blueprints of the Nazis, so too does Yigal take a page from lessons learned in the Warsaw Ghetto: this time, among the Jews, there would be no factions, no competing ideologies, no separate armed groups.

To accomplish that with a normally fractious Israeli population, already viscerally subscribed to political parties with different aims and desires, calls for the application of indiscriminate force. Misha's gangsters and a select group of former cops—a good many are former members of the Border Police, head-busters who were known to strike first and ask questions later—take on this mission with an enthusiasm that the population both welcomes and fears.

In the first twenty-four hours on the job, Misha's specially designated Motivation Squad motivates forty-seven civilians on the spot—no trial, no appeal, no compunction. Whether the ignored prohibition is as small as pissing in the street or as large as displacing a family by force in order to take their corner of some miserably overcrowded apartment, the punishment is the same: a severe beating in full public view.

Mistakes are made, perhaps personal scores settled, and when the area is gray, even the most motivated of the Motivation Squad find themselves wishing to pause. But any pause, any deviation from orders, anything other than drumhead justice administered quickly and on the spot, would have sunk the ghetto into pathetic and fatal dissolution.

Yigal's greatest challenge in re-establishing civil order in Tel Aviv and creating hope among its forlorn residents is logistical. Without printing presses, without radio, without loudspeakers, there is no effective way to bring word of what is to be expected from the population *to* the population. His cabinet has no idea. The army's best minds come up with nothing. Professors of communication from Israel's top universities never faced such a problem.

At the end of the day, and it was indeed at the end of the day, in bed, like every Jew from Abraham forward, Yigal asks his wife.

"Town criers," Judy says.

"There's already enough crying," he tells her, confused by the term.

"Silly," she tells him. "Get a lot of guys out there hollering out whatever message you want."

He considers. "The ghetto is too big. Too much territory to cover."

"Pony Express."

"Horses? There's not one in the city that hasn't been eaten."

"No, no. It's a chain. One messenger brings the message to—I don't know—five others, then they spread out and contact five more, and so on until—"

"On foot? Baby, I don't have enough people strong enough to walk the city, much less run."

"Kids on bicycles," she whispers, then turns over and falls asleep.

In the three days that follow, Tel Aviv does not become paradise, but it is no longer hell. Its population continues to starve, but with dignity.

67

A Syrian lieutenant watches as his men frisk two Bedouin for arms. He is in charge of a reconnaissance patrol belonging to the Syrian Army's Security Corps—an especially feared group built on the lines of the Nazi SS, even down to its uniform. They wear the same double lightning bolt shoulder patches.

"What is your name, filth?" the lieutenant asks almost conversationally.

"Abed Abu-Kassem of the Ghawarna, your lordship."

"And you, piece of shit?"

Cobi offers only a weak smile.

"My mother's brother's son's cousin, sire. He speaks not."

"Shy?"

"Your lordship," Abed says. "He is unable."

"And neither of you with papers?"

"No, my lord. As I explained, we were robbed of them. We journey to Ramle, there to sell the dates in our bags. That we may purchase papers. That we may have them, because we were robbed of them. Thus we journey to Ramle, to sell dates."

The Syrian officer comes so close Cobi can smell the stink of his uniform. "And why is this unable to speak? Does it not hear?" The lieutenant moves behind Cobi and cocks his pistol just behind his head. "It hears. It heard that."

"Sire, he hears certainly. But something is wrong in his brain. He hears, but understands little, like a child. By Allah, I have taken him under my protection."

The lieutenant now stands before Abed. "Have you money, filth?"

"No, lordship. Only dates."

"How then do you live?"

"Upon dates, sire."

"Tell me, then, camel shit. What should I do if my men open your bags and among the dates is found money, or gold, or weaponry?"

"You should kill me, excellency. My lord, you should kill us both."

The Syrian lieutenant spits. "Go. When you sell your dates, return by this route and pay a toll in gratitude that I have spared your miserable lives."

Abed falls to the ground and kisses the lieutenant's boots. "So we shall, nobility. Thank you. Thank you eternally in the name of Allah. In the name of the prophet may your—"

The lieutenant kicks him away. It is not a symbolic kick.

In a moment, the two Bedouin lead their donkeys onward, mounting only when they turn out of sight.

"Abed, how could you debase yourself like that?"

"How would you have wished me to debase myself?"

"There were only six. We could have reached into our packs and killed them all."

"And the sharpshooters above would have cut us down on the spot."

"What sharpshooters?"

"The ones you did not see, Cobi. The ones you are not supposed to see. For a month I have been watching such bastards as these, all the same, trained alike. They never operate without cover." He raises his index finger. "Pay attention: brain, not strain, brings gain."

"Old Bedouin proverb?"

"No," Abed says. "But it sounds good."

68

ABOVE THE SIX SHIPS on a collision course with an Egyptian frigate and two trailing corvettes, a helicopter marked PRESS in Arabic and English hovers like a buzzing witness, a video camera pointed out one window to record what is expected to be a major news event.

On the bridge of the frigate, an Egyptian admiral—the English word is itself derived from the Arabic *amir al-bahr*, ruler of the sea—lowers his binoculars from the press helicopter to focus on the line of six freighters. His executive officer stands by his side and just sufficiently behind, also with binoculars.

"Firing short, excellency?"

"Firing straight on," the admiral says.

"Civilian vessels, excellency."

"My orders are clear. Firing straight on."

The exec speaks into the squawk box. "Bridge to Fire Control. Closing on target. Establish range."

The admiral places one hand on the younger man's shoulder. "Yussef, do this once and done. Then no others will come."

As he speaks, the ship's five-inch 54 cal. guns swing slowly around.

69

ON THE DECK OF CV *Star of Bethlehem*, the hymn singing reaches a fever pitch as the members of its motley crew stare straight ahead at the approaching Egyptian warships.

From the bridge, Captain Frank depresses a button on the loud hailer that is his only means of communication with the ship—the *waa-waa-waa* of the amplified device stops the singing in mid-note. "Yo! Below! This is the captain speaking. Will one of you sopranos hoist the flag per instruction, or do I have to go below and do it my-self? For fuck's sake, the Lord seems to be occupied elsewhere. Raise that goddamned flag!"

70

ON THE BRIDGE OF the Egyptian frigate, a white flag can be seen rising to the top of the communications mast of the first freighter. One by one, the next five ships follow suit.

The executive officer lets hang his binoculars. From this distance, they are no longer necessary. "Begging your pardon, excellency."

"Don't even say it, Yussef."

"But excellency, Law of the Sea—"

"Yussef, who will know?"

The exec points above, where the press helicopter has dropped to hover above the fast-closing Egyptian warships, video camera pointed out its window.

"Take it out," the admiral orders.

"Excellency, I protest. The helicopter is clearly marked. It is a noncombatant. As are the six vessels. These are civilian vessels flying the white flag of surrender."

"Yussef," the admiral says with a mixture of kindness and authority. "Do you wish to spend your naval career scrubbing toilets in a brig in Alexandria harbor?"

The exec switches on the squawk box. "Bridge to fire control. Hold steady on target awaiting command to fire. Repeat, steady on, awaiting command." He pauses. "Bridge to sea-to-air battery. Sea-to-air, come in."

An affirmative noise responds.

"Sea-to-air, acquire spinner at two o'clock, range three hundred meters, altitude one hundred meters and holding."

Another noise, this one longer, and clearly not affirmative.

The executive officer turns to the admiral. "Excellency, sea-to-air battery reports target is clearly marked Press."

"A Jewish trick," the admiral replies.

"Excellency?"

"Shoot it down. Then order gunners to take out all marine targets dead ahead starting with…" He raises his binoculars. "Star of something."

"*Star of Bethlehem*, excellency."

"Indeed, the star. What did I tell you, a Jewish trick."

"Excellency?"

"Yussef, Yussef. Tell me, what is the symbol emblazoned on the Jewish flag?"

"With all respect, excellency. The ships fly the white flag."

"Never mind. The Jewish flag, what is its well-known emblem? The cross? The crescent?"

The exec sees where this is going, but can do nothing other than give the required answer. "The star, excellency."

"The star is correct, Yussef," the admiral says. "The Jews' star. Now do your job without further delay. We are in battle."

71

FROM THE EAST, THREE pink F/A-18 Super Hornets cross from the Sinai Desert and are now over open water heading due west at almost twice the speed of sound. In the lead aircraft, Jimbo opens communications, until now suppressed lest their electronic signatures be picked up by US signal-monitoring satellites overhead. "In four to engage. Reducing to attack speed. How you ladies doin'? Over."

Stan: "Reducing speed. Guys, not too late to turn back. My war. Over."

Chris: "Shut your pie hole. Over."

Stan: "I'll never forget this. Over."

Chris: "Ain't happened yet. Over."

Jimbo: "Happenin' in two. Ourah! Over."

Stan: "Roger that. Ourah! Over."

Jimbo: "We have tally. Repeat, we have visual at nine o'clock. Careful of them cargo tubs, ladies. Ourah and shaalome!"

72

ON THE DECK OF CV *Star of Bethlehem*, the singing continues with a kind of resolute hopefulness, less fervent than earlier but with a good deal more affirmation. If something very bad is about to happen—and there is every indication it will—the mostly Christian crew clearly wishes to die pronouncing words of faith, not fear. They have just broken into "Rocka Ma Soul in the Bosom of Abraham" when Connie Blunt, her producer, and her cameraman scramble up the ladder leading to the bridge and burst in.

"We're flying the white flag. Don't they see it?"

Captain Frank is circumcising a large cigar with a small, very sharp knife. He does not look up from his work except to gaze out at the approaching fleet. "At this range, they sure do."

"Well, what's going to happen?"

"Like I said, sister, there's no telling. I've been Morsing we're unarmed, but they don't reply."

"But what's going to happen?"

"Dunno. Maybe they're waiting for your press friends in the chopper to run low on fuel and leave the scene. Maybe they intend to ram us. I haven't been briefed."

Blunt is losing it. "Ram us? We could drown! Captain, I need for you to contact the press helicopter and get us evacuated immedia—"

A tremendous boom cuts her short, followed by a series of smaller booms as the helicopter's aviation gasoline explodes along its fuel lines.

"What was that?" Blunt shouts. It's as if she needs someone to confirm what she sees. "What's happening?"

She barely completes the phrase before hot steel and flaming plastic begins raining down to starboard.

Captain Frank sticks the cigar in his mouth. "What was your alternate plan?"

"Oh my God. Oh my God! They're going to attack us! You have to get us off this ship!"

"Sister, that was my thinking first time I laid eyes on you." He picks up the loud hailer, carries it out to the deck, and turns on the waa-waa-waa. "Attention, crew of *Star of Bethlehem*. This is Captain

Levine. All hands into lifeboats. Repeat: get your sorry asses into those lifeboats now! To all hands. We are abandoning ship!" He steps back inside.

"But where will we go?"

The captain is rather busy at the moment. He picks up the radio mic. "To all masters, to all masters. This is Captain Levine. We are abandoning ship. We are abandoning ship. According to Uniform Code of Naval Procedure, I cannot order you to do the same, but strongly suggest it. Those trigger-happy Gyppos seriously don't like us. Don't take it personal. Just get your people into those damn boats."

He has not signed off when the ship is engulfed in a rolling boom that comes out of the east and then seems to head up and away as the thunder of three low-flying jets echoes across the sky.

"Holy shit," Blunt's producer says. "It's an air attack!"

Captain Frank picks up the handset. "Attention all masters, attention all masters. This is Captain Levine. Revised orders. Continue to man those lifeboats, but do not deploy. Just stand by. I don't know what the hell just happened, but those planes are friendly. We're being buzzed. Stand by for further information." He picks up the hailer. "To all crew, to all crew. Hold fast those lifeboats. Repeat: don't bother getting your asses wet. All that hymn singing seems to have had an effect."

"What?"

"F/A-18s."

"What? Speak English, for shit's sake!"

The captain shades his eyes. "Super Hornets. Pink ones."

73

THE THREE AIRCRAFT LEVEL off at twenty-eight hundred feet, sufficiently out of range of the frigate's sea-to-air missiles to take evasive action should they be targeted. Likely that will take time. Israel's air

force is known to be destroyed—the Egyptian Navy is not prepared
to defend from aerial attack.

Jimbo: "Stan and Chris, fore and aft. I've got the superstructure.
We'll deal with the small fry later. Ourah! Over."

Chris: "Copy that, Jim. Ourah! Over."

Stan: [Muffled.]

Jimbo: "Stanny, come in. Over."

Stan: "I'm just crying, you big schmucks. Over."

Chris: "Jew-bastard. Over."

Jimbo: "Clipped-dick sissy. Over."

Stan: "You ladies wanna stay the fuck out of my way. Permission
to solo. Over."

Jimbo: "Roger that, Jewboy. Chris, let's give David some room to
tickle Goliath. Party on. Ourah! Over."

74

TWO PINK FIGHTERS CLIMB as the third swoops low over the Egyptian frigate, its 20 mm. cannons blazing at five hundred feet before it
loops to come right back, sending two AGM Harpoon missiles into
the Egyptian vessel's superstructure.

It collapses like tinfoil.

On the frigate, the crew dives for cover, abandoning the very
guns that are its only defense.

On her bridge, the admiral is both surprised and incensed.
"What is that?"

His executive officer is already on the squawk box. "All hands, defensive posture. All hands, defensive posture. We are under aerial attack!"

"By whom?" the admiral shouts above the tumult. "Who has
pink Hornets?"

"Super Hornets, excellency."

"The fucking gays have an air force?"

75

ON BOARD CV *STAR of Bethlehem*, Connie Blunt, abruptly aware she is out of danger, scrambles to the bow for a stand-up. She is in full professional mode, except that absent her French sailor hat her hair is blowing the wrong way as the freighter plows thirty degrees to port to avoid the conflagration ahead. Having turned one way and then the other, Blunt gives up on attempting to have her hair stream behind her and simply holds it back as she prepares to describe the action into a hand mic that will avoid picking up ambient noise, of which there is plenty.

"Hurry up, Buddy!" she screams to her cameraman, who is having trouble keeping his footing on the slippery deck as the freighter hits a swell. "Come on! I'm going to win a Peabody!"

Her producer grabs the cameraman by the waist, stabilizing him sufficiently. "Hooked up to satellite!" he shouts. "Three, two…"

"Damian, this is amazing! You are watching a live attack by unidentified jet fighters on the Egyptian battleship that was bearing down on this humanitarian aid flotilla. Just a moment ago, an Egyptian naval rocket destroyed a BBC-chartered press helicopter, which exploded in midair, almost certainly leaving no survivors. No one on board the *Star of Bethlehem* has any doubt that this was to be our fate too, as well as that of the other five ships behind us bringing much-needed food, water, and medicines to the beleaguered city of Tel Aviv."

A boom.

She turns.

"Life boats on board were about to be lowered after our captain gave the order to abandon ship, when literally out of nowhere there appeared a squadron or whatever you call it of three so far unidentified warplanes, F-16s or F-18s or, and you can quote me on this, F-U's, that have literally saved the day. Behind me, a lone pink—yes, pink!—jet fighter is single-handedly pounding the bejesus out of that enormous Egyptian battleship, which—"

She turns again.

"—which omigod, it is sinking. I repeat, the Egyptian battleship is apparently sinking right in front of us live on CNN. Can you get this, Buddy? Buddy, get the camera off me. Forget what I said! Get the battleship!"

A double boom.

"Omigod, Atlanta, two other pink warplanes have now descended and are apparently taking on the two smaller vessels, which may or may not be destroyers, both of which have been hit by missiles."

At CNN in Atlanta, with the screen behind him filled with the scene five thousand miles away, Damian Smith cuts in. "Connie, we have confirmation the large ship is a frigate, the two smaller vessels corvettes. All three seem to be stopped dead in the water. Connie? Connie?"

On the screen behind him, the three pink jets regroup and come in low directly over the *Star of Bethlehem*. Connie dives for the deck. Her cameraman is already there, with her producer on top of him. On the studio screen, there is nothing but deck, then sky, then deck again, and then sky blacked out as the jets buzz the freighter, dipping their wings.

"Omigod, I think they're about to attack us! I never signed on for this! F(bleep) this sh(bleep)!"

Smith comes in. "Connie, take it easy. It looks like they're just saying goodbye."

Blunt regains her feet. "You think so, Damian?" She turns. "Yes, you're right. The three warplanes are leaving the area, beautiful double plumes of smoke streaming behind them."

"Contrails," Smith says quietly.

"Yes, absolutely, Damian. They are disappearing to the—well, I can't really tell what direction, but they're becoming tiny dots on the horizon."

"Connie, does anyone aboard the *Star of Bethlehem* know whose warplanes came to the defense of the aid flotilla?"

Her answer is drowned out by Captain Frank's waa-waa-waa and then his amplified voice. "Attention all hands, attention all hands. This is Captain Frank. Belay all lifeboats. Repeat, belay all lifeboats. Crew, make fast all boats."

CV *Star of Bethlehem* steams past the listing Egyptian frigate as its corvette escorts burn and lifeboats pick up survivors.

"To all hands: good job all around. Return to normal stations. Repeat: return to normal stations. Next stop, Tel Aviv!"

76

HAVING RETURNED FROM A three-day leave, in her quarters at USMA Forward Attack Squadron Wildcat Lieutenant Colonel Iris McKendrick, her hair in curlers, stubs out a Marlboro, then drains her shot glass. On the television screen before her, a CNN cameraman is panning CV *Star of Bethlehem* as its crew makes fast its lifeboats. Over the sound of the freighter's ancient engines and the pounding of the waves can be heard the joyful song of the miraculously saved. As angry as she is, she cannot help but join in:

Amazing grace, how sweet the sound
that saved a wretch like me.
I once was lost but now am found,
Was blind, but now I see.
Amazing grace, how sweet it is…

77

LIEUTENANT COLONEL MCKENDRICK IS not alone. The song, a staple of the Christian hymnal since it was composed in 1772, will become so popular that everyone from mezzo-sopranos to rap artists will cover it in the weeks ahead. Existing versions are already playing on radio stations while the soundtrack of the crew singing loops over and over again whenever television news reruns footage of the aid flotilla, which every television station outside the Muslim world does with great frequency. The song seems to have touched a nerve even with Russian and Chinese media, which up to this point have shown a sincere lack of interest in the tragedy unfolding in Tel Aviv.

That no onsite reportage emanates from the ghetto itself goes unmentioned even among the most sympathetic news outlets, which hardly wish to flaunt their impotence: so little news gets out of Muslim-controlled former Israel because news personnel find it impossible to get in. Journalists are summarily turned back at their home airports when they attempt to fly into Yasser Arafat International Airport, and the entirety of former Israel is sealed off from access by sea. Without a functioning Internet connection and no electricity to power short-wave broadcasts, Ghetto Tel Aviv is effectively cut off.

Only those governments with satellites have any idea what is going on in Tel Aviv or in the country's huge prisoner of war camps. Primary among them is Washington.

78

IN THE WHITE HOUSE operations room, the president finds himself impressed by the day's events in the eastern Mediterranean.

"Flo, didn't I tell you those Israelians have an ace or two up their sleeve?" he says, tapping his foot to the sound of *Amazing Grace* playing on CNN. "Will you look at that footage. Our flyboys couldn't do it better."

"Should we not be concerned, sir? We had no intel. And still don't."

"Maybe not. But if IDF's got three planes, they've got more, which means those Jews could deliver nuclear. We'd better give 'em that airlift. Anyhoo, there is no more Egyptian blockade."

"Right on it, Mr. President."

"And have Defense mix a little steel in with the vitamins. Otherwise that colored preacher..."

"Gerry Stallwell, sir."

"Otherwise Pastor Gerry gonna piss on our parade."

"Wise move, sir."

"What I want to know is, how did we miss those F/A-18s? And why are they pink? Who knows what else those foxy kikes, no offense, got up their sleeve?"

"They've got nuclear, sir."

"Well, send them that care package. Maybe they'll take a Christian attitude if we send some aid. Forgive and forget. Turn the other cheek and all."

79

AT MARINE FORWARD ATTACK Squadron Wildcat, high-pressure hoses blast the pink paint off the three F/A-18s, whose still-hot engines throw off a cloud of pink steam. In front of the planes on the tarmac, Jimbo, Chris, and Stan pose in their flight suits, their helmets tucked under their arms as Sergeant Major catches the moment with his cell phone camera.

"Sirs, respectfully suggest this here film not be shown in public for a good long while," Sergeant Major tells them. "Like never." He glances back at the base commandant's quarters, whose windows overlook the tarmac. "Colonel's reaction gonna be bad enough."

"Wise advice, Sergeant Major," Jimbo says.

Sergeant Major turns to his maintenance crew. "You handjobs swab my runway down so it's as virginal as the entire fucking US Army. And once that's done, you will not recall it ever happened! Semper fi!"

80

ON CV *STAR OF Bethlehem*, Connie Blunt stands with her back to the bow, beyond which in the distance the low white buildings and glass towers of Tel Aviv's long shoreline glimmer in the sunlight. From this far away, it could be any beachfront city on the Mediterranean.

"Damian, what viewers are seeing over my shoulder is Tel Aviv, known as the White City. It must be a happier city if, as I hope, news has reached its people that aid is less than two hours away. We can't be sure, of course, because as CNN has reported Tel Aviv remains cut off from effective communication with the outside world. But as this brave aid flotilla draws closer, there's no doubt…"

81

SHE IS CORRECT. IN Yigal's office on the fourth floor of the Isracorp building, the chief of staff's spotters have already identified the ships steaming closer. Pinky is there, and Misha, who has taken to wearing a semi-automatic pistol on both hips. If he had a sheriff's star, he would no doubt wear that. The two men seem to have reached a modus vivendi similar to that which appears to have become the rule in the ghetto now that there is a sense of order, if not law. They will never be friends, but they are allies, comrades in arms.

"We need to secure unloading," Yigal says. "Hungry Jews get pushy at a bar mitzvah. These haven't eaten properly for weeks."

Misha looks offended. "What do you think we do all day? Already moving into place."

"You knew the ships would get through?" Yigal asks.

"We plan for contingencies," Pinky says.

"And I was going to shoot him in the nuts," Misha mutters.

"Miracles have been known to happen in this neighborhood," Pinky says. "Manna falling from the sky. A burning bush that isn't consumed. The ten plagues—nobody expected that. And now...Kuwait."

"This is going to work?"

"Yigal, their air force is just sitting there, sixty beautiful F/A-18s, barely used, low mileage, doing nobody any good."

Misha snorts. "And they call me a thief?"

"So it's a go?"

"I don't have any other F/A-18s in my pocket," Yigal says.

"In that case, Mr. Prime Minister, Mr. Minister of Police," Pinky says, grinning for the first time in weeks. "The State of Israel is about to steal itself an air force."

82

ON THE TARMAC AT Marine Forward Attack Squadron Wildcat, eighty-two officers and enlisted men are lined up at attention as Lieutenant Colonel I. C. McKendrick steps up on a wooden box. She has purposefully kept them waiting in the heat of this Middle Eastern afternoon. To underscore her disapproval, she informed her sergeant major not to offer the assembled Marines the solace of stand-at-ease. They have been at attention in the sun for twenty minutes. When she is sure the squadron has been sufficiently roasted, she signals the sergeant major with a nod.

"Ma'am!" he barks. "All hands on deck, ma'am!"

The base commander is mistress of the Marine officer's trick of speaking quietly and slowly. Even so, her voice has all the feminine charm of a 50 cal. machine gun. Her delivery is pointed, humorless, staccato. Lieutenant Colonel McKendrick did not get where she is in the Corps because she is a pussy.

"Marines, I've been informed there has taken place a bit of unauthorized pleasure flying. In case it is not known to any of you assholes, the aircraft on this tarmac are property of the government of the United States of America, which does not look with favor on anyone borrowing same without official sanction. The original price tag on each of these aircraft is $67 million dollars, stripped. Losing one on an unauthorized flight would not only be sufficient for general court martial for the fist-fucker who does so, but would stain the reputation of this entire squadron, of which up to now I have been damn proud."

She takes a moment to light a cigarette, something the commandant of any other base would never do, but this one is so far from official purview she can get away with anything up to but not including shooting several of her pilots in the head.

"Be that as it may, we're in Office Hours." This is the Marine equivalent of Captain's Mast in the Navy, a form of military justice from which there is no appeal, and in which there are few limitations on punishment. "Sergeant Major?"

"Office Hours in session, ma'am!"

"Very good, sergeant major." She looks out at her men with a mixture of anger and pity. "Now all of you gyrene cunts who participated in or aided this morning's excursion, identify yourselves."

At once Stan, Chris, and Jimbo step forward. Two other officers join them, then an enlisted man, then another, and another. Two officers follow. When the sergeant major steps up, the entire squadron joins him.

Col. McKendrick shakes her head slowly. "You sorry palm-fuckers make it so easy. Every gyrene on deck is hereby found guilty of violation of UCMJ Article 86, Unauthorized Absence, and is consequently restricted to barracks."

The colonel pauses for a long time, her scowl slowly melting.

"For a period of two hours. Anyone ever mentions this offense or its level of punishment, I will personally remove his liver with my teeth. Sergeant major, dismiss these Marines. Semper fi! And God bless America."

83

TEL AVIV HAS NO harbor capable of berthing ocean-going ships. At the very center of its beachfront, a large marina shelters several hundred pleasure craft, mostly sail, but the port itself is far too shallow for commercial tonnage. Just to the south, in the tiny fishing port of Jaffa, lighters could be used to offload cargo from a freighter lying at anchor in deep water, but the ancient harbor, which was the region's main port until the construction of Haifa in northern Israel and Ashdod in the south, now has neither the fleet of small boats necessary for the job nor the manpower trained to row them out and back.

Instead, the six freighters of the aid flotilla lie at anchor about two thousand feet beyond the breakers. Crew members on four of the ships pass boxes of supplies to others in lifeboats, who pass these on to a long daisy chains of civilians—male, female, young, old, secular and religious—standing waist deep in the surf. From the other two vessels, tankers filled to the gunwales with potable water, civilians shoulder fire hoses leading to tanker trucks on the beach.

84

AS HER CAMERAMAN SHOOTS the unloading from CV *Star of Bethlehem*, Connie Blunt manages to carry two pieces of expensive luggage to where Captain Frank oversees the unloading.

"Captain."

The skipper scans the horizon with his binoculars. He knows the Egyptian Navy is out of the picture, but this operation is going on in broad daylight, and the only military cover he has is a group of half-tracks on the beach that have brought in female soldiers to punch a hole in the identity card of each person who receives a ration of MREs, Meals Ready to Eat, the US military's solution to feeding fighting men in the field.

"Captain!"

"Jesus, what?"

"Is it safe to go ashore?"

"Safe? Every second this operation continues is one I can't guarantee. So far, so good."

"Well, I'm ready."

He shouts down to the men and women in the daisy chain, "Hey, hold that thing out of the water!" The crew has now started unloading five-foot-long wooden crates marked FIM-92 in black stenciling. "Shit, anybody know Hebrew here? Billy!"

The rabbinical student comes running up with a carton marked *Pharmaco*. "These should go next, captain. Medical stuff. I got a whole crate opened—"

"I said I'm ready," Blunt says. "Captain, we'll need a boat."

"Forget the meds. Get down there in the water, son, and make sure those long crates stay dry."

The kid doesn't have to be told twice. He is over the side and scampering down a rope ladder like a monkey with a skullcap pinned to his hair. He starts shouting at the people in the daisy chain, who stop for a moment, shocked to hear the strange locutions of biblical Hebrew. Billy shouts again. They get it, lifting the boxes above water. It is beginning to develop a chop.

"A boat! I'll need a boat of some sort!"

"What boat?"

"I hope you don't think I'm going to wade ashore!"

"We got no more boats for the unloading, sister, so for fucking sure we got no boats for you. If you're not helping, go over the side!"

"Over the side?"

"Everyone else is doing it."

"Captain, we've got equipment, expensive equipment. And luggage, Louis Vuitton for God's sake. And my hair. I'm about to do a stand-up on the beach."

As he picks up the binoculars once more to scan the skies, he starts to laugh. It comes out a gravelly snort, part amusement, part indignation. "*You've* got expensive equipment? You know what's in them crates? Each one of them crates cost the US taxpayer thirty-eight thousand bucks, though from what I understand we got them at a significant discount from—never mind who from." He turns to the daisy chain. "For chrissake, Billy, tell them to hold that shit out of the water! It don't shoot wet!"

In a split second, Connie Blunt forgets about her luggage. "I thought we were carrying MREs. You don't mean we haven't been carrying humanitarian—"

"Yeah, yeah," Captain Frank tells her, almost laughing now. "We're bringing food and water, sister, but among the meals ready to eat we got a different kind of MREs. Missiles Ready to Engage. Doesn't get more humanitarian than that."

"But this contradicts everything we've been told!"

"War is hell, sister. Now get your fat ass out of the way or start humpin' crates. I got no time to play around." He considers for a moment. "Missiles Ready to Engage—I like it. You got no fucking idea how much I like it."

The next moment he stops laughing. The entire daisy chain has frozen in place, every one of its human links looking up.

From out of the east, five gray jet fighters blast into view, coming in high from over the eastern horizon.

85

IN THE AIR, THE Syrian wing commander surveys the scene below: the six ships at anchor in choppy water, each unloading its cargo to long lines of Jews shifting the supplies to shore like a fire brigade of ants. Two much longer queues converge on a central point on the beach to receive the goods. At 2200 feet, this is the Syrian flight commander's reconnaissance pass, high enough for his Sukhoi SU-24s to evade cannon fire from the beach. But there are no cannons visible on the beach, only several nests of khaki-painted vehicles, some trucks, mostly jeeps. He opens communication.

"Massawi Red to Massawi Flight. Massawi Red to Massawi Flight. Follow my lead, brothers. First the ships, then anything moving on the beach. Massawi 2 the second ship, Massawi 3 the third, Massawi 4 the fourth, Massawi 5 the fifth, and Massawi 6 in reserve. The lead freighter is mine."

Under his breath, he curses his superiors, who refused to give him more aircraft, suspecting a trap. Some trap. If he had more planes, he could simultaneously strafe the lines of people on the beach into a long stain of blood.

"Follow my lead, brothers. As the Americans say, it is shooting fish in an oil drum. In the name of Islam, let us expunge this plague of Jews and Christians. Death to the Crusaders! Over."

86

On CV STAR OF Bethlehem, Captain Frank is desperate, and shouting. "Do any of you people know how to fire one of these things? Are any of you veterans?" He has just managed to pull one of the Stinger missiles out of its box. "I need an infantryman here!"

He gets one, a red-haired diesel mechanic from Kansas City.

"Sir," Taylor C. Briggs says. "You got that backwards. You're gonna shoot yourself to kingdom come if'n you don't turn it around."

"You know how to operate one of these gizmos?"

"Piece of cake, sir. You see this here, this pops up. It's your viewfinder. Gives you general direction. Then you get it up on your shoulder—"

"Jesus H. Christ, kid. Don't teach, do! Grab this pig iron and get ready. Those mothers are coming back. They're turning now!"

A mile out to sea, the Syrian formation performs a graceful unified Immelmann turn and slows to come in low.

87

A STAPLE OF AMERICAN infantry warfare since the 1980s, the FIM-92 Stinger missile is both one of the most complex weapons in the foot soldier's armory and the simplest to operate. Once it is pointed in the general direction of enemy aircraft, its dozens of micro gyrocompasses home in on the heat from the target's engines until it makes contact. The infantry calls it fire-and-forget. With a weight of only thirty-three pounds and an effective range of up to three miles, it is both lethal and, if one knows where to look, widely available on the open market in such places as Pakistan's Hindu Kush, leftover stock supplied by US Special Forces to Muslim insurgents in neighboring Afghanistan. These mostly illiterate fighters used it to send the country's Soviet invaders packing. They then turned the same weapon on the Americans who, in a triumph of wishful thinking, hoped they would not become targets of their own technology. Once taught, any child can shoot a Stinger, and did.

The red-haired kid on the deck of CV *Star of Bethlehem* was apparently paying attention during advanced infantry training at Fort Hood, Georgia. In a matter of moments, others on the deck pry open more crates. Firing Stingers is not only easy. It's fun.

88

As HE BRINGS HIS SU-24 out of its Immelmann, the Syrian wing commander sees the first missile rising to greet him. He dives. It misses his aircraft by inches, but homes in on his portside wing-man, who abruptly ceases to exist. The resultant blast hits the Syrian wing commander's own fuselage with an enormous push, so that his entire aircraft trembles momentarily before recovering. As the wing commander pulls out and heads to sea, he watches two more of his aircraft disappear in mammoth fireballs.

His radio lights up. "Massawi 5 to Massawi Red. Come in, Massawi Red. Commander, regarding the fish in the oil drum. The fish are shooting back! Over."

"Roger that, Massawi 5. This is Massawi Red. All aircraft follow my lead. Back to base. Back to base. It is a Jewish trick! Over and out."

89

OUT INDEED. AS THE remaining four Sukhois shoot eastward over the crippled city back to their base adjoining Yasser Arafat International Airport, a squad of female soldiers, following the lead of a plump nineteen-year-old red-headed sergeant who two months before had instructed recruits in Stinger operation, aim the weapons they have just removed of their crates. The remaining Sukhoi pilots, flying at Mach 1, break the sound barrier over the beach at 800 miles per hour. Flying at 1200 miles per hour, it takes only seconds for the new round of Stingers to catch up.

Debris from the Sukhois rains down over Tel Aviv. No one is seriously injured, but one of Judy's pony express riders takes a nasty cut on his thigh and falls off his bike. He is a seventeen-year-old boy of mixed Moroccan and Polish descent, dark skin, blond hair, green eyes, and sufficient determination to remount and continue on his way bringing the news: "Aid has arrived! Aid has arrived! Everyone to the beach. Keep good order! There is enough for all!"

90

THIS IS HARDLY THE main highway to Tel Aviv, but Alex is a local. She has traveled this route many times on the way back from Ben-Gurion Airport, where immigration always stops her to compare the male visage on her passport with that of the demure figure holding it. The immigration clerks are mostly young girls bored with the endless lines of tired faces and the need to check the identity of every one of them—tourists, returning Israelis, foreign diplomats, Israeli consular officials on home leave. Each passport must be checked electronically against a computer memory of wanted criminals, suspect aliens, draft dodgers, Israeli Arabs, and foreign troublemakers whose names match those in the database. At one time this was done through the visual scanning of lists, but now the computer has taken over, digitally reading the name and face on each passport and comparing it instantly with names and faces in a database.

When Alex flies on a commercial flight, the drill is always the same.

"This is your passport?"

"Yes."

"It doesn't...look like you."

"Bad hair day."

"It's a picture of a man."

"Also the lighting..."

In a moment, two Border Police lead Alex to an interview room.

"There's a note in my file," she tells them.

Nothing doing. In a minute, a senior immigration official comes in. "Alex, what's the word?"

"Inflexibility."

"Yes, well, that's the way we are." He stamps her passport. "I told you the last time, just ask for me. Epstein, David. Remember? I gave you my card. How was Paris?"

"Gay," Alex says. "Entirely too gay."

"You're not…?"

"Just a guy who likes to dress up, David. You?"

Now, standing by the side of this tertiary road that if one knows where to turn will eventually reach north Tel Aviv, Alex is confronted with another kind of immigration barrier as, decked out in his Egyptian officer's uniform, he stands beside the olive-green Cadillac and hears the unmistakable sound of a pistol being cocked.

Without moving anything but his head, he glances behind him to see two Bedouin, both armed. One is about twenty, the other might be his father. Tethered to a stunted mulberry tree beyond them are two laden donkeys.

"Do you mind if I finish?" he says in Arabic.

"Go ahead, Egyptian. It may be your last. Enjoy."

It is a long piss. Alex's mind is racing. He has several hundred Egyptian pounds in the pocket of his military trousers, courtesy of the previous occupant—the fat colonel carried nothing: in Arab armies senior officers have no need for cash—plus the adjutant's watch, a Seiko, and the colonel's, a gold Omega. Alex's own watch, along with other gear, is hidden under the driver's seat. Ever the pilot, he considers evasive action, but the two Bedouin are at point-blank range, so by the time he gets out his own pistol, the colonel's pistol, he will be many times dead. But he can't piss forever.

"Less than friendly," he says, giving his business a good-luck shake, then stops before zippering his fly. He doesn't want to do anything with his hands but keep them at his side. One suspicious move is all it would take. "What is it you desire? Money?"

Abed offers a theatrical sigh. "Why must everything always be about money?"

"I have a watch. Gold. Not plated."

"We'll start with your uniform." He turns to Cobi, and in Hebrew says, "When the moment comes, make sure not to get blood all over it."

"What the fuck? Why are you speaking Hebrew?"

Cobi looks hard at the Egyptian colonel. "Why are we speaking Hebrew? Why are *you* speaking Hebrew? I have to say, it's pretty good."

In one second, Alex has gone from preparing to die to a state of swollen indignation. "It should be, you twat. You're hijacking an Egyptian staff car already hijacked by a downed Israeli pilot."

This time it is the turn of Cobi and Abed to be confused.

"Will you please put those guns away before I get really bitchy?"

Cobi is unsure. "How do we know you're real?"

"Schmuck, your friend's Arabic is better than mine. If you assholes will allow me to reach into this borrowed uniform, you can check my ID. There's a photo."

The two examine Alex's Israeli military ID card, guns still pointed in his direction.

"Air Force major, it says."

"You want my unit number?"

Cobi shakes his head. "I wouldn't know if it's real, or the ID. You could be some sort of spy."

"Oh, yeah, a regular Mata Hari," Alex says, realizing immediately that the two are unlikely to know the name, or its gender. Worse, if they did, it might confuse the issue further. "Look, will you point those guns away? I am an IAF pilot. F-16s. You know, big bird, go fast, save Jewish lives?"

"You really Israeli?" Cobi says.

"No, I'm a fucking space alien. Ask me a question—anything."

Cobi looks to Abed, who shrugs. "Name the starting lineup for Maccabi Tel-Aviv."

Alex shakes his head wearily. "I'm not, you know, big on sports. That's basketball, right?"

"You're from Tel Aviv?"

"Stupid question, kid. Everyone is—now."

"Starting from the south, name all the roads crossing Dizengoff Street."

"Including Buki ben-Yogli? Because that's really small."

Abed shakes his head. "A spy would know that. He'd have the whole city memorized."

"Sing *Jerusalem of Gold*."

"With my dick hanging out?" He sings the Naomi Shemer song, *Jersualem of Gold*, that is practically a second national anthem.

> *The mountain air, clear as wine,*
> *And the perfume of the pines*
> *Carried on the breeze at twilight*
> *Along with the sound of bells.*
> *And in the sleep of tree and stone,*
> *Captured as in a dream,*
> *The city stands alone,*
> *And at its heart—a wall.*

> *Jerusalem of gold*
> *And of bronze, and of light*
> *Am I not a lyre for all your songs?*

> *How the cisterns have dried.*
> *The marketplace stands empty*
> *There are no visitors to the*
> *Temple Mount in the Old City.*
> *And in the mountain caves*
> *The winds wail, and no one*
> *Descends to the Dead Sea*
> *By way of Jericho.*

> *Jerusalem of gold*
> *And of bronze, and of—*

"Enough," Cobi says. "What's with the falsetto?"

"A long story."

Abed keeps his gun leveled. "He could have learned that. I mean, this is what spies do, no?" He takes a step closer to the Egyptian officer.

"*Schindler's List*," Cobi says.

"It's a movie."

"What was the scandal about *Schindler's List* and *Jerusalem of Gold*?"

Alex laughs. "That you call a scandal? It wasn't a scandal, just a fuck-up. A joke."

"I saw it," Abed says. "Good movie. But from my perspective, too Jewish."

"So tell me," Cobi says. "What was the…fuck-up?"

"At the end of the movie, when these people, Jews—you know, from the camps—are leaving, for Israel eventually, the song is played. Israeli audiences howled."

"Why?"

"Because, my young friend, the scene takes place in 1944 or 1945, and Naomi Shemer didn't write it until 1967."

Cobi decocks his pistol. "No spy could know that. Where you headed?"

"Not Cairo."

Cobi and Abed break into broad smiles.

"Kindly put your dick back in your pants," Abed says. "You've got passengers."

91

ON THE LARGE TELEVISION screen in the conference room of what was once the main Jerusalem branch of Israel Discount Bank, a soaking wet Connie Blunt can be seen doing a stand-up from the beach at Tel Aviv.

"As you can see, Damian, aid in the form of food, clean water, and medical supplies is now being distributed to the hungry population of what people here call Ghetto Tel Aviv, a reference to the Warsaw Ghetto where the Nazis concentrated a huge population so that they could be killed off. But today, through the generosity of American private citizens and church groups, the men, women, and children of this ghetto have the chance to live another day."

She presses her earpiece, leaning forward. "I'm sorry, Damian—can you repeat?"

The screen splits. "What can you tell us, Connie, about the footage we've just shown of that aerial attack on the beach?"

"Well, Damian, it wasn't precisely an attack on the beach. It was an attack on innocent civilians. Five or six aircraft, which I'm told are Syrian, attempted to—"

Tupikov cuts off the television. "Regrettable."

General Niroomad is seething. "Syrians are not particularly good at warfare, that is the problem."

Syrian Field Marshall Al-Asadi stands. "When the chariots of Damascus ruled the Eastern Mediterranean, the Persians huddled in caves."

"Always a history lesson. As from my distinguished Egyptian colleague, allow me to quote: 'All Israeli planes were destroyed.' Yet there they were, on television no less, sinking three warships. Not one—three."

"It is unaccountable," Field Marshall Haloumi says, almost sputtering. "Three pink Super Hornets that come from nowhere and return to nowhere. Our intelligence has no sign of them."

"Perhaps you would like also to tell me of the accomplishments of the Egyptians in history. All fiction."

"The pyramids are fiction? You have only to look at them."

"My dear field marshal, the Hebrews built your pyramids. Now they have destroyed your fleet."

"I tell you all Jewish warplanes were destroyed."

"Like the Jewish tanks that wiped out my son's armored division, destroyed, I was assured, by—"

"No Israeli tanks survived!" Marshal al-Asadi shouts. He bangs on the table. "No doubt they were American!"

"Oh, yes, field marshal," the Iranian says. "And then they went back into a hole in the ground!"

Tupikov raises his hand. "Gentlemen…"

"Gentlemen?" General Niroomad says. "Gentlemen do not prevaricate. We are blessed with mysterious planes, mysterious tanks. Now the door is open to a resupply of the Jews we so carefully herded into Tel Aviv to starve. Now, through unspeakable incompetence, our enemy will fatten to create some further Jewish cleverness. We are the victors and they make fools of us. On CNN no less. On world television."

This is Tupikov's opportunity. The only way to unite these disparate forces is through their common enmity. "Then what must be done?"

"There is no question what, my friend," General Niroomad says. "The question is when."

"Exactly," Marshall al-Asadi says. "We have a proverb: a Jew lives, the problem grows."

"So it is agreed?" General Niroomad asks. It is rhetorical, a gesture.

"Syria votes yes."

"The Kingdom of Jordan agrees. As per plan, the Hashemite tanks will have the honor to be the first to enter Tel Aviv."

"Allah go with them," Field Marshal Haloumi says. "Egyptian infantry will follow. The streets will run with blood."

"Our Syrian heroes will seal the city," General al-Asadi confirms. "None will flee. Not an infant. Neither a Jewish cat nor a Jewish dog."

Field Marshal Haloumi turns to the Russian. "The Americans, will they not come to the aid of the Jews? Will they not send the Sixth Fleet?"

"The wings of the American eagle are soaked in oil," Tupikov says. "It is a dodo, a flightless bird. Our satellites display no action, no movement, not even a breeze. The Americans don't care for the Jews, neither for the Palestinians. They care only for oil."

"Again the Palestinians," General Said says. "Squash one bug, up comes another."

Tupikov shakes his head. "The Palestinians are history. Brief history, convenient history, but history nonetheless."

"The Palestinians deserve their fate," General Said says with finality. "They were never a people and never will be." He rises. "The army of the Hashemite Kingdom of Jordan must prepare for the siege of Tel Aviv." His hand on the hilt of his sword, he marches out.

The Syrian commander slowly rises. "Let the Jordanians drown in Jewish blood," Field Marshall Al-Asadi whispers. "Later, at our leisure, we shall deal with them as well." He nods, then he too leaves the conference room.

After his footsteps can no longer be heard resounding in the hall, General Niroomad turns to Tupikov. "Arab heroism. Tanks against pistols. If that. And then treachery."

"The cats eats the mouse," Tupikov says. "The dog eats the cat. Will the lion devour the dog?"

"Iran does not nourish on dog."

"I am sorry to hear that, general."

Niroomad smiles. "But dogs have their uses."

"General, it is an interesting business doing pleasure with you."

"Russia will control the Suez Canal," Niroomad says. "Iran will control the Arabs. And their oil."

"Together," Tupikov says. "We will remake the world."

92

AN ISRAELI BEDOUIN TURNED enemy colonel, in an Egyptian uniform Abed is at least as convincing as Alex, seated beside him, is the picture of feminine beauty. Her transformation astounds the others:

by simply changing clothes and applying makeup, Alex has become someone else, not only in looks, which are external, but in nuance. As the woman's clothes and makeup went on, a woman blossomed from within.

When they stop at a roadblock, which they hope will be the last before moving across the no man's land that marks the border between Egyptian-held territory and Tel Aviv looming to the west, an Egyptian lieutenant salutes. "Good evening, colonel. No traffic beyond this point."

"Were you not informed?" Abed says from the driver's seat.

"Informed, excellency?"

"Secret mission. We are exchanging this Jew bitch for an Egyptian officer." He whispers. "A general."

"I know nothing of it, excellency."

"Remove the roadblock, lieutenant."

Two more Egyptian soldiers approach, looking in at Alex. They appear not to have seen a woman in some time.

"We are required to search the car, colonel."

Abed is no stranger to the Arab psyche, formed from birth in a top-down society that has not changed in a thousand years. "How dare you doubt the word of an Egyptian staff officer? Name, unit, and serial number! Immediately!"

"Your excellency…"

"Move the barrier!"

The Egyptian lieutenant peers into the backseat in a modest attempt at doing his job before yielding to the presence of higher authority. The backseat is empty. He signals the others to do as the colonel commands.

Abed nods. "Upon my return in two hours, this unpleasantness will not recur."

The Egyptian lieutenant salutes. "Yes, excellency!"

Abed returns the salute so casually he could just as well be scratching his forehead, and drives on.

The waning light now has reached that moment of Middle Eastern dusk when abruptly it disappears entirely, but Abed continues to drive without lights until the car has turned out of sight. The land here is flat, signaling their arrival on the coastal plain that stretches from central Israel down to Egypt itself. Here there can be no snipers hidden above. There is no above. In the moonlight, a sign appears, bullet-pocked as though used for target practice, a common incidence everywhere armies pass. TEL AVIV, the sign reads, 2 KM.

Abed stops the car and with Alex approaches the trunk.

"Cobi," the Bedouin shouts. "It's just us. Kindly do not shoot. I am opening the trunk."

The two help Cobi, still in Bedouin robes, out onto the roadway. His body has been compressed for an hour. The pistol in his hand seems frozen in position along with the rest of him.

"Another hour and I'd be permanently bent."

Abed begins changing out of the Egyptian uniform into his Bedouin robes, while Alex retransforms herself, both men watching as if they expect a nude woman to appear. She doesn't. There is only the disappointment of another male body as uninteresting as their own.

"Abed would make a fine Egyptian officer," Alex says. "Total disdain. Feudal in the extreme. Kid, you should have seen it."

"I heard it all," Cobi says. "It was like being inside a loudspeaker. Every minute I was prepared to pull the interior latch and jump out shooting, but the truth is I wouldn't have been able to. My circulation is just coming back. If this is what getting old is like, I don't want it."

"You'll want it," Abed says. "One's perspective changes depending upon where one sits."

"Yeah, well, from where I was sitting, all I heard was an Israeli Bedouin saving the lives of three Egyptians. Three, right? From the footsteps. Were there more than three?"

"Three only. So you are learning to track then? I am impressed."

"If your tribe finds out about this, they'll toss you out on your ass," Cobi says. "You could just as easily have killed them."

"Again killing. My boy, these were merely Egyptian peasants, conscripts doing their job. If ever you have a choice, killing is the last option."

Alex is back in pilot's uniform, strapping on his sidearm. "How about we concentrate on saving the lives of three *Israeli* peasants?" He goes to the flag standard on the right front fender, removes the Egyptian banner, and begins attaching a large white cloth of irregular shape. "Guessing from our location, the next barrier we come to is not going to be Egyptian."

Cobi looks at the white cloth with a mixture of admiration and disbelief. "That'll get their attention."

The staff car is now adorned with a huge pair of boxer shorts formerly worn by a very fat Egyptian colonel. The white expanse is marked like an Israeli flag, but its two horizontal stripes and Star of David are in red, not blue.

"Hate the red, but who wears blue lipstick?" Alex says, getting into the Cadillac. "So trashy."

93

ON A SECOND-FLOOR BALCONY across Ibn Gvirol Street in Tel Aviv, IDF combat engineers secure a quarter-inch steel cable to the concrete building wall, then drop the other end to the roadway, where other soldiers raise it to a parallel balcony on the other side, there to be similarly secured and winched tight. Repeated all down Ibn Gvirol and other broad thoroughfares, the cables are thin enough not to be visible to enemy observers flying high over the city; from street level, they suggest some sort of web, tying the city together two apartments at a time. Few know their purpose, but the civilian population, looking up at the taut cables, surmise the obvious: something is going on, and it cannot be bad. For the disillusioned and disheartened population of Ghetto Tel Aviv, that something is being done cannot be anything but good.

94

WITH THE BEGINNING OF active campaigning only months away, the president is not about to spend his precious time where there are no speeches to make, hands to shake, or babies to kiss—yes, the president has revived that most dust-covered of American political clichés, though his tagline manages to bring it up to date for an economically battered electorate as short on optimism as it is on affordable gas: "Madam, the beautiful child in your arms is the future of America."

Rather than be seen visiting world leaders like a traveling salesman or bringing them together for an emergency conference whose indeterminate results or outright failure might be attributed to the president himself, not a great idea just ahead of an election, the leader of the free world prefers to work behind the scenes. For this he employs the video conference call in dealing with the individuals he terms his "co-world leaders." (Flo Spier has given up trying to get the man to say "world co-leaders"—the president would rather be taken for a smart hick than a dumb Harvard grad.) His security people assure him these calls are as private as if all the participants were locked into a lead-lined closet in the White House sub-basement. The stakes are too high to risk public failure. Few nations are just itching to welcome even a small fraction of an estimated six million penniless Jews.

"So what I got here so far, gentlemen—and ladies, of course, mustn't forget the ladies—is a grand total of, let's see now, give or take, carry the two, about a million five. Here's the bottom line. I know the last thing you folks want is a flood of dyspeptic Hebrews in your country. But I got to say, I mean, a great nation like France, offering to take just two hundred thousand, that's chicken feed. The UK, I see you're down for half that. Italy and Holland, half that again. Folks, we got us six million starving refugees here, and believe me, these people, they get back on their feet and put their biblical heads together, they gonna spark your industries, your sciences, your technologies, your entire economies. Yeah, I know every one of y'all only wants the smarties, the doctors and researchers and so on, and there's quite a few requests I got for air force pilots and top-drawer soldiers. But come on, the cream gets spread around with the milk.

"Anyhoo, first I got to get numbers I can live with. Even my good neighbor to the south, Mexico, not the richest country in the universe, is willing to take two hundred thousand. That's not, you know, the kind of commitment comes easy because my amigos down there are still boot-strapping their nation into the ranks of developed countries. So why are they accepting so many Jews? Because they expect these Jews to help 'em do it. You Scandinavian guys, learn from this. You South American countries, learn from this. Even some of you Asian tigers, think about how a whole lot of Jews can turbo-charge your already impressive success. And my good Russian friend, we got over a million people in Israel just come from your great country twenty years ago. They speak the language, for Pete's sake—it's a natural fit. I got you down for fifty thousand? You gotta be yankin' my chain.

"So looky here. I gonna make you a one-time only offer. Everyone doubles his quota and the US of A will match it, so that means we'll have this problem settled in a New York minute. And, speaking of that city, if you agree right now, for a limited time only, I'll throw in getting the NYPD to cancel every one of your people's parking tickets, I don't care going back how long. No more hassles. That's by way of being a joke, guys, but I'll tell you what I'm gonna do: if you don't have it already, you get most favored nation status for five whole years. That means zero customs duty on most imports to the US of A, which ought to mean quite a lot if your economy is in the toilet, which most of y'all's is. Also, any of you want to meet a special movie star on your next visit to our fine country, I can fix that—just so you keep my role in it on the QT. What do you say, guys? Let's start from the top. Albania, a hundred people—you wanna go to two hundred? What's two hundred people?"

Albania goes to two hundred, Argentina doubles to three thousand, Australia to a hundred thousand, and so on right down the line to Zambia, which agrees to fifty Jews. China and Russia are left for last. Because Taiwan has now agreed to accept four thousand, Beijing signs on for ten times that. Russia, however, isn't budging. Never mind that so many Israelis were until recently Russian engineers, doctors, and scientists trained in Russian schools and familiar with Russian ways. "Russia," its prime minister tells the president, "has too many Jews already. And always will."

With the problem mostly solved, the president needs only to consult with Flo Spier on the best timing for the announcement. She believes it will very helpful to get the new Israeli PM to Washington for a joint statement. Trouble is, communication with what the press is calling the "interim" or "ad hoc" government of Israel is proving difficult.

Less so for an Israeli agent deep in the national security apparatus, who communicates the results of the teleconference—code, shmode—to Yigal Lev via a radio link with CV *Star of Bethlehem*.

"Well, that's settled," Yigal tells Misha. "Where do you prefer, Albania or Zambia?"

"I like it here," Misha says.

"So do I," Yigal says. "The State of Israel isn't going anywhere, not in whole, not in parts."

"Except forward."

"Except forward," Yigal says.

"And then I'll have my favorite cigars again," Misha says.

95

THE THREE IMPOSTERS ARE now close enough to Tel Aviv to imagine the sound of early morning traffic and the sight of exhaust smoke rising over the city. But the morning is silent and the air is clear.

Abed drives slowly; the last thing they need is to come upon an Israeli patrol at speed.

A shout in Arabic from somewhere ahead splits the predawn silence. "Hands in the air!"

Each of the three thinks the same thing at the same time: *shit.* There is no knowing the uniform of whoever is speaking.

"Slowly exit the vehicle, carefully put down your weapons, then move to the front of the vehicle, one man at a time."

When they do, there is a further command.

"Place your hands on your heads."

A half dozen soldiers appear before them out of the morning mists.

Cobi laughs. "Don't shoot," he says in Hebrew. "We're playing for the same team."

"Shut up—not a word!" An IDF captain comes up from behind them, his Tavor leveled at their heads. At this distance, a single burst will decapitate all of them in the time it takes to complete one word of explanation.

A sergeant motions to two soldiers behind him. "Check to the rear, a hundred meters."

"There's an Egyptian forward checkpoint about a kilom—"

The lieutenant swings his rifle butt. Abed goes down. "Your mother's cunt! I said shut up."

The sun is fully up now. One of the squad lights the butt of a cigarette. That is what it has come to: saving butts, relighting them for a last puff. Another squats in the dirt. Time passes with immeasurable slowness, like a clock whose hands have been weighted.

Abed's head is bleeding, staining through the black-and- white-checked cotton of his kaffiyeh. But he stays down.

Cobi tries to read the captain's insignia: Golani Infantry, but no other identifying marks. He wears brown parachutist boots. The two do not go together. Even Golani who graduate jump school do not wear brown boots. Golani troopers and paratroopers get into fistfights over who is tougher. Or they did. Cobi busies himself with solving this puzzle, thinking maybe this is a borrowed uniform, or borrowed boots. Or maybe it is all simply a bad dream. He had enough of them in the cave waiting for Abed to return.

Abed is like the brown boots. A Bedouin, even one who hides his own IDF uniform, should have turned him in for bounty—that was the rap on Bedouin. Why is this one different? Who was to say as soon he got Cobi out of the cave he wouldn't shoot him in the back? But he didn't. Cobi thinks: good Bedouin, bad Bedouin. Just like Jews.

Meanwhile, the captain searches the Cadillac.

"An Egyptian officer's uniform," he says, with no hint of surprise. "Which one of you belongs to it?"

Alex wiggles a finger at the top of his head: permission to speak? She does not wish want to get hit in the face with a rifle butt. Such a pretty face when it is all fixed up.

The lieutenant nods.

"Liberated from the enemy, captain."

"Sure."

It is clear to all three what the captain is thinking: a decision must be made. In Ghetto Tel Aviv there is no room for prisoners, nor anything to feed them. Every calorie that goes to them will not be available to his soldiers. And it is growing light. A reconnaissance patrol on open ground in full daylight might be picked off at any moment. Enemy helicopters are everywhere.

The two soldiers return.

One of them, an Ethiopian whose European face seems to have been soaked in coffee, spits to his side. "Clear to the rear," he announces. "But that's just a hundred meters. For all we know they could be in front of us."

The squatting soldier stands. He knows this much: either they go back with prisoners or they go back without them, but they need to go back now. As though magnetized, the others in the squad take a few steps closer to the three, Alex and Cobi standing, Abed still on the ground.

The captain approaches, peering closely at Alex, whose eyes still bear traces of makeup, his lips a bit too plummy. "Why do you look like a girl?"

"My late mother asked the same question," Alex says. The joke falls flat. "Look, under the seat is my IDF ID."

"Easily forged," the captain says. "Is that eye shadow?"

"Liner," Alex says. "Estée Lauder."

"But you're not a girl."

Cobi can take no more of this. If something doesn't happen, they are all going to be executed by their own forces two kilometers from Tel Aviv. "He's not a girl—he's a fucking cross-dresser, and a damn fine one at that. Look, Captain, isn't there any way to prove who we are?"

"You mean prove you're not Hebrew-speaking enemy agents attempting to cross into Tel Aviv? Let me think. No, I don't reckon you can."

Oddly, it begins with Abed.

"Jerusalem of Gold," he sings from the ground. "And of bronze and…"

Alex and Cobi pick it up immediately.

…of light.
Am I not a lyre for all your songs?

The mountain air, clear as wine,
And the perfume of the pines
Carried on the breeze at twilight
Along with the sound of bells.
And in the sleep of tree and stone,
Captured as in a dream,
The city stands alone,
And at its heart—a wall.

Jerusalem of gold
And of bronze and of—

"Fuck," the captain says. "Why didn't you do that right away?"

Cobi puts his hands down, a relief in itself. "Because we were pissing in our pants you would kill us on the spot, that's why."

"A likely outcome too," the captain says. "You got room for seven more in this boat?"

"Walk in the park," Alex says, grinning. "It's a fucking Cadillac."

96

FOR TWENTY YEARS, SINCE the arrival of General Tawfik Ali, the former Twyford Oliver, uniformly known to his tank crews as Ticky Pasha, the command structure of the armored forces of the Hashemite Kingdom of Jordan has flourished as an independent military fiefdom. While the infantry and air force answer to the minister of defense, Royal Jordanian Armored Command reports directly to the monarch. The relationship between the king and General Ali is considered so unshakeable that only a year earlier a cable to Whitehall from MI6's resident in Amman summarized it succinctly: "Were General Ali to resign, the king would fall—and he knows it."

Like intelligence agencies the world over, MI6 totally gets the past, sometimes comprehends the present, but never even remotely foretells the future. Washington, London, Moscow, and Beijing would be better off hiring fortune tellers. Always and inevitably, the future is complicated—and nowhere is this more true than in the Middle East.

In a desert encampment twenty kilometers outside Amman, the capital, the king is on a visit to the sheikhs of the Bedouin tribes that make up his principal support, the backbone of his army. They are his shield against the growing Palestinian threat within Jordan. Until recently, 70% of the country's population; now, with their numbers swollen by refugees from the pan-Arab campaign to wipe out the Palestinians of the West Bank, the monarch has little choice but to enforce his rule with the sword if he is not to add his name to the list of fallen Arab monarchs. Just as in 1970, when his father ordered the slaughter of Palestinians in Jordan, the current king is determined to do what he must to survive. Of course, if there were some way to deport them all, the task would be easier. But the Palestinians have nowhere to go, certainly not in the Arab world, where they are considered troublemakers. Either they are dealt with now or by sheer numbers they will soon enough depose the monarchy and declare a Palestinian state.

While the British-educated king sits drinking Turkish coffee on a tennis-court-size oriental rug in the vast royal tent, an aide enters to inform him that Ticky Pasha has arrived, presumably to discuss solving Jordan's Palestinian problem for all time.

Within an hour, the two meet in one of seven smaller tents in which the king will sleep that night. Three of the tents are occupied by royal lookalikes. The Jordanian monarch is determined to die of old age.

"Your majesty," General Ali says, speaking the English of Sandhurst and Oxford, of country houses and Whitehall. It is a language they share. Though the British officer is fluent in Arabic, the two always speak English in private. "Your majesty, I ask you to forgive this sudden interruption, but a matter has arisen of great urgency."

"Ticky, please. There is no need to apologize for what is always a pleasurable meeting."

"This one may not be so pleasurable," the Englishman says. "Your highness, I have given to you personally and to the kingdom over which you rule almost twenty years of devoted service. I have dedicated my life's work to the creation and development of the finest armored corps in the Arab world, a force which has permitted you to conquer all of al Kuds." He uses the Arabic name for Jerusalem: *al*

Kuds, the Holy. "As a Muslim, I have wept with joy to see the Mosque of Omar and the Al-Aksa once more in Hashemite hands."

"And as one Muslim to another, I commend your very essential part in causing this to come about. In the annals of Islam, your name will be remembered in glory."

"Your highness, I am now apprised that tanks under my command are to be the vanguard in an invasion of the city of Tel Aviv. Sire, these are weapons designed to destroy military targets, other tanks, armed infantry. Aside from a handful of probably inoperable Chariots that may quickly be swept aside, there are no military targets in the city of Tel Aviv. I am instructed that the targets of my armored corps are to be civilians."

"Jews."

"Your highness, they are unarmed. Women and children."

The monarch smiles. "My dear Ticky, surely as a Muslim you are aware that I am now guardian of the holy sites. My family is descended directly from the Prophet. My first responsibility is to Islam." He nods in affirmation. "First and last."

"Your highness, Jews and Christians are protected peoples. They may not be harmed so long as they do not take up arms against Islam. Even should they reject Allah they are *dhimmi,* who under conditions well defined in Shari'a law may live freely amongst us. The Prophet is himself known to have commanded that women and children and unarmed men must under all circumstances be protected from harm."

"The Prophet stated as well, 'Arabia is Muslim for all time.'"

"Is this then Arabia, your majesty?"

"Ticky, is not my lineage that of the first family of Arabia?"

General Tawfik Ali is now sixty-two years old, his children grown. One is a professor of Arabic at Yale University in the United States, the other proprietor of a London boutique catering to Middle Eastern women visiting England or living in the West; her designs are both modest, in that they cover the arms and legs, and stylish, adaptations of the current trends out of Paris and New York. Ten years a widower, the former Twyford Oliver, holder of a CBE that was never publically announced, has been dreading this moment since he became a Muslim and committed himself to the Hashemites and to their kingdom.

"Your majesty has many times seen the film *Lawrence of Arabia*."

"Many times we have seen it together. It is a tribute to the perfect wisdom of my antecedent, King Abdullah."

"Indeed. But it describes as well the imperfect Englishman who swore him allegiance."

"Only the Prophet is perfect."

"Indeed. But the imperfection of Lawrence is not one I wish to emulate. My faults are great, probably countless. You will recall that at a certain point in the film, the Englishman Lawrence, seething with vengeance, instructs his troops: 'No prisoners.'"

The king listens but does not speak.

"Your majesty, though like Lawrence I was born an Englishman, I am not that man."

"Ticky, I have one fifth column in my country, the Palestinians. Do you suggest I tolerate another?"

"Sire, I respectfully suggest your majesty await the outcome of international attempts to resettle elsewhere the residents of Tel Aviv."

"Yes, of course, that would be the proper path," the king says. "But these are Jews. They rise like the phoenix bird. Their air force has been wiped out and suddenly they appear with three Super Hornets and destroy the pride of the Egyptian navy. Their armed forces are in tatters, most of them prisoners in desert camps. Yet they develop the missile capability which takes out not one but five Syrian Sukhois, as formidable a warplane as exists. Give them another month, another week, perhaps only a day, and they will grow an offensive capability neither you nor I can imagine. Ticky, my beloved mentor, my old friend, these are Jews. They must be destroyed."

"Civilians, your highness. Civilians."

"And did not your own people in the German war firebomb Dresden, also civilians? I believe you have seen the monument in London to the British air marshal who ordered those raids, one Bomber Harris. A statue, my dear friend. Though we Muslims do not erect statues because it is forbidden to make an image, you and I comprehend its significance. The Americans killed millions—unarmed men, women, and children—in Hiroshima and Nagasaki. Why were these acts permitted by Christian leaders who worship every Sunday in a church? In order to save the lives of their own soldiers. It is, in the end, as simple as that. The destruction of Tel Aviv is therefore an act of self-defense."

"Can we not wait a month—a week, even—for the foreign powers to agree a solution?"

"Any such solution will be temporary. My dear Ticky, I promise you the Jews will come back. They always do." For a moment, the monarch looks away. "Let any blame then fall upon my head. You may consider yourself absolved of all responsibility. You merely do my will. Let it be so, and let us forget this conversation."

For answer General Tawfik Ali, soon once again to be Twyford Oliver, and soon to collect his CBE, unsheathes the ceremonial dagger that was presented to him by this same king almost twenty years before, and lays it gently at the monarch's feet.

97

IN THE SEASIDE VILLA in Herzliya that has become the de facto prime ministerial residence, Yigal draws diagrams on the whiteboard in his office. These are not military calculations. Yigal reviewed Pinky's plans for the counterattack and accepted them without qualification. Now he is thinking of next steps, the days after, the future.

Outside, the villa is ringed by troops, with two tanks on the beach to defend it from assault by sea. Pinky understands that the enemy's main thrust will seek the destruction of Israel's leadership, a lesson from the Nazi playbook, where the invasion of every country on the German march brought with it special forces to kidnap or murder its political, religious, and social leadership. After the fall of Berlin, when the list for the United Kingdom was discovered in the headquarters of the SS, its publication drew two kinds of reaction in Britain: relief from those on the list, and indignation from others that they had not been counted dangerous enough to assassinate. Thus the fortifications surrounding the prime minister's villa. The State of Israel, such as it is, cannot again afford to be decapitated.

Judy's concern is more intimate: the health of her husband. It is nearly seven in the morning. Neither has slept. With luck, they can get an hour before the start of the prime ministerial day. "Yigal, please…"

"Almost done," he says. "If I'm right about this, you are going to really love me."

"I already do. Come to bed. I can't sleep without you."

"A few minutes." His eyes return to the whiteboard.

"I want you to know I love you."

"Judy, my Judy."

"Tell me at least what this is."

"National secret."

Still, once back in bed, he tells her. Like all breakthrough ideas, it is as simple to explain as it will be difficult to implement.

"No one thought of this?" she says. "Before?"

"According to Pinky, such a concept does not now exist." He pauses. "It's the kind of plan you don't consider until you are staring into your grave."

Perhaps it is his final phrase. She has been good about not causing her husband unnecessary grief; she knows he has other matters to deal with, matters of consequence. But there is only so much she can take without breaking down. She doesn't want to, not in front of Yigal. But she must.

As tears form, she says it. "I miss Cobi so much."

98

BECAUSE THERE IS NO electric light, the work of the men and women called back to their jobs at Peri Military Industries is limited to the daylight hours—even candles disappeared the first week. When the afternoon sun falls behind the adjoining buildings, it becomes first difficult and then impossible to see. Experienced as they are in the delicate assembly of impact fuses, Alon Peri's workers fall increasingly behind schedule. There is no way to lengthen the working day.

Peri brings the problem to Yigal, who brings it to his cabinet, which consults professors of engineering, efficiency experts, specialists in workflow. Their analysis is always the same: either find a way to light the factory so that Peri's experienced employees can work through the night, or bring in more of them.

Unfortunately, these would require weeks of training before turning them loose on technology that could easily blow up in their faces, to say nothing of destroying the entire factory floor. Without Peri's brass artillery-shell casings fitted with micro-fuses, fully assembled and in working order, the entirety of what is codenamed Operation Davidka will fail.

Named for the original Davidka—Little David—a crudely assembled mortar that became a key weapon in Israel's War of Independence, the technology is far from that of the homemade weapon of 1948. But the stakes are just as high, if not higher. At least 1200 functioning tubes are required. After three days of full-scale assembly, the total ready for deployment is ninety-seven. Somehow eleven hundred more must be manufactured in six days.

While Pinky's staff unsuccessfully struggles to devise a Plan B to provide the same results—the efficient transfer of 1200 Jordanian Challengers to Israel's armored corps, whole, undamaged, fully fueled, and ready to roll—Misha turns up at Peri Military Industries to ask a simple question.

"What exactly does it take to assemble these things?"

Peri had been going twenty hours a day, and now must answer stupid questions from a gangster. But because he was once strapped to a chair on the gangster's yacht, and certainly because Misha Shulman has proved himself as Minister of Police, he turns from the microscope he uses to examine each fuse before it is assembled in its brass tube, and answers the question with a minimum of visible impatience.

"Weeks of training," he says. "The assembler is not working with his eyes, because the parts are so tiny, but with his fingertips. He's like a surgeon doing microsurgery without the benefit of computerized tools and a monitor showing him what he is doing. The best assemblers are not intellectuals, because this is not a job for thinkers. You think about what you are doing, it's all over, because then you get totally confused. Once the sequence is learned, it's all in the fingertips."

"So it can done in the dark?"

"In theory. But most people are not comfortable working in the dark."

"Correct," Misha says. "Let me tell you something from my past. As you may know, yours truly spent some time on enforced vacation in several camps in Siberia. At one of them was a special facility for assembling fine electronics. Amazing, in the middle of Siberia. But it turns out my Soviet masters were not entirely stupid."

"Is this going somewhere?"

"Give me six hours and I'll have your assemblers."

"Very good," Peri says, turning back to his microscope. "I need three hundred of them, maybe four. Even so, it will be tight. And while you're at it, I'd like a steak sandwich and a draft beer. Goldstar if you can get it, very cold. And lights, and air conditioning. And if you can part the Red Sea, I'll have some of that."

Six hours later, Misha Shulman returns with four hundred and twenty-two men and women collected from every corner of Ghetto Tel Aviv, all willing, all sensitive in their fingertips.

"Blind," Misha tells Peri. "A whole camp in Siberia for political prisoners who were blind. Even then, it made me think: for every problem there is a solution."

Peri pulls his assemblers off their workbenches and turns them into instructors, each with ten students. "You know what Ben-Gurion said?"

"The airport?"

"The first prime minister of Israel, for which it was named."

"I knew he was something like that."

"In 1948, when the state was declared and eight Arab armies invaded, he said it. It's in every history book."

"Alon, please don't make me regret I didn't once upon a time break your legs."

"'The difficult we do immediately,' Peri quotes. "'The impossible takes longer.'"

99

An olive-green Cadillac bearing Egyptian military plates and flying a huge pair of white boxer shorts emblazoned with a schematic Israeli flag in red lipstick might have stopped traffic in Tel Aviv less than a month before, but in Ghetto Tel Aviv there is no traffic to stop. The city is eerily empty of cars and trucks, other than those still as roadside monuments for want of fuel.

Cobi drives westward into the northern suburbs, passing on his right the bombed-out clifftop headquarters of the Mossad and on his left the towers of Ramat Aviv, once among the city's most desirable neighborhoods. At the top of each high-rise the vegetation that adorned penthouse terraces is shriveled and brown, the streets below mostly deserted except for the ever-present tent camps shaded in the lee of buildings. It is already tortuously hot, the sun climbing up over the city like the angry muttering of a crazed neighbor, always there, always threatening.

"This is bad," Cobi says. He drives slowly, as though out of re-spect, the way people drive in a cemetery. Only weeks earlier, on this same road, he pushed his motorcycle, a present from his reluctant parents upon graduating high school, to ninety miles per hour, weav-ing through traffic with the casual athletic heedlessness of adolescent males everywhere. "So bad. I didn't know."

"I thought *I* did," Abed tells him. "There was talk. I thought, well, Tel Aviv. It's Tel Aviv. A metropolis, thriving, a beehive. Now..." Abruptly he changes his tone, but not his topic. "Your father is Yigal Lev?"

"How do you know?"

"Google."

"A truck, a television, *and* a computer?"

"Your condescension is underwhelming. Cobi, my wife has a blender. And a microwave. Also one of those devices that shoots water to clean between the teeth. At home there is no shortage of power."

"Not here."

"Cobi..."

"Look at that. People living in the street. Every street."

"Cobi, are there a lot of Yigal Levs?"

"It's not an uncommon name."

"That run a company called Isracorp."

"Only one."

"My young friend, what I am about to tell you may come as a shock."

"After seeing this, I'd be surprised."

"Your father is the prime minister."

Cobi takes his eyes off the road. It is not dangerous. The two have not come across a vehicle since dropping Alex off with the cap-tain and his squad, and that vehicle was some sort of bicycle rigged to pull a wagon. The wagon had a small plastic tank on it, like the water tanks over the outdoor sinks in temporary army encampments. "What do you mean, prime minister? Prime minister of what?"

"The State of Israel."

"The prime minister of Israel is Shula Amit."

"Killed." Abed considers. "Probably. Missing, anyway. They're all missing. The whole government."

"That's crazy. Who says so?"

"The soldiers who rode with us."

"You're saying my father is prime minister of the State of Israel?"

"That's what I'm told."

"Who elected him? He's not a politician. He's…"

They pull up before the villa in which Cobi lived all his life. Sandbags are piled three feet high all over his mother's flowerbeds. The lawn is gray. Military vehicles surround the house, and beyond these, on the beach, two Chariot tanks.

"Stay in the car," Abed says. "It may be that two Arabs approaching the prime minister's house in a car with Egyptian military plates and flying these stupid boxer shorts may spook someone. But if I have to sing *Jerusalem of Gold* again, I'll throw up. I don't even like Jerusalem." He pauses. "Too Jewish. But I used to love Tel Aviv."

Cobi stays. Abed has guided him safely this far. From the driver's seat, he watches the Bedouin walk with exaggerated calm slowly down the path, his hands in the air, in one of them his Israel Defense Forces ID. Immediately three soldiers are on him. He watches the Bedouin point to the car, then to the house. One soldier checks Abed's ID. The soldiers consult for a moment, then nod. There are smiles. One of the soldiers slaps Abed on the back. Even from where he sits, Cobi can see, or perhaps only imagine, a puff of dust rising from Abed's robes. They have been on the road for almost a week.

Accompanied by a major—paratroops, brown boots, red beret tucked in his left epaulet—Abed approaches the driver's side window. "We are cordially invited," Abed says.

The rest happens quickly.

Still in charge, Abed knocks at the door. There is a doorbell, but of course without electricity it is merely a button in the stucco wall. After a time a woman in a robe opens it, looks out at the two Bedouin, the one behind partly obscured by the first. Out of habit, Cobi's face is partially shrouded by the filthy keffiyah that hangs down around his face like curtains in a slum window. The woman is middle-aged, still attractive, but tired, as if she has not slept in a long time.

"Good morning, dear lady," Abed says. "Good news. I bring you a gift."

Judy looks past the two Arabs to the major, who hangs back, grinning. "I don't..."

"Despite my attire, I am Staff Sergeant Abed Abu-Kassem."

"Yes?"

"And this, I believe, belongs to you." With flair, as though revealing a work of art, he uncovers Cobi's face.

She falls upon her son, engulfing him, staring at his face and then holding him again as though he is a small child who has wandered off, wandered off and been found. Suddenly she turns into the house.

"Yigal, come down!" she shrieks "Yigal!"

100

PLANNING THE CONQUEST OF the State of Israel posed special problems for Iran's theologians. Not since 1453, when the Ottoman sultans took Constantinople and converted wholesale its mostly Christian population, has Islam been compelled to come to terms with implementing its very raison d'etre, the conversion of an entire population and their absorption into the Muslim polity. Certainly Islam is no stranger to the role of conquerer: Mohammed brought all of Arabia to Allah; his descendants carried Muslim civilization from North Africa through southern Europe to India and the Far East. But those converts were pagans, induced to accept Islam by the opportunity to participate fully in a new world order, with all the rights and privileges thereof.

Israel presents a different problem.

Like Christians, throughout history Jews were afforded special status as protected peoples or *dhimmi*. But leaving in place six million insincere converts to Islam would be demographically untenable and politically impossible. A few mullahs insisted the Jews be offered the chance to live as Muslims, but this solution would still leave such new Muslims a majority in the holy city of al Kuds, which the Jews call Jerusalem, and in Tel Aviv and Haifa and throughout the land. The conflict was in Shar'ia law itself: these Jews must be permitted to live, but by force of numbers would remain a threat. Left in place, the clever Jews would win again. Thus principle warred with pragmatism.

Pragmatism won.

Having spent over fifty years decrying the evil of these sons of dogs and monkeys, that the holy warriors of Islam should be defeated by trickery could not be permitted. Thus, after years of debate and research—the reconquest of the Holy Land was hardly spur of the moment—the mullahs concluded the evil the Jews had wrought could not simply be wiped away by conversion, which most likely would be as superficial as their conversion to Christianity in the Iberian Peninsula in the fifteenth century.

Let nature then take its course in Tel Aviv.

If Allah willed the Jews life then the One God would provide them manna, as He had the Jews in the desert upon their exodus from Egypt. If Allah wished them life then clean water would spring from the ground. If Allah wished them to survive then Allah would come to their aid.

In the absence of such divine intervention, it was only charitable to cut the Jews down so as to spare them suffering a slow death of thirst, starvation, and disease. In this, Islam would treat its enemies with humane generosity.

101

FRESHLY SHOWERED AND SHAVED and wearing white terry robes, Cobi and Abed sit at the kitchen table with Yigal. Ordinarily Judy would be hovering with food, as she always did when Cobi brought home friends from high school, or the occasional girl.

"Cobi likes cold chicken sandwiches, with too much mayonnaise," she says to Abed. "Or just hummus with olive oil floating over it and French bread to mop it up. MREs," she points, "don't make for much of a homecoming."

The two can barely take this seriously. They have been surviving on stale pita and dates, dates and stale pita, for the past five days. Once they descended from the highlands surrounding Jerusalem, there was orange and grapefruit, somewhat dry because there was no one to irrigate the plantations, but fruit nonetheless. Here and there was carob, also known as St. John's Bread, which hangs dry in trees growing wild by the roadside as they have for thousands of years, the long pods, tough and fibrous and tasting of molasses, that kept them chewing for hours.

So about the meal set before them they had no complaint.

"Meals ready to eat are a sin against nature," Judy says.

"And a very welcome one," Yigal counters. "Though if we don't get resupplied we're going to turn into cannibals ready to eat." The bounty of the aid flotilla is limited. In a day or two, it will be gone. But in the meantime, the population is merely half starved, which is an improvement on starved completely.

"It is very tasty, madam," Abed says, attempting to read the English on the package. "What is a veghi burjer in barbessue sauke?" He looks up. "Not pig?"

"Not pig," Yigal says. "You are an honored guest, staff sergeant. We take care of our guests, just as you do." He looks to his son, scrubbed clean, appearing to his father to be all of twelve years old. "Just as you did."

"It is my honor to be of service," Abed says, then puts down the plastic fork that comes with the MRE. He has already finished two helpings of "chocolate banana muffin top wheat snack bread" smeared with "seasoning blend cheese spread." He pauses. "Mr. Prime Minister, I am of the Ghawarna. Though a mere staff sergeant, I feel confident that I speak as well for the Abu-Idris and the Ibn-Harad. In the name of your servants, I ask a favor of the government."

Yigal is drinking tea. They have a lot of it. Judy liked to collect all kinds. Normally it just sat in the cupboard, exotic blends with catchy names that would be ignored once they were tried out. Now Judy and Yigal are going methodically through the stock. Yigal is drinking "Orange Pekoe Pick Me Up." No sugar. Each MRE comes with packets of sugar, but these are gone.

"Promotion?" Yigal says. "Reward? Name it, staff sergeant. When things improve, we'll dig you wells you can swim in."

"Only this, prime minister. That when the time comes for you to fuck the repulsive invaders from the front, that we Bedu of the Jordan Valley should have the honor to rise up and fuck them from the rear."

From far off, there is the sound of thunder. But there is no thunder in Israel during the summer, nor rain. The skies will not open up until late October, perhaps November, the downpour continuing sporadically through March. It is not thunder, but grows louder, closer, imminent.

As one they run out to the kitchen terrace, beyond which is an empty swimming pool.

Above them a vast flock of what at first seems to be migrating birds darkens the sky, which then abruptly explodes into something else: the heavens are filled with thousands of cargo parachutes dropped from hundreds of planes.

Over the next week, these aircraft, C130s mustered from US bases in Germany and England, Turkey, Greece, Italy, Djibouti and even indirectly—routed through Cyprus—from Saudi Arabia, will deliver more food, water, and medicine than during the entire Berlin airlift, two Asian tsunamis, and four Central American earthquakes. Also in the huge crates that come down like wholesale deliveries of manna are radio equipment and heavy-duty batteries.

From the ground, Yigal is not yet aware of all that is in the crates, but it is certainly one hell of a good sign one day before the counterattack is set to begin. Now he need not worry about starvation at home.

"Cobi, suit up," he says. "If things work out, very soon you'll be a tank commander again. And get our guest a clean uniform from my closet." He looks up again. "God bless America. Staff Sgt. Abed, our time has come."

102

OVER DECADES, THE INSTITUTION of the president's cabinet had come to reflect not only the size and complexity of the American government but its relation with the corporate world that is its principle stakeholder. Though more than 90% of United States tax revenues derives from individuals, corporations retain massive power and influence in Washington. Very few individual employees have the leverage to make the mind-boggling campaign donations of American corporations and their special interest groups. Thus the American paradox: individuals finance the vehicle of government, corporations drive it. So it is hardly a wonder that the White House has come to look like the corporate world. The president's cabinet, once a panel of advisors expected to contribute across a broad range of issues, is now made up of specialists, as in any large business: secretaries of the treasury who would not dare comment on national security, secretaries of defense with no interest in housing or health or education. Because of this, when the president makes decisions, he relies upon a close inner circle outside the cabinet, and in the end upon two individuals: Flo Spier, whose shrewd knowledge of the electorate got him to the White House, and Felix St. George, who never stumbled upon a world crisis that could not be ameliorated by the forceful application of cynicism. Thus every major decision in the White House comes down to delicately balancing the requirements of domestic politics with the demands of America's role in the greater world.

"So what you're saying, Felix, is that we know what the A-rabs are about to do, but we don't know how the Jews will counter?"

Like many presidents before him, the leader of the West instinctively and mistakenly includes Iran in the Arab world, just as Israel becomes "the Jews." In the Oval Office, no one bothers to correct him.

"We know the Arabs are gearing up," Felix St. George says. "They're calling it the Siege of Tel Aviv."

"And we know this how?"

"CIA, DIA, NSA—all in accord."

"But nothing from the Jews?"

"Nothing, Mr. President. The Israelis have gone low-tech on us. Or they just don't want to talk."

"Sigint?" The president loves to use the lingo.

"Signals intelligence works rather well when there are signals. As to humint, the damn CIA pulled its assets from Tel Aviv when the writing was on the wall. They claim their people in Jerusalem were picked up early in the war and never heard from again. Probably they're in Tehran. The agency preferred their people in Tel Aviv not suffer the same fate." St. George carefully adds a note of detachment. "That's what they say."

"Satellite?"

"DIA has nothing. Just pictures of a severely overcrowded city. Nothing moving. Like a still photograph."

"And the mysterious pink planes?"

"They are working on that, sir."

"And those missiles the Jews used to take down the Syrian whatchamacalls?"

"Sukhois, sir. It appears Israel may retain some missile capability. But Stingers don't work very well against tanks. In fact, they don't work at all. And tanks are what's going to roll into Tel Aviv."

"And the nukes?"

"Those don't work against tanks either. Even if Israel uses them, it won't save Tel Aviv. To hit Iran, they'd need long-range bombers. We know they have none."

"They have jets," the president says. "Three at least. They could—"

"Jets could conceivably deliver the weaponry, indeed." St. George makes sure he interrupts the president at every meeting, if only just once. He likes to keep the president in line. St. George is a baseball fan. His favorite pitchers always brush batters back. "We've seen evidence of only those three fighters, sir. Super Hornets. But if they're in Israel, our satellite cameras can't find them. It's not like they have any ground facilities left. There's a small field just outside of Tel Aviv, Sde Dov, but it doesn't have the runway length. Still a mystery, though there is speculation the pink paint may be anti-radar—we know the Israelis were working on this. Best guess: the three planes probably crashed in the sea for lack of fuel. A suicide mission. But it hardly matters. Pink or green or purple, the planes are gone." He fixes the president with his translucent gray eyes. "What is clear, so far as can be deduced, is that Israel, what's left of it, is backed into a corner. There's no way we can see they can use their nukes, other than in a giant suicide. No armor, no air force, no reserves of fuel or ammunition. Not much food or medicine either."

"Except for what we've just dumped on them."

"Mr. President, very few countries have gone to war armed only with MREs, antibiotics, and field radios."

"The radios were a nice touch," the president says. "I see your fine Hungarian hand in that."

St. George hates to be called Hungarian. Even "European" galls him. He has been an American citizen for over forty years. "The radios will enable Israel to surrender in an orderly fashion."

Flo Spier is not pleased. *Damn,* she thinks, *I light the fire, and now the pest from Budapest is frying his fish on it?* "Mr. President, my idea was we don't want to be caught with our electoral pants down. By sending aid, we look like we care—"

The president is offended. "We do care."

"Yes, sir, of course. But in terms of perception, it's important to leave a care trail. You will recall my mantra for success in November: Jewish money, Christian votes. What we've dumped on Tel Aviv makes a year's foreign aid look like Halloween candy. A very impressive attempt to intervene without endangering US forces. Plus, we have offered to take three million refugees."

"Which we may not actually have to take," the president says. "When do we announce it?"

Flo Spier has clearly taken back the reins. *Fuck you, Hungarian sleazebag, and fuck your realpolitik—when it comes to real politics, there's nothing like a woman.* "Mr. President," she says coolly. "We announce it when it's too late."

103

AT PRECISELY 3:49 AM, as soldiers of the Quartermaster's Corps paint the last of five blue-green Israeli Egged buses a dull khaki and others follow to stencil on Egyptian insignia, an IDF jeep leading two similarly disguised Humvees rolls through the gates of the bus cooperative's main installation on Begin Street. The chief of staff returns the sentries' salute, then dismounts to enter a makeshift meeting room that normally functions as Egged's repair center. Only a few buses are inside, the rest scattered around the city, out of gas, most functioning as broiling shelters for those refugees who cannot find better.

Two hundred IDF personnel, armed to the teeth, stand to attention, their folding chairs, arrayed in precise rows, shrieking on the concrete floor. Pinky shakes hands with the colonel at the front of the room. He is in his late thirties, a fireplug whose dark curls, cut close to his head, are shorter than those rising out of his shirt. His muscles strain the fabric of his uniform sleeves, which according to IDF regulation are carefully rolled to an inch over his elbows. When war broke out, the colonel headed up the chief of staff's commando unit. Half the personnel here are his, together with selected individuals from the navy's special operations group and a similar team from the air force. In better times, the chief of staff's commandos would be more than sufficient to the job, but most are gone, either prisoners of war or, as the military euphemism has it, missing.

"Be seated," Pinky says. "We'll make this quick. I'm informed by Col. Lior that you've been well briefed, both those of you in the insertion team and the pilots. If you have questions, ask now."

The uniformed men and a few women, among them Alex, are silent.

Pinky expects nothing less. "In one hour, the paint on the buses will be dry. Let's hope we can say the same for your pants."

He salutes, cutting short their laughter.

"Good luck, and safe home."

The assembled force rises as one to return the salute. The chief of staff leaves as abruptly as he entered.

Col. Lior takes over. For a man of his imposing physical presence—he began his military career as an instructor in *krav maga*, the IDF's contribution to hand-to-hand fighting—he speaks softly, the assembled soldiers leaning forward to pick up his words.

"It is precisely four hours. In thirty minutes, you will be appropriately suited up. From this point until the conclusion of stage one of Operation Davidka—the successful conclusion—the language of ops is Arabic. Those of you who speak no Arabic will be mute under any and all circumstances. I expect the Arabic speakers among us to think in Arabic, be anxious in Arabic, if necessary kill in Arabic. As has been pointed out, upon the success of this operation depends the entire future of the State of Israel. Now be good Arabs and get dressed for the party. Dismissed."

104

AT THEIR BASE JUST south of Jerusalem, 1194 tanks of the Royal Jordanian Armored Corps are lined up like a child's toy army, but one with the greatest destructive potential of any armored force in the Middle East: 400 upgraded British Challenger I tanks, 250 updated British Chieftains, the remainder modernized US M60s. As their commander's olive-green Rolls Royce Silver Shadow Landaulette begins slowly to roll past, each tank commander starts his engine, so that what begins as a single roar gathers cumulative force until the noise is so great it is as if the roar of engines is all, the massive 1500 and 1200 cc motors creating their own universe of percussive sound. But as the command vehicle rolls by to take the salute of the tank crews arrayed precisely in V formation in front of their tanks, not one tankist is ignorant of the fact that it is not Ticky Pasha standing in the open back of the Rolls but his second in command. The superstitious Bedouin tank crews know that Ticky Pasha has never not been there to take their salute before an attack. In the dark cloud rising from the smoke of burning diesel, many wonder what this portends.

105

FROM THE TERRACE OF a second-floor apartment, Cobi peers up and down Ibn-Gvirol Street, the would-be Park Avenue of Tel Aviv were it not for the design of the apartment houses that line its six lanes. As in the Italian city of Bologna, its apartments are cantilevered over the sidewalk, so that pedestrians shopping at street level or

drinking espresso outside the cafés are shaded from the Middle Eastern sun and protected from the long winter days of rain. Now there
is neither shopping nor coffee drinking, but there is shade, beneath
which tens of thousands of Jews sit on the cracked pavement and do
what refugees do. Nothing.

Apart from the pistol strapped to his waist, Cobi is armed only
with a foot-long brass pipe, once a spent artillery shell, sealed at both
ends. A ball-peen hammer is tucked into his military web-belt.

As expected, the first of a long line of Royal Jordanian tanks
appears from the south, making its way slowly down the divided
boulevard. Not one shot is fired from their cannons. Apparently their
intent is to take up positions along its entire length so as to seal the
long roadway from end to end.

Cobi tests the cable strung tight across the boulevard.

Like the other cables, it is taut as the string of a violin, the white
sheet pinned to it announcing surrender—a surrender that everyone
in the city understands will not be honored by the victors. Their
tanks are not here in some imperial gesture or show of strength. They
are not here to proclaim victory, but to execute it. Tel Aviv is about
to be blasted to bits.

As the endless column moves down the boulevard—named for
the medieval Spanish poet who wrote in both Arabic and Hebrew, a
detail which could not possibly interest the invading force—the lead
tank's commander scans the street through binoculars. Sure of the
city's surrender, he stands in his turret. He sees nothing but white
sheets. Satisfied, he re-enters his Challenger, seals the hatch, and orders his driver to continue until the very end of the street, which his
digital map shows terminating at a rather flimsy bridge over the Yarkon River. After the buildings on either side are destroyed and their
inhabitants annihilated like cockroaches, he will order his brigade to
bypass the flimsy bridge, cross the river, little more than a wet ditch at
this time of year, and then attack the northern suburbs, whose high-
rise apartment buildings can be expected to collapse. After that, they

must only wait for Egyptian infantry to pour into the open wound that was Israel's first city and mop up the surviving population.

106

As the sun rises over Highway 2, which links Tel Aviv to the international airport and then continues east to Jerusalem, the commander of a division of Egyptian mechanized infantry, some ten thousand men in two hundred vehicles, spots an Egyptian Humvee and several truckloads of personnel coming straight at him.

The commander opens communication. "Eastbound force, identify. This is Eagle Green. Identify."

"Eagle Green, Eagle Green, this is Reconnaissance Group Gamal, this is Reconnaissance Group Gamal."

"Gamal, I know no such formation. Over."

Laughter erupts from his headset. "Nor were you to know. Eagle Green, we are an independent unit, very hush-hush, attached to Field Intelligence HQ. We expected to be out of your line of fire an hour ago, but ran into small Jewish resistance. Over."

"Gamal, Jewish resistance? I am informed the entire city has surrendered. Please amplify, over."

"Eagle Green, this appears to have been a dissident group. You know our cousins: two Jews, three opinions. Small arms. Nineteen men. I personally counted the bodies. Neutralized. Repeat, neutralized. Over."

"The city is wide open, then? Over."

"Like a beautiful woman on the cold steel table of a gynecologist," the voice on the phone comes back. "We are returning now to Field Intel HQ, adjacent Arafat International Airport. Please stand by for signal to proceed west. Over."

"Copy that, Gamal. Over."

"Eagle Green, Force Gamal now moving out of your trajectory. Happy hunting! Over."

The Egyptian commander watches through his binoculars as the reconnaissance unit pulls onto an exit ramp marked with the sign of an airplane. The Hebrew and English for *Ben Gurion International Airport* have been painted over, but no one has re-lettered *Yasser Arafat* over it in Arabic and English. "Allah willing, Gamal. See you in former Tel Aviv. Over."

The reconnaissance unit has moved beneath the road to an underpass and is temporarily out of sight.

"Eagle Green, Eagle Green. Don't kill all the Jews, my brother. Leave some for us. Over."

"Not to worry, Gamal. We have before us many days of hard work. Your assistance will be welcomed. Thousands of blond Jewesses await. Over and out."

107

LIKE ALL THE MAJOR roads in conquered Israel, Highway 2 is controlled and administered by Iran. This came about because it was quickly seen that only an outside authority could be trusted to maintain the roadways snaking in and out of territories administered by four other nations. But Iran has little interest in maintaining the highways of a country split into four sectors, none of which is Iranian. This is why the highway sign leading to Yasser Arafat International Airport is blank.

By contrast, the sign over the security checkpoint leading into the airport itself is a freshly painted red and black over a dazzling white, the color of the Egyptian flags that line the long drive to the terminal buildings. These flags caused yet another dispute among the nations: should not all the victors' flags be flown here, at the gateway to the holy land? But the Egyptians are adamant that the airport is as much part of Egypt as Alexandria or Aswan. Did not the Egyptians demand their national banners be flown beside the Jordanian flags over Jerusalem? And what was the answer of the Jordanians under whose aegis it has fallen?

Though united in religion—except for the Sunni-Shia rift, which remains persistently in the background—the administrators of the former State of Israel are hardly of one mind on how it is to be governed. In the north, the Syrians and Iraqis continue stealing everything not bolted down; in the east, Jordan concentrates on renaming in Arabic all of Jerusalem's streets; to the south, Egypt, seeing itself as the legitimate heir of the ancient land from which its Hebrew slaves escaped, are determined to make the farmland of former Israel an Egyptian garden, irrigated by Israel's National Water Carrier originating in the Galilee—but in the north, Syria and Iraq immediately redirected the water to their own countries. In retaliation, Egypt closed to those countries the port of Ashdod, and refused to use its Mediterranean fleet to help clear the wreckage of scuttled Israeli vessels from the Syrian-controlled port of Haifa.

If defeat is an orphan, the many fathers of the victory over Israel have settled in for the same sort of dyspeptic discord that marked the neighborhood for centuries as stubbornly unstable, virulently fanatic and rabidly chaotic.

In keeping with its sense of pride in controlling the aerial gateway to former Israel, Egypt makes it a point of honor that Yasser Arafat International Airport be as presentable as it was under the Jews. The entryway is repainted daily, as are the red and white markings on the black asphalt leading to the checkpoint, whose military personnel are as polished and pressed as the Egyptian president's own palace guard. However, these soldiers have little to do other than look spectacularly turned out. Under the Israelis, the checkpoint was manned by Border Police, a no-nonsense entity whose soldiers thought nothing of searching a suspect vehicle for an hour before admitting it to the airport proper. But now there is no threat of terrorism.

As a result, the Humvee-flanked convey of buses carrying Reconnaissance Group Gamal is waved through without so much as a pause for rudimentary questioning. The soldiers at the checkpoint might just as well be the Queen's Guard that pretends, for tourism's sake, to protect Buckingham Palace, unmoving, unswerving, unnecessary for anything other than showing up.

The convoy proceeds slowly down the mile-long approach road until a point where the road bends around to the left. The convoy does not bend around to the left. It continues straight on, tearing through the chain-link fence that cordons off the runway, where a Kuwait Airways 717 warms up for takeoff.

In a matter of seconds, the soldiers of Reconnaissance Group Gamal are out of their buses and surrounding the plane. Using a nautical loud-hailer, their commander barks an order in Arabic-accented English to the curious captain peering out through his port window.

"Kuwait Airways captain, you are commanded to lower stairs for security inspection."

The captain slides open the window, managing to get most of his head out. He has red hair and a pug nose, so that when he twists through the opening his aviator glasses slip down and he has to force his arm through the open window to adjust them. "Only three passengers aboard, colonel," he shouts. He is clearly an American from the deep South. "They've cleared security."

"Kuwait captain, lower stairs!"

The captain has been through this before. He has been flying in the Arab world for twenty years. It is always something. In a minute, the oval door of the 717 opens. The Kuwait Air captain has a schedule to keep.

In a flash, half the Egyptian force has scrambled up the aluminum stairs and are moving from the first-class cabin straight through to the rear. There is no one in the rear. In first class, the commandos secure the crew and the plane's only passengers, a blond woman and two men.

"What the hell's going on?" Connie Blunt wants to know.

The Egyptian commander does not even hear her. "Passports, please," he says in Arabic.

Connie just looks at him.

The Egyptian commander tries English. "Passports, please. This is a security check."

"Aw, fuck. Your people have inspected us three times."

Connie's producer is not happy. For fear of terrorism leaking from the Middle East, only Muslim countries and Russia and China are accepting flights from Yasser Arafat International. There are no direct flights to the US. "Look, we've a real tight window in Kuwait for our flight to Atlanta."

The Egyptian commander can barely restrain a smile as he returns the passports. He then removes his Egyptian uniform shirt, under which is an IDF shirt rolled up tightly over his biceps.

"Atlanta?" Col. Lior says. "I am afraid you may miss that connection."

The second half of the crew in the buses now clambers aboard, removing their uniforms to reveal Israel Air Force flight suits. They pile their Egyptian uniforms into a rear toilet.

Col. Lior moves forward with two of the IAF officers.

"Captain, I have the pleasure of introducing you to your new first officer, Major Halevy, and navigator, Lieutenant Marks. Your crew will fly this flight as passengers. This ship has been commandeered by the Israel Defense Force, which expects you to cooperate in every way on your regularly scheduled flight."

"You are fucking kidding me."

Lior unholsters his pistol and puts it directly to the head of the Kuwait Air copilot. "Anything other than full cooperation will result in summary execution of your aircrew, beginning with senior personnel and proceeding down the line. In case you believe yourself to be safe, please be aware that three of my men are reserve Israel Air Force officers who regularly fly 717s as commercial pilots. Yes or no, do I have your cooperation?"

"What d'ya say your name was?" the captain asks, so quietly it comes out a hoarse whisper.

"Col. Lior."

"Well, colonel. Just so's y'all keep from killin' my people, you got my word I'll fly this crate to hell and back."

Col. Lior nods. "That, captain," he says, "is precisely our flight plan."

"Roger that, colonel." He switches on the cabin loudspeakers. "Good morning, folks, this is your captain speaking. We're cleared for takeoff here at Yasser Arafat International and after some delay, which you may have noticed, or caused, we're now taxiing for take-off. Weather is clear all the way through to Kuwait City, cloud cover high and light. So far as we can see, we've got great flying weather ahead, so settle back in your seats, pay attention to the instructions of our chief steward, Ms. Peggy Springfield, and her wonderful cab-in crew, and have yourselves a great flight this morning on Kuwait Air 201. Our estimated time of arrival is 10:23 AM Kuwait time, God willing. Now y'all relax and have yourselves a real nice flight."

108

BECAUSE THE PRESIDENT IS a country boy at heart, or sincerely believes he is, he likes to get out of the District of Columbia as often as possible, especially in summer. The presidential retreat at Camp David, Maryland, is an hour's drive from the White House, but only ten minutes by helicopter. The president's schedule over this week-end, as printed by his private secretary, is as follows:

8 AM: Breakfast, overnight briefing
9 AM: Skeet shooting
11 AM: Lake swim
1 PM: Working lunch [w/ F Spier, Congressional Leaders per appendix]

3 PM: Nap
5 PM: Trail riding
7 PM: Security update [F St. George, Joint Chiefs]
8 PM: Continuing through dinner
10 PM: Movie: Dead Sure [Leonardo di Caprio, Holly Mawn]
Midnight: TV news highlights, tomorrow's daily papers

The president is especially interested in tonight's film, a version normally shown only to movie industry insiders, in which the fellatio scene is unedited, uncut, and—according to the president's Hollywood liaison—fucking unbelievable.

109

As COL. LIOR AND his staff go over diagrams of the target site, Connie Blunt and her producer step into first class.

"Hate to be a party pooper, colonel," she says. "But it happens CNN bought us three seats in this section. You and your men are in them."

Col. Lior is amused. "And?"

"We've been deposited in business."

"I'll see you get a refund. Please return to your seats."

"Come on now, colonel."

"Or we could lock you in a toilet."

Like Blunt, her producer did not get where he is because he is easily contained. "It's just the three of us," Terry says. "For cryin' out loud, we're press. Unarmed." He smiles. "Except for cameras."

"You know what it means, *chutzpa*?" Col. Lior asks.

"Audacity," Terry says. A Puerto Rican, he grew up with Jews in New York. "Impudence, outrageous nerve. We have a proposition."

"*You* have a proposition?"

So it is that a visual record of Operation Baby Candy—as in the taking of the latter from the former—will come to exist, a collection of digital B-roll whose fate at the moment is as uncertain as the out-come of the mission itself.

"This is Connie Blunt aboard Kuwait Air flight 201 en route, we have been told, to Kuwait. Myself and my CNN crew were awaiting takeoff from Yasser Arafat Airport in former Israel when the plane was stormed by Egyptian commandos."

Buddy Walsh, Blunt's cameraman, pans business and coach—by agreement, first class is out of bounds—picking up soldiers and pilots napping, playing cards, cleaning weapons, before returning to Blunt.

"The commandos were not Egyptians. They are in fact Israelis."

Buddy picks up an IAF pilot zipping his pants as he leaves a toilet.

"So far I have not been permitted to interview anyone aboard, including the flight crew. You should also know that as a condition of being able to shoot aboard this aircraft, our footage is to be handed over to Israeli military censors in Tel Aviv. This suggests that our plane will be returning to Tel Aviv. Such a situation is simply impos-sible to imagine. As is widely known, Israel's former first city, its New York as it were, is now its only city. Surrounded, short of food and—it is widely believed—with no viable military capability—"

Blunt's assessment is interrupted by three electronic chimes.

"Ladies and gentlemen, this is your captain speaking. We are preparing for our scheduled landing at Kuwait International Airport. It is imperative that passengers cease moving about the cabin, return your seatbacks and tray tables to their upright position, and pray to God Almighty that someone here knows what is going on, because I surely do not. We are on schedule and cleared for landing. Air crew: emergency procedures are now in place. I am advised that fore and aft hatches may be opened before the aircraft comes to a full stop, along with emergency exits port and starboard. God save us all."

Seeing that the commandos and air force personnel are strapping themselves in, Blunt and her cameraman and producer scramble for their seats. She attempts to make sense of the landscape through the window but the airport shows nothing unusual as the plane extends its flaps and prepares to land.

If Blunt could see what the captain sees as he makes his approach, it would be this: the standard airport runway, with jetliners and cargo carriers lined up to the right, and ahead of the plane and a bit to the left, a military airport. This is Al-Mubarak Air Base, home to the pride of the Kuwaiti Air Force, sixty F/A-18s in ready formation beyond a chain-link fence topped with barbed wire.

On instruction from Col. Lior, the 717 captain has kept the circuit to the cabin open, so that everyone in the rear of the plane can follow events as they happen. Col. Lior prefers to keep his people apprised. Should there be a problem, he does not want to have to waste even seconds with an announcement.

The 717 captain's voice comes on. "Kuwait Air 201 to Tower, we're at 1500 feet beginning approach Runway Two. Request final clearance. Over."

The tower officer has an English accent, not unusual in Arab aviation, where experienced expat personnel are normally responsible for airport operations from tower to maintenance. "Tower to Kuwait 201. You are cleared for Runway One, repeat Runway One. Pull up and come around. Over."

"Kuwait 201 to Tower. Negatory on that. Landing gear is descended and seems to be locked. Permission for Runway Two. Over."

"Tower here. Roger that. Kuwait 201, you are cleared for Runway Two. Repeat, now cleared for Two. Good luck. Over."

"Roger that, Tower. Looking good at 700 feet and descending. Over."

"Looking good, 201. Over."

In the cockpit, the 717 captain switches off his radio. "Colonel, you get us out of here in one piece and I'm going to buy you a really nice bottle of wine."

Col. Lior braces against the doorway. "You know what you have to do, captain. Just do it. Or none of us will ever drink wine again."

The aircraft touches down smoothly, the kind of landing that normally would bring a scattering of applause from passengers.

Col. Lior picks up a mic and turns back into the first-class cabin. "Boys," he says quietly, his voice reverberating through the plane, "this aircraft is stuffy. Ventilate it!"

The commandos are already on their feet, the pilots among them remaining strapped in. As the 717 rolls down the tarmac, they fling open all its doors and emergency exits. The plane continues to slow—and then abruptly speeds up, the aircraft shuddering momentarily as it breaches the fence between the civilian and military airfields, and slows again, its powerful brakes whining. On either side are the parked F/A-18s.

The 717 is still rolling when its emergency slides descend and inflate, the commandos gliding down the soft plastic like manic children in a swiftly moving playground, some setting up machine guns in static defensive position while others aim their guns at the barracks and admin buildings to the right. From these buildings there is no reaction. Either they are empty or the base personnel are still asleep.

In her seat, Blunt now hears the tower officer's voice relayed through the plane's loudspeakers. "Tower to Kuwait Air 201. Have you gentlemen been drinking? You've overshot into military area. Taxi back. Over."

"Kuwait 201 to Tower. My bad, y'all. Sun in eyes. Rolling back. Over."

But Kuwait Air 201 is not moving. Instead Blunt watches in fascination as the aircraft empties, the pilots now sliding to the ground and, under cover of the commandos on the tarmac, sprinting for the parked F/A-18s. She is glued to the window, not unaware that doing anything else is likely to get her killed. She must be scared, she knows, because she is hallucinating: one of the pilots sliding right under her window appears to be wearing bright red lipstick.

Alex would have preferred heels as well—nothing slutty, just three inches or so—but then she would not be able to sprint to the third F/A-18 on the right. Unlike most of the other pilots, whose only experience with that aircraft is from intense instruction in Tel Aviv's central bus garage, Alex is familiar with the plane, having evaluated it at its production facility in Fort Worth. He was one of the instructors in a two-day ground school as the pilots worked simulated dashboards made of cardboard and bits of plastic.

Kicking aside the chocks, Alex clambers onto the wing, enters the cockpit, surveys the instrument panel, and begins flipping switches. Ordinarily, no IAF pilot would take up a plane without running through a checklist, but there is nothing ordinary about these circumstances. As if to underscore this, a siren sounds, and then gunfire. Alex fires up the twin GE turbo-fan engines.

They roar to life. The plane moves forward.

"Such a relief," Alex sighs to no one as she locks the canopy. "Just like getting my period."

Now the gunfire is one blanket of explosive noise.

In the 717, cameraman Buddy Walsh kneeling beside her, Connie Blunt leans out of an emergency exit, describing into a hand mic the scene before her as it transpires.

About twenty Kuwaiti airmen, most still in their underwear, are on the ground, returning fire, with more gunfire pouring forth from the barracks' second-floor windows. This is answered by blanketing 50 cal. machine-gun fire from the commandos.

From the other side of the runway, a lone marksman at the base of a Kuwaiti Air Force service shed fires freely until he is silenced by an RPG.

The shed shudders, then collapses as the last group of F/A-18s takes off.

The 717 captain has his head out the window. "Colonel!" he shouts. "For Chrissake, Boeing didn't make this aircraft to fly with holes. Swiss cheese don't fly!"

A bullet whizzes by his ear. He ducks back in.

Col. Lior enters the cabin. "Two minutes to takeoff, captain."

"Aye-aye, sir!" He tosses off an easy salute.

Col. Lior looks at the man. He could be sixty-five, maybe older, too old to fly an American flag aircraft, his red hair faded to white at the temples and thinning on top. "US Navy?"

"Three tours Vietnam. But I ain't never seen nothing like this!"

Col. Lior returns the salute, crisply.

Under cover of machine gunners already aboard, the remaining commandos scramble up rope ladders. As the 717 begins to taxi, the slides hanging from the aircraft are slashed off.

"Neither have I. Captain, you are cleared for takeoff."

"Not exactly," the captain says quietly.

Through the windshield, he has seen them coming as the 717 gathers speed: two Kuwaiti Air Force Apache Longbow helicopters rising directly ahead.

Immediately Col. Lior slides open the side window, pushing the captain against his instrument panel as he leans out, firing his Tavor rifle in studied desperation.

In the first Apache, its pilot has just enough time to tell his wingman, "Mohammed, on my signal" before the helicopter explodes, debris flying over the field like so much metallic trash, its forty-eight-foot main rotor spinning off of its own momentum as in an instant the second Apache disintegrates in the air.

Through the flying debris and smoke, a lone F/A-18 seems to be headed directly for the 717 when it zooms up and over it, avoiding a collision by little more than inches.

No one on board can see it, but the pilot of the F/A-18 rising over the airliner at what seems to be an impossibly steep angle of ascent is at the same time reaching into his external vest pocket. In lipstick, he draws two bright red X's on his windshield.

Kuwait Air 201 has just begun to level off when it is joined by first one and then a second F/A-18 riding shotgun on either wing.

Its radio comes alive. "Tower to Kuwait 201. Tower to Kuwait 201. What the hell is going on out there? All I can see is a lot of smoke. Kuwait 201, you are not cleared for takeoff. You are on a military runway. Turn your aircraft around and return to Kuwait International. You are cleared for Runway Two. Kuwait 201, do you read me? Over."

"Tower, I read you loud and clear." The captain looks over to his Israeli co-pilot and navigator. "Regret Kuwait 201 is no longer operational. Over."

"Tower to Kuwait 201. Bullshit. I have you on radar. Hell, I have you visual. Turn your aircraft around. Over."

The ex-Navy pilot is enjoying this more than any flight he has commanded since Vietnam. Flying a commercial airliner is no different than driving a bus. This is different: it brings back memories. Pressing a button, he suppresses voice on the radio. "Where the hell we going, colonel?"

"Ben Gurion International Airport. You know it?"

"I know it's been Yasser Arafat Airport for a month. We get close, them Gyppos'll shoot us down."

"Captain," Col. Lior says quietly in the brusque whisper that is his trademark, "as you call it, negatory on that."

The 717 captain shrugs, then flips on his mic. "Tower, this is former Kuwait Air 201. Over."

"This is Tower. What the fuck do you mean, *former*? Over."

A flight attendant squeezes into the cockpit. "Captain…"

He raises a forefinger. "Tower, I am pleased to report this aircraft is now designated El Al 201. Over and out." He turns to the flight attendant. "Peggy?"

"Captain, they won't return to their seats. And they're smoking."

He chortles. "They sure are, baby." He hits the announcement switch. "Attention passengers. This is your captain speaking."

He turns to look back into the cabin through the open door. The commandos are carousing, spritzing beer and chasing each other around first and business as the cabin crew tries to settle them down.

"It appears you people are out of control back there. Such behavior is contrary to regulations of the International Air Transport Association. But since none of us gives a shit, let me further announce that this is a smoking flight, and that if you'll give the cabin crew half a chance, they'll rustle up some breakfast. One more thing. The bar is open and drinks are on the house. Cabin crew, y'all take good care of our passengers. We're bringin' em home."

110

THROUGH THE DUST OF his office window, Yigal sees the first wave of F/A-18s flash across the morning sky over Tel Aviv, then head out to sea before turning back to cross the city once more. There are fifty-eight. In twenty-five minutes, two more will appear, escorting what is now El Al 201. For the less well-informed citizens of Tel Aviv, who are aware that an attack on the city is inevitable, the planes spark resigned panic, very similar to the reaction of Londoners during the Blitz, who moved quickly to the shelter of Underground stations in determined desperation.

But there is no subway in Tel Aviv, and though by law each apartment house must contain a below-ground shelter, in total these are designed to protect the population of the city, not the entire country. Still, chaos does not ensue: like the residents of wartime London, the people of Ghetto Tel Aviv hurry, for the most part stoically, to previously chosen locations as though they are simply late for a date: the lee of abandoned buses and trucks; the underground shelters of public parks and office buildings; beneath the city's trademark white apartment buildings, which are built on pillars so as to provide parking spaces; within cafés and shops whose doors were forced by the endless flood of refugees seeking shelter and anything they might barter for food.

By the time the waves of Kuwaiti aircraft double back over the city, there is no one on the streets but Misha's police force, together with medical teams already well distributed in first aid stations across the city. There is no other way to deal effectively with the huge numbers of expected wounded; no vehicles are available to bring the victims to the city's hospitals. In groups of three, doctors and nurses are stationed where the wounded are expected to be.

There are no wounded.

One by one, the city's residents poke their heads out from their hiding places as the F/A-18s return east.

"Phase one, check," Yigal says to no one, though Misha and Alon Peri are with him. He turns to Peri. "This is really going to work?"

"Absolutely," Peri says. Then: "All things being equal."

"I never know what that means," Yigal says. "What if their tin cans take other routes?"

"On the narrower streets, their turrets can't turn," Misha says. "All they can shoot is the tank ahead. Unless they're totally incompetent, they'll stick to the boulevards."

"And the...devices?"

Peri beams with confidence. "Couldn't be lower tech. They'll be fine."

"If not, this guy's dead," Misha says.

Yigal turns back to the window as the last of the F/A-18s flashes by. "If not," he says, "we're all dead."

111

THE PRESIDENT IS AT the lake, popping open a bottle of Peroni Nastro Azzurro. He prefers this Italian brand, but can never drink it anywhere but Camp David. Where there are photographers, which to the president's great annoyance is everywhere else, he makes a point of drinking Bud, Lone Star, Sam Adams. Election day is right around the corner.

With him are the members of an ad hoc war room, none of them in bathing attire.

"The Arabs are ready to roll," Admiral Staley says. "No doubt about that."

"Big?" the president asks. He dips a toe in the water. It is not quite as warm as he would like, but he still intends to swim out to the platform a half mile out. Two Boston Whalers—engines idling, each holding four Secret Service agents, one of them equipped with oxygen—stand by to accompany him.

"We invaded Iraq with less," Staley says. "Over a thousand tanks, Jordanian, backed up by mechanized infantry, Egyptian those. Strung out all along the western border, there's enough Syrian and Iraqi ground forces to surround Washington D.C."

Shielding his eyes from the sun with both hands, Felix St. George peers out onto the lake—this is as artificial as his gesture, which is meant suggest he can be depended on for the long view. "Mr. President, if Israel has the capacity, this is the time they'll effectuate."

"You're talking what, Felix—Armageddon?"

"Mr. President," the security advisor says. "Do you recall the story of Samson?"

"Delilah gave him a haircut, that one?"

"That one, Mr. President. Sir, he pulled down everything around him."

No slouch at gestures himself, the president hands Flo Spier his watch. "Flo?"

"Sir, if this goes nuclear, a radioactive cloud will cover the globe. Mr. President, I hate to sound cynical..."

"No, you don't. Because you're so good at it." Now both the president's feet are in the water. "Go ahead."

"Mr. President, those Jordanian tanks better take out Tel Aviv before Tel Aviv takes out the world."

The president stretches his arms over his head, then straight out, then stretches again. "Admiral?"

"Mr. President?"

"What are the odds? Am I going to get to see that blowjob movie tonight?"

"Mr. President, aside from the nuclear option, which doesn't seem like they've got any way to deliver, Israel's down to a few tanks, and they're strung out in an easily punctured line. Sir, by the time you finish that film this evening, the State of Israel, such as it is, will no longer exist."

The president chugs the last of his Peroni and, in a final gesture, hands the empty to Admiral Staley. "Well, I always said they should have put it on a travel poster," the president says, turning to the lake. "Israel—see it while it exists."

The president dives in, his smooth, even stroke barely disturbing the surface of the water as the two purring Boston Whalers full of Secret Service personnel follow at a discreet distance. Aside from the two small boats, the president has the entire lake to himself.

112

WITH NO HELICOPTERS OR observation planes, no drones and no access to Israel's five orbiting satellites, Pinky and his senior staff have little choice but to climb as high as practical in one of Israel's modest skyscrapers to view what is officially known as Phase II but which everyone involved in its planning thinks of as the Battle of Tel Aviv.

The building rises forty-five stories above the Diamond Exchange on the border that defines Tel Aviv proper from the municipality of Ramat Gan. Once separate geographical entities, the two have agglutinated, as Tel Aviv has with its other suburbs. From their observation post on the tenth floor—going any higher would isolate the IDF leadership should they need to descend quickly—Pinky and his officers have a 360-degree view of the city and its environs, including the Ayalon Highway which slices south to north. From here, they see the first of hundreds of Challenger tanks moving by fours on both sides of the divided highway, some branching off onto the broader streets leading west to the sea. As predicted, the tanks stick to the wider thoroughfares.

Pinky eases down his high-powered binoculars and turns to the others. "Those who are religious, you know what to do," he says. "In fact, all of you. It's an order. Pray."

113

As four Royal Jordanian Apache helicopters hover at two thousand feet, seemingly endless columns of Jordanian armor push through the flimsy barriers of bed frames, derelict refrigerators, and abandoned cars surrounding Ghetto Tel Aviv and enter the city. From the point of view of the tank commanders, who toggle between front, rear, left, and right views on their screens, Tel Aviv is a ghost town, its boulevards empty, nothing in motion. Thirty feet above them, at regular intervals, white bed sheets serving as flags of surrender hang from taut cables. Indeed, the only movement is the sheets themselves as they stir in a light breeze coming off the Mediterranean.

Enclosed in their tanks, the officers and men of the Royal Jordanian Armored Corps are at once gratified and puzzled. There is nothing alive, not so much as a stray dog or cat. There wouldn't be: all but the quickest have been eaten. The sheets give the city a strangely festive look as the tanks move into position.

114

From his perch on the terrace of the second-floor apartment overlooking Ibn-Gvirol Street, his harness clipped to the cable, Cobi tightens his gas mask and launches down until he reaches the moving

Challenger below, slips the clip from the cable, and drops to the roof of the slow-moving tank. Were he less focused on what he was trained over and over to do, he would see copies of himself alighting on every tank on the boulevard; were he in one of the Jordanian Apaches soaring over the city, he would see hundreds more. He clambers to the tank's ventilator in the turret, pulls the foot-long brass tube from his belt, and smashes it down into the ventilator with his hammer.

By this time, the tank crew may be aware something untoward is happening, but like most main battle tanks, Challengers have 360-degree viewing capacity on the horizontal plane but are blind to anything happening immediately above or below. What is happening above is an example of the primitive overcoming the sophisticated. The ABC (Atomic, Biological, Chemical) filter on the intake vent of the Challenger is a soft multi-tissue membrane—it must be in order for clean outside air to enter the otherwise sealed tank cabin. Once that membrane is pierced, such as by a brass tube struck by a ball-peen hammer with sufficient force, the cabin is no longer secure.

The IDF planning group responsible for this breakthrough—and it is a breakthrough in more than figurative terms—first examined the feasibility of inserting a grenade into the cabin and thus neutralizing its crew of four on the spot, but since the objective is to utilize the enemy armor immediately, it was decided to use CS, commonly known as tear gas. The problem then was how to pierce the filtration membrane and fill the cabin with CS at once. Alon Peri provided the answer: a simple tube that, when hit in its center, engages a firing pin, while at the same time tearing through the filtration mesh.

From his office overlooking Ibn-Gvirol and—though he is not at the moment aware of it—his own son's part in the operation, Yigal watches with Alon Peri as the choreography unfolds: IDF personnel sliding down the taut cables between the buildings, dropping to the tank roofs, inserting the brass tubes, striking them with hammers.

"How long will it take?" Yigal asks.

"Three," Peri says, watching with him.

"Three what, minutes? That's too—"

"Two," Peri says. "One. Blastoff."

In an operation that seems to have been designed by Busby Berkeley for a military training film—though minus the music—from one Jordanian tank to the next the same scene repeats: hatches fly open as the coughing, choking tank crews climb out, a good many falling off their tanks in a blind attempt to find clean air. Immediately, from storefronts and apartment house entryways, IDF soldiers sprint out to throw the retching tank crewmen to the ground and cuff their hands behind them with plastic ties. It is not so much a battle as a harvest.

While this is happening, IDF tank crews in gas masks enter the Challengers. These will be hot zones for at least an hour. Hatches open to air them out, the tanks move forward immediately, their new commanders riding above, for the moment able to remove their masks. What they see at street level is what the four Jordanian Apache pilots see from two thousand feet.

The empty boulevards swarm with people, a whole city come alive as the shelters empty. From the apartment house terraces, the white sheets are pulled down—one enthusiastic civilian even sets one alight, the flaming fabric falling to the street and nearly setting an IDF tank commander on fire. On every street, spontaneous dancing breaks out. Someone plays an accordion on his balcony. Here and there, as on the Jewish New Year, a ram's horn sounds, a kind of tenor bellow, its pizzicato notes celebrating the joy of deliverance.

Then the Apaches drop down.

As one the celebrants look up, their happiness evaporating into fear as they stampede for cover. For dozens of civilians, it is too late—the Apaches' twin 30mm machine guns plow through the crowd, spewing death in long lines like sewn seams as the helicopters swoop down the boulevards, aiming their Hellfire missiles at the tanks still bear the flying pennants of the Royal Jordanian Armored Corps. Two tanks are taken out immediately, their armor exploding in a wide radius, killing the tank crews and causing further civilian casualties.

But the attack does not last long.

From apartment house roofs, IDF infantry, among them a nineteen-year-old red-haired girl sergeant who last used a Stinger missile a week earlier on the Tel Aviv beachfront, take them down with an efficient dispatch that is at once angry and professional.

Little is left of the Apaches other than their forty-eight-foot rotors, which spin off over the city until they crash into the tops of buildings and, in one case, fly through the windows of an office tower, some twenty feet of rotor blade sticking out into the still air like a flagpole. Later that day, an enterprising teenager will crawl out and attach to it the blue and white flag of Israel.

115

WHILE CLOSE TO TWELVE hundred captured tanks move eastward out of Tel Aviv in four columns, the sixty ex-Kuwaiti F/A-18s have already struck three significant targets: the Egyptian military field adjacent to what will soon enough return to being called Ben Gurion International Airport, the Jordanian field outside of Jerusalem that shortly will again be called Atarot, and a constellation of four smaller former IAF airfields in the north that were taken over by Syria and Iraq. In each case, most enemy aircraft are destroyed on the ground, black smoke from the planes and the asphalt burning beneath rising in columns that can be seen as far away as Cyprus. There casual observers note the fires before American intelligence specialists underground in the island's British bases can detect it via satellite.

The few enemy pilots able to get their planes in the air take one look at the masses of Kuwaiti Super Hornets and decline to engage. All are pursued and brought down, some over enemy territory where anti-aircraft operations were terminated a month earlier. After all, Israel has no air force.

Under the command of General Ido Baram, the newly Israeli tank force is focused on seven distinct objectives:

[1] Pierce the wall of Syrian troops surrounding Tel Aviv that is meant to prevent its population from fleeing eastward;

[2] Bypass the Egyptian force waiting for Jordanian armor to secure the city so they can enter and begin cleansing operations, then prevent the enemy fleeing south and east, an IDF tactic first used in the Yom Kippur War to bottle up Egypt's Third Army in Sinai;

[3] Secure the international airport so that food, medicines, and ammunition can be airlifted in;

[4] Punch through Syrian troop concentrations north of Tel Aviv to reach Israel's main power station at Hadera, hard by the ancient Roman port at Caesarea, so that Israeli military engineers and civilian employees of the Israel Electric Company can reconnect its twin turbines to the power grid supplying Tel Aviv. The Iranian Revolutionary Guard commandos who moved in early to take over the power station are now outgunned. Those who do not die in battle are collected in Caesarea's restored amphitheater, before the war a popular venue for concerts.

[5] Meanwhile, newly re-mechanized infantry is tasked to find the point where the pipeline bringing water from the north has been truncated and reconnect it. The effort fails until Persian-speaking interrogators identify an Iranian officer who knows the spot, and by two the next morning water begins to flow in Tel Aviv—brown at first, heavy with rust flushed from the unused pipes. By first light it is clear. To the people of Tel Aviv, no event of the past twenty-four hours is more significant. So many people bathe between 6 and 8 a.m. that in much of the city there is only a trickle. No one cares.

[6] Liberate six POW camps, four in the Negev, one close to Jericho, and one just outside of Netanya at Beit Lid, where a prison meant to hold twenty-two hundred convicted Palestinian terrorists

now holds over thirty thousand Israeli prisoners of war. And zero Palestinians. These were summarily executed by the Jordanian *mu-habarrat*. Indeed, as they move forward, Israeli intelligence officers are surprised to see no guerilla resistance from either Hamas or Hezbollah; only later does it become clear both Palestinian groups were early on massacred by their Muslim brethren in order to stifle any Palestinian claim to conquered Israel.

Conditions in the POW camps are horrific. Mass starvation, little to no drinking water, and lack of latrines have brought about an epidemic of typhus and amoebic dysentery. With no medical facilities on hand, and no medicines available to members of the IDF medical corps who fell into captivity, some 70,000 of the 380,000 Israeli prisoners have perished, the death rate multiplying up to and even past the hour of liberation. Because Arab prison camp commanders provided no facilities for burial, not so much as a shovel, bodies are found simply stacked up in corners of the camps to deteriorate in the sun. The stench is so bad the first tankists to arrive are forced to re-don their gas masks. Immediately, water taps in the Arab guard barracks around the camp are opened for the POWs—it is clear there is no shortage of water, merely a shortage of interest in keeping the Israeli prisoners alive. Those guards who have not fled face gruesome deaths as the skeletons in their charge take revenge.

It is a mark of how closely the camps resemble those of an earlier attempt to solve the Jewish problem that senior officers arriving on the scene turn their backs on the dismemberment of the guards. At one camp in the Negev, guards are executed next to the single tap available to the prisoners before liberation—the tap had been set up merely to drip water, so that the POWs were compelled to queue up for hours to receive the equivalent of a teaspoon each before returning to the rear of the long lines for their next taste. From captured documents, it is learned that reducing the flow to a trickle was meant to keep the death rate at manageable levels—were all the POWs to die at once, the mess might be visible from orbiting Western satellites.

[7] After fulfilling their primary missions, two hundred tanks, among them Cobi's, are detached from the main force to make straight for Jerusalem. Here there is resistance from Jordan's disciplined Arab Legionnaires, some under British officers. But blessed with intimate knowledge of the capital, the Jewish tankists carve Jerusalem into segments, liberating one neighborhood after another. By day's end most of the Legionnaires surrender, the remainder fleeing east across the nearly dry Jordan.

The Old City is left for last. It proves no challenge. Not only have its defenders melted away, but the entire population of the Muslim Quarter has decamped as well. The ancient Jewish, Christian, and Armenian Quarters are of course empty, their houses having been reserved for later use by Jordanian government officials. Like the rest of Jerusalem, the Old City is empty.

Within its walls, six major churches are found destroyed, including the Church of the Holy Sepulchre, along with a dozen monasteries and nunneries. Most synagogues have been used as toilets. The single exception to the destruction of non-Muslim holy sites are Russian Orthodox churches, a concession to Moscow for providing intelligence and logistical support, to say nothing of its role in the Security Council, where it vetoed even minimal efforts to succor the population of Tel Aviv and provide food and water to Israeli prisoners of war.

The Western Wall of the Second Temple, Judaism's most holy site, is found to be demolished. Its massive rectangular stones, one measuring forty-one by eleven by eleven feet, are strewn like children's blocks about the plaza where Jews of all persuasions, from ultra-Orthodox to Reform, prayed since the Old City's liberation from Jordanian rule in the Six Day War of 1967.

At the sight of this wanton destruction, IDF discipline, which has held through the entire day, breaks down.

The first tank to reach what is left of the wall is commanded by an Orthodox Jew whose family, of Yemenite origin, has lived in Jerusalem since the fifteenth century. The second tank is commanded by the son of a paratrooper who died in the Israeli conquest of the Old City in 1967. No record of any communication exists between the two—at the subsequent court martial, their actions that day are termed "autonomic and unplanned."

But only seconds after the two tanks arrive at the rubble that was the wall, they climb together to the plateau known to the Muslim world as the Noble Sanctuary, a flat plaza built over the ruins of the Holy Temple itself.

The first tank levels its 1200mm gun at the Dome of the Rock, not truly a mosque in that none worship there, but a shrine, and at point-blank range destroys it. The second tank joins in. In a matter of seconds, what is normally referred to as Islam's third holiest site is flattened, a cloud of dust rising above what were once walls of brightly colored hand-painted ceramic tile, the blue, green, violet, and yellow of its façade rising with the red and yellow of the interior, all of it tinged with a corona of gold dust from the dome.

As the two tanks swivel toward the second structure of the Noble Sanctuary, the Mosque of Omar, General Ido's command tank moves up to insert itself between the two Chariots and the mosque.

The words he uses as he opens communications are by now among the war's most quoted, less a military order than a spiritual aspiration: "Enough! Remember before Whom you stand."

116

WITH BEN GURION INTERNATIONAL Airport opened again, Connie Blunt is more than aware her unique situation as the only Western television correspondent is about to end. Unfortunately, when she arrives in Israel with El Al 201 her satellite phone is seized, along with the digital footage from the raid on Kuwait.

Even in time of war, IDF military censorship moves quickly, but this is no ordinary war. No one she speaks to can even speculate where her precious footage and satellite phone have been sent. And she has no way to get around. There are military vehicles on the roads, but few are heading to Tel Aviv. In the massive mobilization taking place, no one has time to worry about a blond correspondent complaining that her equipment has been stolen.

By great good fortune, a civilian taxi shows up at the airport—where the driver acquired gasoline is anyone's guess—and for a small fortune, its driver agrees to provide transportation to Tel Aviv. Connie, Terry Santiago her producer, and her ever-capable cameraman Buddy Walsh pile in.

With a tiny digital video camera he held in reserve, through the taxi window Walsh is able to record the rebirth of an entire city, an entire nation really. To save precious pixels, the record of their journey into Tel Aviv is shot in black and white, and to this day remains the only documentary evidence of the first hours of Israel's redemption.

At first their driver takes them to IDF headquarters in the Kirya. This is a dead end in every sense of the term: it is leveled.

Then the driver, who has driven foreign press before, thinks to bring them to Sokolov House, home of Israel's Journalists Association, where before the war editors and reporters from the Hebrew dailies hung out in the small café on the ground floor. Amazingly, Blunt finds the café functioning—after a fashion: there is no whiskey or beer, nor coffee, but with water now available, it is possible to brew tea. The place seems to have regained its attraction for Israel's fourth estate. With the promise of electricity, Israel's newspapers are preparing special editions, and as before, the nation's reporters gather here to trade rumor, innuendo, fabrication, and the occasional misplaced truth. A woman with a cigarette dangling from her lip—smokes have become available, though at very high prices—directs her upstairs to the office of the IDF spokesman.

To Blunt's relief the office is functioning. With the Kirya destroyed, the spokesman's office has returned to the modest chambers it had abandoned several years before. A clerk brings her to the officer in charge, a petite major. The woman speaks South African accented English. Blunt's equipment is on her desk.

"Thank fucking God," Blunt says.

"Thank fucking Col. Lior," the major says. "Military censorship has reviewed the footage you recorded on the plane to Kuwait and the subsequent military engagement."

"Great!"

"None of it may be released."

"You're fucking kidding me."

"All such footage must be approved by the IDF censor before it may be transmitted abroad. Your material has not been so approved."

"But it's great stuff. Your people are heroes."

"Yes, of course," the officer said. "That is our job. But IDF regulations forbid the identification of serving personnel engaged in military operations. You are welcome to reclaim your equipment provided you agree to comply with standard procedure for journalists in a warzone—"

"It's not a warzone—you won!"

"It is a warzone until the chief of staff directs otherwise. As to the existing footage, it shall remain here until such time as you find a way to dis-identify the military personnel involved."

"Dis-identify?"

"Technology may be employed."

"What, black out faces? That could take days."

"Exactly. Meanwhile, I have the pleasure to inform you that so far your crew is the only accredited foreign news organization in liberated Israel."

"Jesus, we are?"

"Does the word 'scoop' mean nothing to you?"

Without so much as another word, Blunt grabs the video camera and satellite phone and is out the door of Sokolov House and into her taxi.

She tells her producer, "I'm not just going to get a Peabody, I'm going to have a Pulitzer." Then she realizes the gaffe. "You too, Terry. You too."

117

AT DINNER THAT EVENING in Camp David, the president, Flo Spier, Felix St. George, Admiral Staley, and Marine Commandant Arthur Hefty are among the millions of people around the world, including the personnel at USMA Forward Attack Squadron Wildcat, watching as Connie Blunt does a 3 a.m. stand-up on the tarmac of the military airfield adjacent to Ben Gurion International Airport. For the Marine aviators, as for Americans as a whole, watching Blunt's footage produces either suppressed tears or tears outright.

At Camp David, it produces reservations.

"As we've seen, Damian, Israel is even as I speak rising phoenix-like from the ashes of its own destruction. With electricity and water supply now returned almost to prewar levels, and access to limited supplies of gasoline, the country is back on its feet. The mood here is not so much celebration as relief, and across the board a dedication to getting Israel going again.

"According to military sources, Israel's situation on the battle-field can best be described as a turnabout win for David over Goliath. However, because I am compelled to follow the guidelines of Israel Defense Forces censorship, I can provide only sketchy details. We do know that Jerusalem has been liberated and that the port of Haifa is expected to be functioning sometime later today, Israel time. I am given to understand that about half the occupying Muslim forces have melted back over Israel's borders, while as many as three hundred thousand, let me repeat that, three hundred thousand Arab and Iranian troops are bottled up in several so-called pockets, completely surrounded by Israeli forces. What their fate is, no one will say, but according to the IDF spokesman's office these will be treated as prisoners of war according to the Geneva Convention, with full access by the International Committee of the Red Cross. I spoke earlier this morning with Dr. Heinz Wortzel of that organization, who tells me he expects full cooperation from the IDF.

"To sum up, Damian, nothing better illustrates the situation here in Israel than the scene just behind me, where as you can see bombed-out Arab aircraft have been bulldozed out of the way and Israeli-piloted warplanes carrying the markings of the Kuwaiti Air Force have been taking off and landing for hours. How this strange situation came about is something I expect to reveal exclusively to CNN viewers as soon as technically feasible. However, I can assure you, Damian, the full story is likely to go down in the annals of military history as—"

"Connie, let me jump in here. We're getting reports from other sources, so far unconfirmed, regarding the Arab invasion's tragic effect on the Palestinians, with reports of mass executions by the Arab armies and wholesale flight from these persecutions. I know it's very late for you, Connie, and that you and your crew have been working without sleep in order to bring CNN viewers here at home and around the world this startling exclusive coverage. But is there something you might add concerning what may emerge as a significant political, if not humanitarian, problem as the days wear on?"

"Damian, I attempted earlier to reach the office of Yigal Lev, who is identified as Israeli's acting prime minister, but on this question a spokesman would say only, and I quote—" She reads from a sheet of paper. "—'*The government of Israel remains sympathetic to the deplorable suffering of the Palestinian people at the hands of the neighboring Arab regimes, but considers this to be an internal problem of the Arab world.*' As to if and when Israel's borders will open to Palestinians who fled Arab attacks and may wish to return to their homes, I was told only, and here again I quote, '*The return of Arab citizens of Israel to their homes in the—*'"

"Is he saying, Connie, Palestinians who are not citizens—"

"Damian, if you don't mind. '*The return of Arab citizens of Israel to their homes in the State of Israel according to its biblical borders is assured.*' I can't confirm this, but it does appear Israel intends to formally annex the West Bank and possibly Gaza now that both areas have been nearly completely depopulated of Palestinians by the invading Arab armies. If so, I'm afraid we are looking at another perilous development in the rather unpleasant history of Israel-Arab relations." She pauses, leaning forward. "I'm sorry, Damian, I didn't quite get that."

"Sorry to interrupt, Connie, but we now have news that may make the Middle East situation even more complicated. According to information just received, Ayatollah Nasr Sadiqi, president of Iran and also its leading cleric, has declared a fatwa, or religious edict, calling for Muslims to enact a death sentence on the State of Israel, which he claims has intentionally destroyed the Dome of the Rock in Jerusalem, said to be Islam's third most holy site. The fatwa specifically stipulates that all Israelis are to be destroyed, including women and children, and I quote, '*So that they may not propagate their evil.*' Iranian authorities have now vowed to destroy Israel with nuclear weapons. Here's an excerpt from a news conference in Tehran which ended only moments ago."

On the screen behind Smith, the bearded mullah's high-pitched rant opens at full volume and then is reduced so the halting voice of a simultaneous translator may be heard. "The Jewish trickery will be...solved...fixed. And this...invites, will cause a second and final holocaust upon the Hebrew sons of monkeys and dogs, even the infants. Therefore we have commanded...invited the Muslim armies and all Muslim peoples to leave Palestine so that our sacred bombs will fall only upon the Jewish Nazis and their Christian allies. In a matter of hours this sacred soil will be...cleansed...in vengeance, in the vengeance of God, against those beasts who destroyed the sacred holy shrines of Islam."

"Jesus H. Christ," the president says, buttering a slice of cornbread. "I thought those Eyeranian assholes don't have nukes." He clicks off the television with a remote emblazoned with the presidential seal. No one else is authorized to use it.

"You will recall, Mr. President," Felix St. George says, "as early as two years previously I very strongly urged not to accept the word of the mullahs on the nuclear question. It is firmly within Muslim tradition that in dealing with the infidel—"

"Have we got anything from Tel Aviv?"

"We keep calling, but they're not answering," Admiral Staley says. "The Israelis are toying with us. They don't want a ceasefire this time. They're going for the whole nine yards."

Flo Spier is all over this. "At least Israel hasn't gone nuclear, sir. Mr. President, your airlift will go down in history as having averted an atomic war on the part of Israel. This recent development certainly can't be laid at your feet."

"Yeah, well, we restrained the Jews all right," the president says, salting his cornbread, "but we can't restrain the towelheads. All it takes is one bomb to take out the whole of Israel—what is it, the size of Rhode Island?" He thinks about this. "Or New Jersey, somebody said. I think it's New Jersey."

"Mr. President," General Hefty says. He has barely eaten. "As you yourself noted, we are committed to defend Israel in case of nuclear attack. Ipso facto the US is treaty-bound to hit Iran. Sir, the fuckers are *announcing* a nuclear attack. There's six million Israeli civilians packed in there about to be kosher barbecued. Mr. President, we have the means to stop it. Is it a go?"

"Felix, break it to him gentle-like."

"If you look closely at the treaty, General Hefty, we're committed to defend Israel in the event of a nuclear attack, not in advance of one."

General Hefty is about to lose it. "Mr. President, that is the most cynical sentence I have heard in Washington in my lifetime, and this is far from my first rodeo."

The president considers another slice of cornbread. "Might well be, Arthur. But let me ask you this: What's one pissant country compared to ensuring that we and our allies do not run out of the lifeblood of democracy and the American way of life?"

"Sir, my letter of resignation will be on your desk in the morning."

The president decides to go for the cornbread—he can swim it off in the morning. "Arthur, I like a man with ideals. But should we attack Eyeran, the US is at war with the whole Muslim world. Which means no oil. Zip. We're not just talkin' high-priced gas—our pumps will go as dry as a widow's pussy."

"In an election year," Flo Spier adds, as if she must.

The president genuinely likes General Hefty, probably as much as he likes cornbread. Both have that gritty, down-home quality. "See, Arthur. Israel's got holy sites and all that history, and brave people, real brave people. But what it doesn't have is what we need."

"It's a fact of life, sir."

"That's right as rain, Felix. Now, Arthur, I sure am glad those Israelians didn't take out the Arabs with their nukes, even if now it means Eyeran is going to take out Israel with theirs. Sometimes life just ain't fair. Y'all want to pass the jam down this way?"

118

IN THE WARM WATERS of the Persian Gulf, an Israeli submarine rises to the surface, joined a half mile to the east by a second. In both, the same exercise is worked through step by step: confirmation of code, confirmation of source, confirmation of target, confirmation of onward orders. In each submarine, the captain opens the hatch to step out on deck to have a last look at the world before it is bent into a new shape, permanently altered, transmogrified.

After the missiles are launched, both vessels gently submerge beneath the waves for the long voyage home.

119

THE ISRAEL TO WHICH they return will be familiar, and not. Still fractious and almost ferociously opinionated, the Israeli in the street, like all survivors, is forever changed, but ultimately the same. Coming back from death's door is for the individual Israeli a transcendent experience, but once it is shared this most personal of emotions becomes nationally affirmative.

The extent of the damage is unfathomable. Israel's medical facilities, overburdened with caring for the sick and wounded, become an assembly line as thousands of Jewish women and girls, some as young as eleven, line up for abortions. Israel's Chief Rabbinate, which otherwise condemns the practice, turns a blind eye.

No other people experiences so many funerals per capita in so short a period. Israel's supply of rabbis qualified to lead prayers at gravesites proves to be insufficient. When it becomes clear how many dead are piled up like rotting logs in the former prisoner of war camps, rabbis from around the world are invited by the IDF Chief Rabbinate to fly in to help. They do so in droves, many for the first time putting aside their skepticism about a Jewish state that in their eyes is insufficiently religious.

Yet, as always, Jewish humor prevails, and as usual it is black. Television comedians quickly see the possibilities: the Muslim invaders have finally given Israel's cities an opportunity for broad-scale urban renewal; the Knesset, with no members, has never been more efficient; the ultra-Orthodox, who before the war dedicated their lives to study, eschewing labor, have at last joined the workforce.

Jewish money pours in from abroad to finance the rebuilding, so much so that, as the comedians put it, the country's second major import—after cash—is brass plaques to commemorate the donors.

With labor in short supply and no Palestinians to take up the slack, Christian fundamentalist and Jewish college students flock in to hammer nails, pour concrete, and repave roads.

The Knesset building is reconstructed in six months. Rebuilding the western wall of the Holy Temple takes longer: some of its stone building blocks weigh five hundred tons. Bulldozer after bulldozer breaks down in the effort; how the ancient Israelites brought them to the site and lifted them into place remains a mystery to this day.

120

BETTER TIMES ARE NOT slow in coming. The massive defeat of five Muslim armies and the Iranian theocrats who planned the war does not immediately turn the Muslim lion into a Jew-loving lamb. But the plan Yigal worked on while Pinky and his generals prepared the counterattack removes the lion's claws, and teeth.

And balls.

To Yigal, a student of history, it might have appeared that charity following victory would accomplish more than brutal vengeance. The examples are classic, well known, and an article of faith in every Western doctoral course in international relations. After World War I, the victors so emasculated the vanquished enemy that Germany's obsessive dedication to revenge brought forth a second, even more horrific world conflict. Learning from this, after the fall of the Axis powers in World War II, the West took a more humane tack, actively assisting Germany, Italy, and Japan to rebuild, in the process creating three long-lived democracies so opposed to war that their armies became mere miniatures of what they had been, purposeless by design and in posture merely defensive.

Yigal rejects this model.

As he tells Judy the night of the first day of the counterattack, "After the Second World War, the West was dealing with the West. The victors and the vanquished shared a common secular civilization, so compassion made sense. Here we are dealing with people whose worldview does not accommodate other religions, and who approach the secular as even worse."

"They're our neighbors."

"Geographically," Yigal says. "But if your neighbor's very essence, his every urge, is to destroy you because you are different, then the only way to deal with this is to disarm him, reduce him to impotence, and then simply ignore him. For a thousand years, the Muslims stewed in their own enforced ignorance—this after centuries of being the light of the world. Do you know how many Western books were translated into Arabic from 900 AD to today? A thousand. It's the same number Greece translates from other languages in one year. Our neighbors are intent that Islam rule the world, and they wish the world to look like them. That being the case, I don't care what they wish for. I don't care if my neighbor hates me. I care only to make sure he is disarmed. What is their weapon? Oil. With oil, we gave them strength."

"But that's geography again, isn't it? You can't take away their oil. They're sitting on it."

"Honey," Yigal says, "just watch me."

121

THE DAY AFTER THE counterattack, Israel begins repatriating the first of some 300,000 Muslim prisoners of war. The total may be significantly higher, but the IDF has better things to do than take names and numbers, or to build POW camps to house and feed the enemy. There is no sense in it: because the Muslim armies had removed no Israeli prisoners of war to their own countries, there are no prisoners to trade. Short of mass execution, exporting Arab captives is the only solution.

Only the day after her clean scoop, Connie Blunt loses her exclusive as hundreds of foreign correspondents arrive in Israel on the first planes to land at what is again Ben Gurion International. Like Blunt, they are doing their stand-ups on the low rise overlooking Allenby Bridge, where a seemingly endless line of Arab prisoners of war, tied neck to neck, marches into Jordan, some going home, others eventually to reach Egypt, Syria, Iraq, and Iran. No observer can determine their nationality by their dress. The prisoners are, to say the least, out of uniform.

"Damian, this line of naked men must be a mile long," Blunt reports from the ridge. "Clearly the Israelis mean this to be a humiliating lesson to the enemy, whose combined armies only two days ago had Israel on its knees. As you can see, or can't see because FCC standards and good taste prevent us from shooting up close, if you look at the faces of these prisoners you may be seeing the end of Islamic dreams to destroy the State of Israel. However, Iran, which military sources here call the instigating and organizing force behind the attack, seems to have gotten off scot—"

"Connie, sorry to interrupt, and please stay with us as we break away for startling footage, just in, of developments in Iran, where the oil port of Bandar Abbas has become one enormous fireball. Other reports describe nuclear-like explosions in remote—"

122

IN THE PRESIDENTIAL BEDROOM at Camp David, the president clicks off the television. He has already been apprised of the situation in Iran. All in all, this night has left him at once frustrated and gratified. He had hoped that the first lady might be inclined to emulate Holly Mawn in the previous evening's film, but she dozed off in the Camp David screening room just before the crucial, uncut scene. This accounts for his frustration. His gratification is less personal.

"At least," he says to no one in particular, "it wasn't us that did it."

The first lady stirs softly in her sleep. Maybe, the president thinks, looking at her, the night can be win-win after all.

123

BECAUSE REPAIRS TO THE prime minister's residence in Jerusalem are not considered a priority in a capital where entire ministries must be rebuilt from the ground up, Yigal chooses to remain at the villa in Herzlia and commute to Jerusalem. In truth, he does not wish to live where his predecessor died, especially after her mutilated body was discovered in the Jerusalem city dump. Besides, his home suits him, and Judy, and Cobi. His son has just taken off on his motorcycle for some sort of party at the same beach that so recently was a slum on its way to becoming a graveyard. If anything, Yigal is aware how slim is the line between vibrancy and rot, hope and despair, attending the funeral and being the corpse. Yigal Lev is determined Israel will not be the corpse.

The phone rings.

Judy looks in. "Good luck," she whispers. Then shuts the door.

"Good day, Mr. President," Yigal says into the phone.

"And a good evening to you, Mr. Prime Minister. Yogi—may I call you Yogi?" A pause. "Yi-gal, of course. My Hebrew's a bit rusty. Barely made it through Spanish in high school. I'll tell ya, every time I stand up to say something to a group of Messicans I'm thinking, 'Dear Lord, help me not to say *fuck* instead of *luck*.'"

When this is greeted by silence, the president merely continues: not everyone has a good sense of humor.

"Yi-gal. Bible name, is it?"

124

IN THE LIBYAN DESERT two hundred miles southeast of Benghazi, a truck marked BP driven by an oilfield foreman bearing a striking resemblance to Col. Lior churns through the sand until it comes to a second BP truck with drilling equipment attached. On the horizon, hundreds of derricks pump like nodding birds. After men in yellow BP coveralls unload a heavy black cylinder, three feet long and a foot thick, gently setting it into a drill hole, a technician screws a long antenna into the top of the all but buried cylinder. Others gently cover the antenna with sand.

125

"It means God will redeem, Mr. President."

"Well, if you don't mind me saying so, Yi-gal, your God didn't bring much redemption to them Eyeranians."

"Mr. President, may I call you Dwayne?"

"Wouldn't have it no other way."

"Dwayne, yours didn't bring much redemption to the Japanese."

Another pause. The president was briefed, but not enough is known about the Israeli prime minister for a proper assessment. Central Intelligence was reduced to interviewing business associates and rivals. Apparently the man is a straight shooter, but not easy.

"Yigal, let's look ahead instead of back. I'm gonna lay it on the line. The world would feel a lot better if Israel cut back its nuclear arsenal."

"In the spirit of peace, as it were," Yigal says. It is a good thing the president cannot see his face.

"Point taken. But you and I know there's no reason you need so many nukes. Can't we reduce that a bit, for the sake of safety and easing tensions? Frankly, I'm looking at a close election. By golly, you are too."

126

From an unpaved road twisting through wasteland, a convoy of US Army Humvees descends onto an even rougher track ending at a metal gate marked in Arabic and English:

Halliburton Iraq
NO ENTRY

The US Army major in the first Humvee dismounts, unlocks the gate and swings it open. In the light of the Humvee's headlights and despite the unfamiliar uniform, he looks very much like the Israeli gangster and sometime chief of police Misha Shulman.

Eventually the convoy comes to a lone tent over which a US flag snaps in the wind. The tent is guarded by Hebrew-speaking soldiers in US Army uniforms, who salute, then part the tent flaps to reveal what appears to be a grave, shovels still in the ground. Speaking in Hebrew, the US Army major orders a black metal cylinder, about three feet long and a foot thick, brought into the tent and placed gently in the grave.

127

"EXACTLY, DWAYNE," YIGAL SAYS. "I agree. We *should* do something about our nuclear arsenal. And if it will help you at the polls, how can I say no?"

Now the pause is longer. "Well, sir, I'd hoped for your cooperation, but I didn't expect it to be this easy. You people got a reputation for driving a hard bargain, am I right?"

At this point both sides are pleased the conversation is limited to voice, the president because he is surrounded by advisors, the prime minister because he is alone—with others in the government present, there would of necessity be a record of the conversation, and even released after the statutory thirty years this might cause problems.

"Naturally Israel must be compensated for the destruction caused by this war, not least because American weaponry was used against us. And the United States did wait a very long time before delivering humanitarian aid." Yigal stage-coughs. "We do have a shopping list, mostly military."

The president mouths the word silently to Felix St. George: *Jews.* "Yogi, I'm sure we can work something out. How about we make a joint statement here in Washington to announce this reduction plan—"

"Dwayne, there may be some misunderstanding here."

But the president, buoyed by the prospect of electoral victory, is moving right along. "I'm thinking late October. Howzat? Leaves time for your folks and my folks—"

128

IN THE SAUDI DESERT, a camel caravan moves past a forest of oil rigs to a small oasis, where armed Bedouin sit around a fire. The two groups greet each other formally before the caravan leader, who is in fact a Bedouin, though not local, is taken to a pile of rocks arranged in a rough pyramid, a traditional marker. A heavy black cylinder, three feet long and a foot thick, is unloaded from one of the camels. The Bedouin leader watches it being buried beneath the rocks. IDF Staff Sgt. Abed Abu-Kassem of the Ghawarna, a small clan in the north of Israel, smiles broadly. He has waited this long to fuck the enemy in the rear, and properly.

129

"DWAYNE, ACTUALLY OUR PLAN is not exactly to *reduce* the number of our nuclear weapons. It's more like we're storing them, for the safety of all concerned."

"Well, Yi-gal, I'm sure that would be fine." Another pause, this time with whispering. "Uh, where precisely were y'all thinking these weapons might be stored?"

Yigal has been waiting to say these three words since he devised this plan in the middle of the night, scribbling on a whiteboard in this very office. "With...our...enemies."

"Beg pardon?"

"That's correct. In exchange for our Arab neighbors taking possession of our nuclear arsenal, Israel proposes to take possession of their arsenal. It's the oil weapon that counts, isn't it?"

This time a lot of whispering. "Yogi, you want to run that by me again?"

130

THE NEXT DAY, THE president has a phone conversation with the King of Saudi Arabia, this time with video. The king feels more comfortable seeing the faces of those who approach him for favors. The two leaders speak English, though a pair of translators stand by in the palace should there be confusion. The president's English is known to be bizarre.

"Yo, your highness. How ya doing?"

"Thank Allah, my good friend."

"Amen to that," the president says. "Your highness, you may not be so familiar with the practice, but every four years we here in America have what our Asian friends call an erection?" Because it is the White House photographer's night off, the president has fortified himself with two Peronis, not enough to dent the presidential judgment, but just enough to stimulate what the first lady calls his "inherent friskiness."

The king does not so much as hear the joke. "I am familiar with elections, Dwayne."

"Well, your—say, would you mind if I call you Abdullah?"

The silence that greets this is so glacial the president eases back.

"Your highness, the American people been paying through the nose for oil for decades. They need a price at the pump they can live with."

"Dwayne, as always we do our very best."

"Yeah, I'm sure you do. But there's been a development."

"A development?"

"Yes, sir. Seems that while you been doing your best, our friends in Israel been doin' theirs."

"Dwayne, to characterize these people as my friends is not, how shall I put it, suitable. But please continue."

"The sons-o-guns gone and installed their nuclear devices in your oilfields."

The monarch signals for his translators. "Would you mind, Dwayne, repeating that?"

"They got nukes in oilfields all over the Middle East. Sort of a stealth thing? You know: surprise!" The president is at once pleased with himself and concerned about the effect of that second beer. But not that much. "It's changed the equation."

"Excuse me, my dear friend." The king has never studied mathematics—others count his money. The royal translators are challenged. One suggests *situation*; the other tries *formula*, then realizes this is no better than *equation*. He chooses *playing field*.

The monarch gets the picture. "If true, it is an act of war."

"Jesus, king. You folks don't really want another one, do ya? If so, those Israelians gonna open up a can of kosher whup-ass. And they ain't gonna stop until they visit whatever palace you plan to be sleepin' in that night."

"Mr. President, I hope I do not understand correctly that you approve this act of…of piracy."

"Your kingship, how do I say this delicately? You people been flyin' the skull and crossbones for eighty years. Anyhoo, to cut to the chase, we're talking two bucks a gallon at the pump. Regular."

The king needs no translators for this, nor mathematicians. Oil is now selling at over $150 a barrel. The new price would cut that by two-thirds. "My dear friend, that is simply not possible."

"Yeah, well, then you can expect the Jews to blow up your oil, and you won't have none at all."

The king learned to play this game before the grossly smiling man on the other end of the telephone was born. "My dear Mr. President, neither will you. It is a...standoff, no?"

"Hmmm," the president says. "Let me think on that." He mimes thinking, the tip of his index finger to his lips, his face screwed up as if in intense cogitation. "Uh, actually, no. Number one, we made you king and we can unmake you. Number two, the US of A is not about to sit still until we get to the point where some damn Jew with a itchy trigger finger blows all that oil to kingdom come. Number three, let me put it to you direct. The price of oil is always going to be an internal political problem in my country. Your highness, Abdullah, whatever, oil goes up over two bucks there'll be so many American military in your oilfields you'll have to salute some nineteen-year-old corporal from Mississippi just to take a leak." He signals for another Peroni.

"Mr. President!"

"And some of them military gonna be women. And by golly, by executive order I'm gonna make sure every goldarned one of them ladies be wearing short shorts!"

"Mr. President, I have never been addressed in this manner! By anyone!"

"And Abby, by the way," the president says, "don't *ever* be fuckin' with a sitting American president in an election year."

131

OVER THAT YEAR, MANY changes are to take place.

Connie Blunt is promoted to CNN anchor, replacing Damian Smith, who becomes presidential press secretary after Don Beadle moves on to the private sector. Smith has an easy job: with gasoline at $1.93 a gallon (regular), the president barely has to campaign at all. Blunt brings with her to CNN a certain IDF Special Forces colonel who commandeered a certain plane to Kuwait to be the network's resident military analyst, on the side co-authoring a book on the operation with the Air Kuwait 717 captain who never lost his cool. The movie does $170 million in its first week. But only in North America.

In the rest of the world it bombs, reflecting a sociopolitical antipathy whose roots precede Islam and Christianity, and which date back at least to the time of the Pharaohs. Though cheering for the underdog is normally seen as instinctual, a curious reversal takes place as it becomes clear the oil weapon is now in Israeli hands, controlled by what many European newspapers and websites unabashedly term "malignant special interests." These special interests, rumored to control the world economy, are said to be manipulating the price of oil in order to stimulate business, and thus generate even more wealth for themselves. Or something.

As though the near annihilation of a second six million Jews is little more than a fast-dissolving early-morning dream, the image of Israel returns to *status quo ante*. This is nowhere more evident than in the image of the Palestinians, who once again have taken their place in the front rank of international martyrdom. What is left of their leadership assiduously labors to present evidence to the West that the recent decimation of its people has occurred not by their fellow Muslims but at the hand of Israel.

The Palestinians demand a return to their native land, which—through the bloody efforts of their Muslim neighbors—is now by and large empty of Palestinians. The population of Israel's own Arab citizens, slaughtered wholesale in retribution for decades of "collaboration" with their Jewish fellow citizens, declines from two million to one half of that—this genocide is also blamed on Israel. In the West Bank and Gaza, the death rate is even higher; the actual number will never be known because Palestinian spokesmen, once adept at exaggerating the population of living Palestinians, now invent similarly magical numbers for the dead, all ostensibly victims of Israel.

UNRWA, the United Nations Relief and Works Administration, an international welfare office dedicated to preserving the refugee status of all Palestinians, living, dead, and fictional, quickly establishes new camps in Egypt, Syria, Lebanon, and Iraq. (The king of Jordan refuses to offer Palestinians even temporary shelter.)

Armed with funds supplied by the same Western governments that ignored the Palestinians' slaughter, UNRWA returns to its traditional policy of providing generously for its clientele, even to the point of publishing new textbooks demonstrating the continuing diabolical culpability of "the Zionist enterprise," replete with caricatures of hook-nosed predatory Jews. These become standard in Palestinian schools.

Faced with the electoral clout of a flood of Muslim immigrants, most European democracies undertake what comes to be known as a policy of "progressive balance" with regard to the new reality of the Middle East. The sclerotic French left, ever opportunistic, presents the recent conflict as a war of self-defense by the five Islamic attackers, who struck first on evidence of Israel's plans to attack *them*. To this upside-down version of the truth, a spoonful of anti-Americanism sweetens the pot: it is clear the US and Israel colluded in an anti-Muslim war. A new term, *islamicide*, becomes the rage among European leftists, and some in America as well. On university campuses, it is considered a fact that massive numbers of US troops were engaged on the ground on behalf of Washington's neo-colonialist junior partner.

The Muslim governments of the Middle East play a double game. While continuing the Islamic propaganda campaign against Israel, they are careful about doing no more than making noise at the UN. With Israeli nuclear devices hidden in their own countries, a return to war is unthinkable. Nor may they raise the price of oil.

Depressed energy prices affect Russia as well. With little to sell but diamonds and petrochemicals, Russia's economy is now shriveled to below that of the Communist era: churning out unexportable automobiles and nesting babushka dolls is hardly a solution. Russia remains a leading manufacturer of arms, but this trade is limited to those countries that have seen their weaponry destroyed or captured by Israel, and these are no longer bottomless pits of hard currency. In the short term, dumping diamonds on the world market might bring revenue, but eventually oversupply would undermine the price of gem-quality stones. At giveaway prices for crude oil and natural gas, *The Economist* notes, "Moscow has nothing to sell but rubles, and thus has nothing to sell." As a result, Russia pulls back from attempts to disrupt the new international order.

Big oil is unfazed by the drop in petroleum prices. Able to sustain profitability at any price, the American petrochemical industry not only continues solidly in the black, but for the first time in decades benefits from an outpouring of public goodwill. Share prices for big oil rise to historic highs. At the same time, Detroit, so recently emasculated by its inability to offer cars economical on gas, roars back with a new generation of big-engine mega-mobiles, some with fins. The price of oil is so reasonable electric cars become a standing joke on late-night television. Not only is there a V8 in every American garage, V12s make their appearance as the standard of luxury. At these prices, Americans have oil to burn, and do.

As the price drops for industrial power and commercial transport, industrial America rebounds to such an extent that Wal-Mart, once almost exclusively the retail agent for 90% of Chinese consumer exports, moves to buy only American. As a result, the US develops a labor shortage: there are too few workers to man the new machinery. Congress acts quickly, creating a new visa classification under the Guest Labor Act—critics in organized labor call it the Gomez Labor Act. With the US-Mexican border open to a flood of documented *obreros huespedes*, American manufacturers abandon China en masse to establish factories in Mexico, as well as new facilities close enough to the border for documented day laborers to cross through turnstiles activated by electronic visa-card readers. Seemingly overnight, the US Border Patrol morphs from a police force to an employment agency.

Considering the almost universal benefits of low-cost energy, the rise in anti-Israel sentiment becomes a kind of litmus paper of illogic, but anti-semitism was never dictated by reason.

Once again missiles (this time supplied by Russia) begin raining down on Israel from Palestinian bases in Lebanon, Syria, and Egypt, yet world public opinion persists in seeing Israel as the imperialist, if not racist, villain of the peace.

132

CONSIDERING THE HUMILIATING DEFEAT of the Islamic Liberation Force, surprisingly few heads roll.

General Niroomad is convicted of treason in a Tehran show trial in which a group of Iranian Jews are compelled to testify that the architect of the Muslim invasion was all along in the employ of the Mossad. The mullahs make sure the world sees in televised close-up that the faces of Niroomad's Jewish co-conspirators show no signs of violence. Not shown are their families, who are promised a horrible fate if the accused Jews do not cooperate. When Niroomad is hanged in Tehran's Azadi Square, these so-called "partners in treason" swing with him, each convinced he is giving his life to save his wife, his children, and his parents. The next day, the families of these martyrs, men, women, and children, even infants, are discreetly liquidated at a military base near Isfahan.

But Iran is exceptional.

In all the Arab nations taking part in the attack, the military high commands are forcibly retired, but in every case permitted to live out their lives in luxury as comfortably pensioned senior officers. As opposed to theocratic Iran, which considers failure in jihad a sin requiring capital punishment, the Arab reaction to failure within its ruling class is by tradition tolerant. Anything less would bring the existing power structure crashing down.

The search for scapegoats extends even to Israel, but is more subtle.

Because the government responsible for the intelligence failures leading to the near-termination of the State of Israel was itself terminated—there is no one to vote out of office; they are all dead—the country's citizenry turns obscenely on the very individual who saved them. One columnist compares Yigal Lev to Churchill, noting that the British prime minister was recalled by his own traumatized nation after World War II, like Israel a nation yearning for better times. As with Churchill in Britain, the fickle Israeli electorate associates the name of Yigal Lev not with salvation but with hardship.

Ever hopeful for an idyllic rapprochement with the Jewish State's eternal enemies, the resiliently optimistic Israeli left crafts a campaign that ruthlessly works both sides of a particularly nasty political street. One plank in its platform is meant to appeal to those for whom the thought of endless war is intolerable: in order to negotiate a lasting peace, Yigal Lev must go, because the Arab nations will never sign a peace treaty with the man responsible for their shameful defeat. The opposition's other argument appeals to the emotional instability of the average Israeli: the discipline imposed on Ghetto Tel Aviv is angrily decried to have been needlessly authoritarian. In televised debates, Yigal is labeled to his face a Jewish fascist whose storm troopers went so far as to beat a man for urinating in the street.

Yigal's measured response militates against him. He stresses the need for discipline in time of war, a principled defense but not one that arouses sympathy for the man compelled to make such decisions. Likewise, he is accused of seizing power from the lawful government at gunpoint. A business executive and not a politician, his response is as dry as it might be in describing the dismissal of an incompetent manager: "I learned early in business that the general good means more than the protection of some fool's resume."

Perhaps most damaging, Yigal is unable to go on the offensive regarding his opponent's credibility—his own character questioned, he has no counterattack: the left-wing nominee spent the war as a prisoner of the Syrians in one of the most notorious POW camps, where he lost an arm to gangrene. The absence of this limb is on display before the nation. Yigal's most cogent argument is a question: "In my place, what would you have done?" In reply, his opponent manages only partially to disguise a sneer: "I would have negotiated an honorable peace."

After what can only be called a cataclysmic defeat, Yigal dedicates his energies to rebuilding Isracorp and to spending more time with Judy. They take a second honeymoon in Provence, under an assumed name renting a house overlooking a vineyard near Aix. The couple is so enamored of the peaceful setting they consider buying a second home in the area. But on a tour of available properties, they are interrupted by the arrival of three carloads of officers of *la direction générale de la sécurité intérieure*, the French equivalent of the FBI, who politely but firmly insist the couple must return to their villa and pack. Paris has learned that an Islamicist group centered in Marseilles has targeted them. The DGSI will provide protection until they return to Israel. After making a phone call to Jerusalem, Yigal tells them Israel will provide for their security. But this is not enough to satisfy Paris, which is less concerned about the lives of Yigal and Judy than the embarrassment of a violent incident in French territory—tourism remains the country's main source of income.

In the private jet the DGSI provides for the flight from Nice to Ben Gurion, Yigal allows himself a moment of deep despondence in the knowledge that their life together will never return to what it was. But he says nothing: there is a good chance the two-person cabin crew serving them are French agents who speak Hebrew.

"Sweetheart," Judy tells him. "Don't be sad."

"Arlingday, ethay abincay isway iredway."

"Otay otequay Igalyay Evlay: Ifway ouyay esireday eacepay, eparepray orfay arway."

"Ethay onnectioncay?"

"Ifway ouyay avehay otay otectpray ourselfyay, ependday onway ouryay ownway."

He laughs. "Ethay Ionistzay anifestomay."

"Iway ustjay antway otay ebay omehay." She squeezes his hand. "Unnyfay, onlyway away ortshay ilewhay agoway Iway idnday'tay eelfay afesay inway Israelway oneway inutemay. Ownay Iway onday'tay eelfay afesay anywhereway elseway."[4]

132

ON THEIR RETURN, JUDY establishes a foundation to benefit the families of those killed during the war, both civilian and military. It becomes Israel's leading charity, and for good reason. The numbers are staggering. With so many men killed, widows with young children are compelled to find work, of which there is plenty, but the national childcare system—with government kindergartens for children from the age of four—now must be expanded to include even infants. The government is not up to the challenge.

Judy enlists Hadassah, the worldwide Zionist women's organization. With an international structure already in place, Jewish women everywhere contribute money and time. In a matter of months, infant care centers are set up in the big cities; within a year, there is

---

4 "Darling, the cabin is wired."

"To quote Yigal Lev: If you desire peace, prepare for war."

"The connection?"

"If you have to protect yourself, depend on your own."

He laughs. "The Zionist manifesto."

"I just want to be home." She squeezes his hand. "Funny, only a short while ago I didn't feel safe in Israel one minute. Now I don't feel safe anywhere else."

not a village without one. Calling on Yigal's connections with Israeli business leaders, Judy insists large companies set up crèches at the worksite. Where this is not possible, mothers are welcomed into the labor force through innovative schemes that include telecommuting and even home assembly of electronic components.

Under Judy's guidance, Hadassah sets up a nonprofit bank to offer loans to war widows starting small businesses of their own. When it becomes clear that war *widowers* with young children find themselves in a parallel situation, Hadassah enlarges its safety net to include benefits for men. The second most popular name for Israeli daughters becomes *Hadasssah*.

The first is *Judy*. No one is more proud than her husband, though he sees his beloved so little he calls himself an honorary war widower.

Discharged after the war, Cobi declines to re-enlist and, in the tradition of many young Israelis following their military service, travels abroad before beginning university and annual reserve duty that will last until he is forty-eight. In Nepal, he meets a red-haired girl, also Israeli, also recently discharged. It turns out she knows a thing or two about Stinger missiles. Via Skype, their engagement is announced from Fortaleza, Brazil.

Staff Sgt. Abed Abu-Kassem of the Ghawarna retires from the IDF to become a member of Knesset on a far-right ticket—like most Bedouin, he is a born reactionary. Bedouin despise change.

Abu-Yunis, the Christian barber and entrepreneur, opens a restaurant with a Jewish partner. The restaurant is called *Cousins*. Between Jewish visitors and Christian pilgrims, there is never a day when its parking lot is not full of tour buses.

Ticky Pasha returns to England, where he spends his days in country pursuits—fly-fishing is not an option in Jordan—and his evenings writing his memoirs. Suppressed under the Official Secrets Act, they are not published. He never returns to Jordan.

There would be no point. Two years after the war, the Jordanian monarch is assassinated by a Hamas suicide bomber. Civil war breaks out between Jordan's Bedouin and Palestinian citizens. The latter, aided by Palestinians flooding in from neighboring countries, are victorious. The Hashemite royal family is deposed and the country renamed the Republic of Palestine. In emulation of Zionism, it opens its doors to Palestinians from all over the Arab world and from as far away as South America.

Because the Palestinian leadership finds itself fully engaged with the construction of new towns and the infrastructure of a modern state, including such details as sewer systems and roads, it finally comes to terms with Israel. Under a secret memorandum of understanding, the Republic of Palestine will forego a standing army, its (once Jordanian) tanks, artillery, and missiles to be purchased by the IDF. In return, Israel pledges to defend Palestine's borders from aggression by any neighboring country, its Red Sea port of Aqaba to be protected by the Israeli Navy. Moreover, a land corridor is established so that Palestinian agricultural and manufactured goods may be exported through the Israeli deepwater harbor at Ashdod, where Palestinian customs officials operate out of their own dedicated section of the port.

Muslim holy sites in Jerusalem continue to be administered by the Waqf, the Muslim religious council. Along with the blue and white flag of Israel, the newly designed flag of Palestine, a solid green banner, flies over the Mosque of Omar and the Dome of the Rock, which Israel has rebuilt.

The King of Saudi Arabia dies in his eighty-seventh year and is replaced by his thirty-six-year-old grandson, who faces enormous challenges. The flow of oil continues, but the riches have ceased, a situation that prevents the royal treasury from continuing to support the multitude of regional sheikhs on its payroll. The country quickly fragments, returning to the primitive tribalism that was its natural state before Saudi Arabia was formed after World War I.

Kuwait sues in the International Court of Justice at the Hague for return of its sixty F/A-18s—London's *Daily Mail* gleefully summarizes the charge sheet as "Grand Theft Air Force"—but the judges rule for Israel after documents are entered into evidence proving Kuwait a veteran financial supporter of international terror in general and anti-Israel terror specifically. The aircraft are termed spoils of war.

133

ALEKSEI TUPIKOV, THE RUSSIAN general in charge of GRU operations in the Middle East, is transferred to Washington as nominal second commercial secretary. One evening, at a diplomatic reception, he comes face to face with Misha Shulman, now director of covert operations for the Mossad. Though Misha never met the Russian during the war—the GRU mission in Jerusalem was helicoptered out before the first Israeli tank entered the city—Tupikov's role, and the role of the GRU, becomes public knowledge when Israel releases video of the meetings of the Islamic Liberation Council in the boardroom of Israel Discount Bank in Jerusalem. In their hurry to leave, the Russians neglected to remove the cameras they installed.

Ten days after the reception, Tupikov's body is found by a jogger in Rock Creek Park, his penis stuffed in his mouth.

The Mossad launches an investigation in parallel with that of the District of Columbia Police Department and the FBI. The American cops come up with many suspects but no indictments. The Mossad immediately identifies the killer, but its objection is not to the crime but to the concomitant flouting of bureaucratic principle: no one authorized the hit. Rather than return to Israel to face disciplinary action, Misha elects to resign from the agency. He moves to Los Angeles to produce action films where the crooks invariably outsmart the police. *Variety*'s headline is succinct:

GANGSTER FILMS GANGSTER FILMS

With Pinky retired, General Ido Baram takes over as IDF chief of staff, surprising everyone, considering his background in armor, by setting about building up the Israel Navy. Eight nuclear-powered submarines are ordered from a hastily formed shipbuilding conglomerate led by Isracorp. To head the effort, Yigal chooses a pragmatic engineer named Alon Peri.

Perhaps as a result of the shortage of available young men after the war, Alex finds a very understanding and enthusiastic girlfriend. She marries him on condition that he retire from the air force. Together they set up a fashion house based on designs Alex often sketched between flights. Within five years, the name Alex joins that of Dior and Chanel in the highest ranks of haute couture. Beyond high profits and praise from the fashion press, the House of Alex wins the ultimate in recognition: knockoffs appear in shops all over the world.

Of the three Super Hornet pilots at USMA Forward Base Wildcat, Captains Stanley Field and Christian Thurston re-enlist; Jimbo leaves the service to attend Yale Divinity School, where he speaks standard English.

Israel's ambassador to the United Nations remains on the job in New York and later becomes director general of the foreign ministry. But Shai Oren's career will never reach a higher point than on the day Jerusalem is liberated, when he stands before the General Assembly to deliver, in sixteen words, the shortest speech ever given at the United Nations, and perhaps in diplomatic history.

"Distinguished representatives," Ambassador Oren says, before even one of his colleagues can reach the exit. "The State of Israel is pleased to confirm its existence. Get used to it."